I0557447

THE HOLLOW SEA

A Novel by Geoffrey Jenkins

CALIBER
BOOKS

A Twist of Sand
The Water Place of Good Peace
The Disappearing Island
The River of Diamonds
Hunter-Killer
The Hollow Sea
A Cleft of Stars
A Bridge of Magpies
South Trap
A Ravel of Waters
The Unripe Gold
Fireprint
In Harm's Way
Hold Down a Shadow
A Hive of Dead Men
A Daystar of Fear

THE HOLLOW SEA

Caliber Books is an imprint of Caliber Comics.
For further information visit the Caliber Comics website:
www.calibercomics.com

Cover image by: Dubya2x

AUTHOR'S FOREWORD

The disappearance without trace of the crack liner *Waratah* of the Pondoland coast of South Africa remains one of the great mysteries of the sea.

I have built my novel into the facts of this mystery and have not bent history to suit my fiction. Several years of intensive research have brought to light a number of fascinating new facts.

I believe that in the remarkable sea phenomenon experienced by the British cruiser HMS *Birmingham* during the Second World War off the Pondoland coast, and subsequently by several large British and Dutch liners, lies the true solution to the *Waratah* enigma.

Pretoria
1971

PROLOGUE

Last entries from log of missing yacht *Touleier*:

July 28th, 1971

5 p.m. Ship out of control.
   Latitude, unknown; longitude, unknown.
   Course, unknown.
   Visibility, nil.
   Position (dead reckoning) - 400/500 miles north-northeast *Waratah* hulk.
   Furious gale unabated (6th day). 65 m.p.h. estimated, anemometer blown away. Beaufort scale, southwest/10.
   Run of sea — mountainous southwest, high and short, waves approx. 35/40 ft.
   Barometer at lowest, 985 millibars.

5:30 p.m. Gale eased slightly, wind approx. 55 m.p.h. Overcast lifted temporarily westwards. Tremendous heavy cross-sea. Ship still burying herself, lee deck completely under water. Attempted to cut away mainboom wreckage which fouled self-steering gear at onset of gale. Unsuccessful. Rudder useless. Stump of mainmast started to thrash. Feared heel would knock a hole in hull. Managed to secure it. Left hand out of action, flesh stripped from thumb, third and fourth fingers, severe pain from spilt acid of dead radio batteries.

5

6 p.m. Gale resumed its fury, southwest/10, gusting 70 m.p.h, Dumped last polluted food overboard. Sampled remaining fresh water tank. Undrinkable. Heavily contaminated with salt. Ship taking large quantities of water aboard. Doubtful whether she will survive tonight.

July 29th, 1977

7 a.m. Course, position, drift, unknown. Woken dawn by crash of mainmast stump previously damaged at deck level. Mainboom and self-steering wreckage also carried away. Starboard cabin ports blown in, destroying everything in cabin. *Waratah* records in top galley locker still safe. Ship covered in spray and lying on her side. Scores of dead and dying mollyhawks and albatrosses caught in rigging tangle. No craft can take such punishment. End very close.

7:20 a.m. Ship's motion wilder. *Waratah*...

CHAPTER 1

What made her come aboard that first evening?

There was no compelling reason for it that I could discover later. There was no suggestion, as far as she knew, that I was in urgent need of the chart. I was sailing that night for Durban and I had told Mr. Hoskins that I required a chart, but she was not in the chandler's at the time. Mr. Hoskins had always been obliging and somehow—because of the three-barreled name of the firm, perhaps—Merry, Baggs and Hoskins—I had thought of him more in the light of a benevolent lawyer from Lincoln's Inn than a ship's chandler. The name reeked of old briefs and faded documents, not of charts, rope, ships' stores and sail-making, nor of Dock Road, Cape Town, within biscuit toss of the great array of ships which have made the port, since the closing of Suez, again worthy of the name Tavern of the Seas. Since I had taken command of *Walvis Bay*, I had fought a running battle with officialdom about stores and equipment for her: the Weather Bureau preferred its 'official channels' and I Mr. Hoskins, who seemed to sense the wants of a ship as unique as *Walvis Bay* on her strange occasions among the great hectic wastes of the Southern Ocean.

I wonder now whether she came less because of Mr. Hoskins' benevolent wish to cater for an unusual client of a skipper than under compulsion to what she was to call those strange forces which have surrounded the *Waratah* and her fate? Now that the whole long history of the ship has been laid bare, I have been able to trace a step-by-step inevitability which doomed her, and doomed those who sailed in her, and doomed those who came near her. The fates of men and of ships come down to these forces, they say, and the *Waratah* was fated. She was the first ship ever to be claimed as unsinkable—before the *Titanic* even—and I know now that even after the ship was dead, those vaunted watertight compartments of hers still carried the power to strike. I am prepared to believe, after all that has happened since, that it was indeed the forces of the *Waratah* which brought the girl to the docks that evening as I got *Walvis Bay* ready for sea.

I was aft watching the two Weather Bureau technicians unhouse some of the radiosonde equipment we used for balloon ascents at sea, which we would not want on the coast-wise passage from Cape Town to Durban since there are plenty of shore stations and our route would be close inshore. It was almost dark and we were working by floodlight. There was a thin speckle of rain from the northwest, but the Port Met. Officer and I had decided that there was not much to it and *Walvis Bay* would not have to put up with a winter's gale round the Cape of Storms. Nonetheless, I did not wish to risk the radiosonde gear when the ship was not on station: it had taken us, when *Walvis Bay* had been converted from a whaler to South Africa's first weather ship, too much ingenuity to install. The radiosonde gear had not been specifically designed to operate at sea from a ship, but we had got round that by shifting the mast forward and constructing a makeshift balloon-filling hut abaft the funnel—and it worked. *Walvis Bay* was, in fact, a compound of ingenuity, improvisation and enthusiasm by a small working group from a number of formidably-named state and semi-state organizations. Now we were bound for Durban to try and increase her weather watchdog usefulness by equipping her with special radar and other apparatus for observing the new American Itos weather satellites. From Durban I had been ordered to make a series of special observations along the line of the Agulhas Bank deep down south towards Bouvet Island and the Antarctic ice shelf, and then swing back towards my station between Gough Island and the Cape via the Discovery and Meteor Seamounts, where further scientific investigations were scheduled. Durban was where the whaler had been converted and, since it might be necessary to alter the ship still further, I wanted the shipbuilders there who had worked on her previously with such success. Cape Town, moreover, was so jammed with shipping, including the massive supertankers, that to enlist a shipbuilder for a relatively small but tricky job was virtually impossible.

I did not hear the Mini pull up on the dockside because of the noise of the electric drill we were using; the driver was invisible anyway to eyes blinded by the floodlight. The first I knew of her was when the bo'sun Fourie thrust his long sideburns into our circle of light and said, "Lady to see the skipper, sir."

Now, thinking of it, I see one of those tiny, inevitable, fateful steps, the first on the dark road to our venture. Why did she simply not hand over the oilskin-wrapped chart to the bo'sun with the request to pass it on to me? I would have thanked Mr. Hoskins, who knew of the ship's projected sweep into waters hardly ever frequented by any but an occasional whaler, next time I saw him; he might have, if the interval had not been too long, passed on my appreciation to her. Perhaps I should have met her then, perhaps not. But she had asked to see me, and I walked for'ard to the starboard side where the gangplank to the shore was still in place. We were not due to sail until the *Shell Mammoth* was well clear of the Robben Island channel; I had no wish to tangle with a 200,000-ton supertanker on a murky night.

Outside the strong floodlight, I could not see her face clearly, and I asked her to my cabin under the bridge. The cabin also served as a chartroom to the little ship (only 600 tons). She was wearing slacks and a thick grey yachting sweater with loose raglan sleeves and a complex pattern knitted into the wool. Strange, that it was to have such a place in our lives!

My attention when I came to the ship's side was certainly not on her or else I would have realized that she had made a special effort to get me the chart I had asked Mr. Hoskins for. And I certainly had no idea, as she told me afterwards, that she had gone home, changed, and then motored seventeen miles to Kalk Bay, near Simonstown, to collect a chart from a friend of Mr. Hoskins who had a yacht there, and then motored back again to the docks. It was so trivial a thing to involve so much coming and going—and yet she did it for a skipper who was a complete stranger. All I recall is my surprise and pleasure at this new evidence of Mr. Hoskins' helpfulness, and the rain-dappled pattern from shoulder to neck of her sweater. I have no recollection of what she said and what I replied, nor of the first picture of her face.

The dockside was alive with all the movements of sailors going ashore; behind lay the murky bulk of Table Mountain, hazed out of its habitual dominance by the screen of rain, except for a house light here and there or a string of sodium-yellow street lights up its slopes; the broad waterfront driveway of the Heerengracht was flanked by the pallid wateriness of skyscraper lights, while a blue neon restaurant sign atop one concrete minaret called the faithful to eat.

She ducked under the steel-lintelled doorway of the cabin. I was behind and could not see what impact the starkness of my steel box had made upon her. I might have guessed, though, from the reserve in her voice.

"She's a very tiny ship."

I took off my cap but not my oilskins, I scarcely expected her to stay. "It's a very big ocean."

Her eyes went to the wind-gauge repeater, then to me, and back again to the instrument. It was that scrutiny which, I think, first brought her face into sharp focus for me. Her cheekbones were quite high and exquisitely molded, and the slightly thin nose and fine line of her lips contributed to an ascetic quality of loveliness which became more exciting when I came to know that it reflected an inward counterpart; my first comparison of the sea-green-blue eyes was an instinctive one: with the Minch off Skye, clear now that the sky was clear, but thoughtful always of the great Atlantic storms at its back which come to trouble its pellucid depths. The people of those coasts are an admixture of Celt and Viking; she was of the same fine-boned breed, and I was to discover that my instinct had not been amiss in placing her among those who sometimes seem to have less than one foot in this world. Her hair was short and light, emphasizing the lovely contour of her face. For a moment she had an abstracted, concentrated expression which I later came to know meant that something had moved her, and at the same time puzzled her. She started to say something, half to herself, but cut it short. She did not let me see her thoughts, then.

Instead, she said, "Mr. Hoskins thinks you must have about the loneliest job in the world."

I avoided the clear eyes. "He's very kind to me. Gets me all sorts of things you can't hope for from officialdom." I gestured to the wrapped chart which she held close to her left breast and the strange pattern of her sweater.

"Why do you say officialdom?"

I had been fretted by a host of small details in preparing the ship for the trip to Durban and the long voyage south, and my reply was sharper than intended.

"So many committees have had a hand in this ship that it's a wonder she got beyond the planning stage," I retorted, but I pulled myself up. "No, I'm being unfair. Anything like a first-ever weather ship in a small country like South Africa, and a great ocean like the Southern Ocean, requires a lot of things which don't strike the eye, especially the layman's eye. True, many organizations are involved, but there's been plenty of clear thinking too."

"I thought you were a sort of floating weather station?"

"Correct. But the problem was to get that weather station floating—and to keep it floating."

I wished she would hand over the chart. I hadn't a drink to offer her, and I had scheduled only an hour and a half for dismantling the radiosonde gear before sailing.

"Mr. Hoskins says you are mainly responsible for that."

I should have thanked her and let her go. Instead, I went on to explain.

"A couple of years ago, SANCOR—that's the South Africa National Committee for Oceanographic Research—got together with the Weather Bureau and the Council for Scientific and Industrial Research..."

"Officialdom!"

I thought for a moment the interjection was mere frivolity, but she seemed too serious for that. She was staring at two big photographs screwed on to the steel bulkhead.

I went on, a little uncertainly. "There are more: Fisheries Division, Oceanographic Department of the University of Cape Town. I don't know if you want to hear about..."

She said, irrelevantly, still looking at the photographs, "It takes courage."

I didn't know her context then, so I said, "And money. We—that is, the various bodies concerned who wanted a weather ship or some sort of automatic weather device stationed in the Southern Ocean..."

She placed the chart on the glass face of the wind repeater, balancing it neatly.

"I can't make out why you weather people must have your own special ship when there are plenty of other ordinary ships which can send you weather reports."

I thought of my meetings in hot Pretoria committee-rooms. I had learned to fence, to explain, to argue, that same question while the fans hummed and a torpor of heat seemed to hang over my listeners, jacketless at the chairman's permission, or wearing cool "safari suits" which are the civil service fashion in the capital.

"Surface and upper air observations from a weather ship stationed slightly south of the Gough Island meridian and between Gough and the Cape itself are especially valuable. This is a part of the South Atlantic bordering on Antarctica where even surface observations of current weather conditions are extremely rare..."

She looked at me puzzled, disappointed even. Was I talking by rote, I asked myself, a bore addressing a group of unresponsive civil servants? Her glance went quickly to the two photographs and then to the wind repeater. I could see that in her mind something somewhere didn't tally.

She did not reply, but waited. She had a strange power of waiting, a way of building up forces to make things go her own way when they seemed to be taking a wrong channel. In the silence I heard the heavy boom of the *Shell Mammoth*'s siren and the adolescent shrill of the tugs' sirens as they started to move her out of her berth.

For the first time, I responded to her quiet guidelines.

"What I mean is, most ships stick pretty close to the South African coastline, and for our professional purposes they don't tell us much we don't know about the weather. They can give us only symptoms; we need a basic diagnosis, and that comes from regular, quick and reliable news of weather from deep down in the Southern Ocean. That is where the South African weather is really born. The occasional ships which cross to South America don't go as far south as the areas from which we want reports. Understandably. The

Roaring Forties aren't the place for pleasure cruises."

She seemed easier, more relaxed at my colloquial explanation than my earlier jargon. I could see the rain droplets in her fine hair under the electric light and was about to say some politeness about them, but the clear, searching scrutiny of her eyes stopped me.

"How long have you been—out there?"

"Nearly a year. We radio back observations every three hours."

"You haven't been out there a year! At sea!"

The puzzlement, the slight disappointment, were gone. She seemed satisfied at our rapport, and it brought the beginnings of a luminosity to her lovely face, like the first nimbus of light round a lighthouse seen in fog.

"No. I meant, I first took up station a year ago. I bring the *Walvis Bay* back to Cape Town once a month for bunkers and stores. It means being off station for a week at a time, but I'm afraid that can't be helped."

"Afraid it can't be helped!"

I went on, warmed by her challenge, and too absorbed to realize how odd it must sound to her shore ears, to describe the need to keep up the continuity of the weather watch.

"Coming back to port really means that we lose one week's weather out of every four—on the spot, that is. We naturally take readings and observations on the way back to port and out again, but it's not quite the same."

"I read somewhere that during the Napoleonic wars Admiral Collingwood blockaded the French port of Brest for twenty-two months without ever once stepping on to dry land," she said. "You're not doing too badly for yourself—once a month!"

She turned to the two photographs and stared hard at them, as if she had come to some decision. Her voice was subdued, warm in its sincerity.

"Now it's my turn to be unfair. I said just now, it takes courage. A year—that's what I really meant."

I might have dodged into some conventional repartee, but her sincerity forbade it.

"No one has ever described it as courage before," I replied a little wryly, wondering what had made her choose to work for a ship's chandler. "Screaming boredom, insufferable separation from the bright city lights, way-out type of living, hermit existence—it's been called all that, and more. But courage—no."

She waited. The electric drill was still and I guessed the crew was busy with the crating. Since she had begun to talk, perhaps I felt a little differently. It was their job. They could do it well enough by themselves. They didn't need the skipper to nursemaid them on every minor function connected with the ship.

Her eyes dropped to the wind repeater, as if silently urging me to go on.

"In many ways it's better to be in a ship than be stuck on one of the weather observation islands down in Antarctica," I said. "The sea is always alive, and you have something to occupy yourself with all the time. They tell me that one of the biggest problems for men on Gough is boredom—off watch, during leisure time."

"I don't understand why there has to be a ship to observe the weather as well as the island stations."

"The trouble is that Gough is 1400 miles from the Cape; Tristan da Cunha, still nearer South America, is 2000," I replied. "On the east, the opposite side of Africa, we have a weather station on Marion Island, but it's 1200 miles from land. To the south, in Antarctica itself, there's the South African base—2300 miles from home. It's no good reporting a storm front passing over Gough and expecting as a matter of course that it will strike the Cape. Between cup and lip, so to speak, a lot can happen in 1400 miles. A storm front can sheer off to the north or the south of the main land mass, or change its whole character and form what we call a secondary low...anyway, most of the storm systems which give the Cape its bad name start east of Gough towards the Cape—in other words, after they have passed over the island."

"What about weather satellites?" she asked. I had begun to find my tongue; it was strange, and a little exciting, to be talking weather outside the sterilities of synoptic readings. "There was a radio talk about them the other day. It seems they are able to photograph the build-up of storm-cloud formations over any part of the ocean."

She flicked a quick glance at me, wondering whether her question might kill the conversation. "All you have to do, it would appear, is to sit tight in your office safely on land and wait for a satellite photo to come in—without going to sea at all."

I smiled a little at her seriousness. "You're trying to talk me out of my ship! No, weather satellites are valuable, but they're not the whole answer. From them you can see vast stretches of ocean and its weather. If I had some of the photos here I'd show you how you can actually watch the great battalions of cloud taking up storm formation as a front approaches South Africa from the southwest, from Antarctica. The storm may extend for a thousand miles. But we weathermen need a great deal more than a photograph. We want upper air temperatures, wind speeds, barometric pressures—a whole lot of technical things we lump together under the term synoptic reading. If we have these readings we can also work out, far more accurately than from a satellite photo, when and how a big storm system will strike the Cape."

"It seems an awful lot of effort to go to in order to tell people whether or not to go for a picnic or a swim."

"Fortunately, those people are at the bottom of our priority list," I replied. "Ships in coastal waters and aircraft are our main concern— farmers next. For them, however, I suppose we could have got by without the *Walvis Bay*. It's oil rigs which make this ship important. Without them, she wouldn't be here tonight."

"Oil rigs?"

"The weather ship's main function is to supply accurate information for the big floating rigs drilling for oil on the continental shelf off the southern Cape coast. Our forecasts are of prime importance to them—there's a great deal of money involved in missing just one day's drilling, or having expensive equipment smashed because the oilmen didn't know what sort of seas to expect. When this little *Walvis Bay* starts to cavort in a southwesterly swell 600 or 700 miles out on the high seas, it's a fairly good bet that three or four days later the huge drilling platforms on the coast will likewise cavort. In fact, it was oil which really clinched the whole weather ship project. Without finance from the backers of the oil rigs, none of the other bodies concerned could have afforded a ship like this with her special expensive equipment. When you arrived, I was dismantling some of it to make sure it wouldn't get damaged on the passage to

Durban. It's a great responsibility, all this special apparatus, and it's a major part of my job to see it doesn't get smashed at sea. I sail *Walvis Bay* on a very light rein in the Southern Ocean, with one eye all the time on my equipment."

"And this is your whole life?"

"I'm used to it," I answered. Then it slipped out. Why should I have told her? I didn't need a confessional, but those steady, provocative eyes were on me.

"Single-handed yacht racing is a loner's game," I said a little self-consciously. "I graduated in that school. Whalers first. To the Antarctic—but that was more a bit of schoolboy fun than serious sea-going."

She asked no questions. She simply waited, in that quiet, serious way of hers.

So I added. "I raced *Touleier* in the Cape *en* Buenos Aires race. It was a sort of curtain-raiser to the big Rio race this year."

"And won—I know," she answered. "The whole world heard about *Touleier*'s exploits—they even learned to pronounce her name." She ran it round her tongue, as if it gave her pleasure to do so. "*Tow-layer.*" She ran her finger round the dial of the wind gauge repeater, as if vicariously sampling those great gales which had swept me across the empty ocean between the two great continents of the south. "You call it a curtain-raiser, the papers called it sorting the men from the boys."

I remembered a field of ice as I neared the winning post, the gale blowing the spicules of ice so that they scored the face of the compass.

"If you can stand forty-four days alone in a yacht at sea, it's easy to take twenty-one days each month in a ship like *Walvis Bay*, which is thirty times her size, surrounded by men, in touch with the land every three hours by radio, discussing all the time things like pressures, wave heights, wind direction and force, plotting..."

"Mr. Hoskins didn't tell me it was the skipper of *Touleier* I was bringing a chart to tonight."

"He was my backroom boy for the race. That was the first time he fathered my needs for a special outfit; *Walvis Bay* is also special. You get used to this sort of life. It has its compensations. Who do you know gets one week's holiday every four? That's what happens to my crew. Three weeks at sea, one in port. It's also got its rather imponderable academic rewards. No one has ever yet sat in continuous watch over the weather in the Southern Ocean where I'm stationed. Already some extremely interesting new developments have come to light which we could not have known without on-the-spot observations."

She did not reply, but took three steps across the cabin, as if pacing it for size. From the inward-angled bookshelf—designed to prevent my books falling out in a seaway—she picked out a blue-covered one.

"I suppose a hermit finds compensations in his cell," she murmured, as if to herself. "Compensations!" She turned to me and quoted the title. "'The Antarctic Pilot, comprising the coasts of Antarctica and all the islands south of the usual route of vessels.'" She did not look up from the print, but put it back among half a dozen others of the same ilk, reciting their titles volume by volume.

The irritation which I had felt earlier from the pressures of getting the weather ship to sea returned, and I was on the point of asking her whether she expected me to spend my leisure hours at sea listening to mushy radio programs or gazing at pin-ups. But her action stopped my comment. The bookshelf had been only a ploy, a kind of vestibule, as it were, to her true purpose.

She went quickly to the big framed photograph of a ship on the bulkhead, turned, and faced me.

My eyes, she told me afterwards, went blank like iceblink in the sky when the great bergs haze a blue Southern Ocean sky with their dead reflection.

She waited, but this time I did not respond. She stared at me, and I at her. I should have let her go then.

She had taken another inexorable step,

She had stepped under the photograph of the *Waratah*.

She frowned and dropped her eyes from their long penetrating assessment of mine.

"I have been very, very presumptuous," she said softly. The slight shake of the head was more a plea in extenuation than in defense. She rapped the glass face of the wind gauge with a finger. This time it was

17

not to share, but to probe, its secret. "One cannot see an altar and not be awed, even if the altar of someone's life is..." It was half a question, half an assertion "...the wind?"

I remained silent. She turned and stared at the photograph of the *Waratah*. I heard the clump and thump of the crew on the deck above, and somewhere a gull screamed in rage. The points of her hair in her neck, short like a boy's, curled where they touched the polo collar of her jersey.

She ran her left fingers round the heavy frame of the photograph, speaking more softly still, addressing it almost, not me.

"Can it really mean so much—simply this photograph of an old high-funneled liner with a signature in each corner?"

I seemed to hear myself reply; I kept my voice level. "You can't read the name—photographers weren't that good in 1909. If you could, you'd see that it was—*Waratah*."

Only on rare other occasions in my knowledge of her did she give that quick jerky sigh, half intake of breath, half a smothered exclamation. Still she did not turn from the ship.

"*Waratah!*"

The sound of the name spoken by someone else was unreal to me; I had lived with it, buried, for so long; now it seemed to stir in its grave-clothes at her startled exclamation.

"I suppose more has been written about her fate and more speculations let fly than about any other ship which ever sailed the Seven Seas," I ventured.

She replied hesitatingly, but her concentration was on my reaction, not on her own words. "There was some appalling tragedy connected with her—I don't know the details—"

She told me later that I spoke mechanically: the words seemed to have been learned by heart.

"The *Waratah* was one of the finest ships of her day—before the First World War. She was big for those days, too—10,000 tons. She was brand new, on her second voyage only. She sailed from Durban bound for Cape Town one winter's night in 1909 with 211 people on board. Next day, nearly a couple of hundred miles to the south, off the coast of Pondoland, she was spoken to by another steamer. *Waratah* exchanged signals; there was no hint of trouble. Then, a few hours later near East London, she disappeared. Vanished. She was never seen or heard of again, and no wreckage of bodies were ever found, not so much as a matchbox. Just like that. In broad daylight. In sight of the coast. Ships behind and ahead of her. It remains one of the greatest mysteries of the sea."

I wanted to hide my tenseness from those clear eyes. So I gestured. "Read the signatures on the photograph."

She read, "'J.E. Ilbery, Master.'"

"Go on."

"'Douglas Fairlie, First Officer.'"

Someone tapped on the cabin door, but we ignored it.

"There's no need to go on, is there?" she said.

I shook my head.

"I repeat, I was very presumptuous," she went on. "I had no idea I was treading into a place of such grief."

She looked startled at my unnatural laugh.

"Douglas Fairlie was my grandfather. I never even saw him, nor did my father, for that matter. Douglas Fairlie was lost in the *Waratah* over sixty years ago."

The line of her lips was puzzled. "But you—it's sixty years—is it grief, still?"

I said brusquely, "Look at the other photograph."

"It's an airliner—South African Airways."

The cabin seemed hot, and I slipped off my oilskin. I did not join her at the photographs.

"I'm sorry, I forgot the signature's on the back. I'll tell you what it says: 'Ian, what do you think of my flying *Gemsbok*? Love from Dad.' Do you follow?"

She said slowly, "The South African Airways airliner *Gemsbok* crashed while coming into land at East London. All on board were killed."

"The pilot was Captain Bruce Fairlie," I added. "No bodies or wreckage were ever found."

She looked from one photograph to the other and said very deliberately, "Those are *Waratah* words."

"The *Waratah* vanished near East London without trace," I said. "The *Gemsbok* vanished without trace near East London. Bruce

19

Fairlie commanded the *Gemsbok*. Douglas Fairlie was first officer of the *Waratah*."

"The papers were full of it—the *Gemsbok* was the worst air crash until then in South Africa."

"It's four years ago now."

"Wasn't there something about the pilot dying at the controls...? I'm sorry, I mean your father..."

I heard myself talking in that flat, official jargon again. To hide—what?

"The court of inquiry found that the possibility of my father having died of a heart attack at the controls as the Viscount came in to land could not be ruled out..."

She gave a slightly perceptible, impatient toss of her short hair and frowned. She had lost me for the moment; it warmed me to be wanted back.

So I said, "What I am trying to say is that my father and my grandfather died at roughly the same place, at an interval of over sixty years, one in a fine ship and the other in a fine plane."

She added, "And from neither were any bodies or wreckage ever found. Yet the son—the grandson—is at sea, on as hazardous a job as is possible in these days of push-button safety."

"I told you, it suits me."

"Did he—your father, the pilot—approve of your singlehanded ocean racing?"

"*Touleier* came after the *Gemsbok* crash. The sea comes first with the Fairlies. In my father that love mutated into flying. He acknowledged that it was so. My brother too."

"Your brother, too?"

"I have a younger brother who is a South African Air Force pilot—Buccaneer sea-jets. They say that if you can handle a yacht, it gives you a feeling to handle a plane. Perhaps there's really not much between us either way."

I thought then she was breaking off at a tangent, tactfully trying to end the overcharged conversation. "You've told me about the *Waratah* and the *Gemsbok*, but can I ask you a question about yourself?"

"There's nothing much beyond what you already know."

"Why do you live with a wind gauge repeater in your cabin?"

From anyone else it would have been prying impertinence. She was too deep for that.

"It's part of my job—an important part—to know the direction of the wind."

"Day and night? Where you sleep? Where you relax?"

I replied, "You see, the big fronts which come up from Antarctica and affect the weather round the Cape and the oil rigs I told you about are from the southwest..."

Suddenly I wanted to sail, to be at sea. Later, she was to tell me that my voice changed and the iceblink blankness was back in my eyes. But she had the key she wanted—southwest!

She waited only a little, not pressing a reply, and said she must go when I paused on the word. Her voice was restrained; she did not look again at the two photographs.

I moved from the doorway and in doing so brushed off my oilskin from the chart where I had shed it. Her chart lay still unopened on the wind gauge repeater. She stared at the one the oilskin had laid bare.

"You have my chart already!"

It was impossible to explain to her, then.

"Yes, I have one chart of the Pondoland coast. But I wanted another."

She frowned a little as she bent to read the superscription on mine. I noticed that her lips moved more towards their right-hand corner than the left. "'East London to Bashee River, S.A. surveying ship *Africana*, 1934/35.' It's marked full of lines and arrows which I don't understand."

I was tired. I nearly said, I don't understand them either, but instead I covered up. "There are too many lines and markings on this chart of mine. I wanted a clean one for *Walvis Bay*'s trip. That's why I asked Mr. Hoskins for a new one."

"I think he might be a little hurt if he knew you'd had one all along," she said.

"He's never been in my cabin."

"So he hasn't seen the *Waratah*?"

"I think we should let it go at that, don't you?"

She went.

I did not leave the cabin.
I did not know her name.

CHAPTER 2

"Green Point light bears zero-six-three."

"Distance?"

"One and a quarter miles, sir."

"Ground haze or fog?"

"Not tonight, sir. Clear as a whistle."

"Steady as she goes, then."

"Aye, aye, sir. Steady as she goes."

Young Smit, who held the imprecise status of second officer of the weather ship, was enjoying the formality. He, like me, was a yachtsman and knew the approaches to Table Bay like the back of his hand. This was a new course to him, for usually on taking *Walvis Bay* to her Southern Ocean station, I headed westwards into the open sea; now, Durban-bound, the weather ship would first have to make her way round the thirty-mile projection which is the Cape Peninsula and then follow an easterly course past the notorious Cape Agulhas, and then parallel to the country's southern shore. I was keeping a bright watch for fog on this winter's night, as it has an evil trick of hanging over a very limited area of low-lying ground which are Green and Mouillé Points and ambushing any unwary shipmaster who sees the bright lights of the port all around him and heads for them. The fine ships whose bones lie on the reefs are proof of the folly of taking that final short-cut into the great port.

The peaks of the Twelve Apostles were misty to port, and I decided to keep closer inshore than the *Shell Mammoth*, ahead of me in the night, could do with her deep draught. I went over to the port side of the bridge and took a look at the receding land.

Chart-bringer!

Had I thought of that quiet but disquieting presence which still lingered below my *Waratah* photograph as someone to be sought out again, I should have chafed now at the thought of my long absence from Cape Town during my deep probe southwards beyond Bouvet and past those two seamounts which are more real on a chart than in the actuality of the wild sea-desert of the Southern Ocean and, departing, I would have wondered where she was among the blaze of lights abeam which was Sea Point. I might have even picked out a block of flats as her possible home and told her of it when next I met her. I might have rejected Sea Point and let my mind hover, helicopter-like, over the sprawling welter of suburban lights glistening in the rain under the great mountain and speculated again where she did live. With parents? From whom had she derived that strange withdrawn look, that quiet fervor at the back of those deep eyes, which had touched—me or the *Waratah*? Or both? I side-stepped that uncomfortable thought. I might have asked too, had the mood of pleasant fantasy been upon me as I watched the lighted land and the darker clefts and kloofs of the mountain slide away, whether she ever watched the ships come and go? Being a weekend, was she partying among the lights, forgetful of her encounter with an odd skipper who was making his way to sea in the darkness, maybe some unaccountable darkness of his own mind?

I might have had these thoughts, but I did not: it was not of herself, but of me, that she made me think that night. She held up a mirror to me, and it was at my own image, not hers, that I looked as the shoreline became progressively less illuminated until only an occasional light shone out to sea, or a car's headlights search-lighted the magnificent Marine Drive which swings again and again as it follows the shoreline the length of the Peninsula. I was twenty-eight. She was perhaps twenty-five. Command of the *Walvis Bay* was my first real job. I had been born in Cape Town, educated there, and had graduated from Cape Town University. Before university, as I had told her briefly, I had spent a season in a whaler in Antarctica as a youthful adventure. I think the influence of the head of the university's Oceanographic Department had something to do with my

24

appointment to the command of the weather ship, plus my ocean-racing experience. I had raced *Touleier* ("the one who leads the oxen") to South America—and won. That night off the Peninsula I had not yet heard the soft inflexion of her Welsh name, so unusual to South African ears. Tafline! Had I known it, and known something of the ancestry which had shaped that finely-molded face, it might have given her more substance; there was nothing of her in my cabin but a presence and an oil-skinned chart. There was no lingering perfume, even. She had called the cabin a cell, her curiosity compounded with compassion; I handed over the bridge for a moment to Smit and went below and tried to look at the cabin with her own eyes and project the image of myself which had clearly intrigued her, but I found it uncomfortable, and I went back to the darkness and the disappearing land.

Mine had begun as a life much the same as thousands of others, but then came the acclaim and publicity over the ocean race. It was true what I had said, that it was boredom which killed on the weather-station islands; at sea, especially in a racing yacht, there is no time for it. Under the self-scrutiny which she had provoked, I realized that subconsciously I had made the weather ship into a substitute for the yacht: for the endless vigilance of sails, helm and wind I had replaced the regular three-hour readings, the barometric pressures, wind velocities, temperature charts and radiosonde balloon ascents, but the essential matrix of aloneness remained unchanged. *Walvis Bay* and *Touleier* were different, but the same. This I realized as the cold sea swished by and the land became more ill-defined. The long voyage ahead from Durban, the complex of scientific observations involved which, until she came, had occupied all my thoughts, were, I saw on the silent bridge that night, a further step towards isolating myself from human contacts.

In themselves they need not have been, but she had gone unerringly to the heart of it all—*Waratah*.

My own father had never seen First Officer Fairlie of the *Waratah*, his father. Dad was born in January 1910, and the *Waratah* had been lost during the last days of July 1909. By the time I came to discuss the *Waratah* with Granny Fairlie it was history, and she talked of it impersonally, without sorrow. One thing she asserted, however, and that was that the ship had not been lost the way the ineffectual court of inquiry had found. "Douglas Fairlie knew ships," she used to state. "Captain Ilbery was the same. They knew how to handle them, even if they were—as everyone said after the *Waratah* vanished—different. Captain Ilbery had graduated in the wool clippers and he used to tell some hair-raising stories of them running the easting down to Australia with decks awash, carrying all sail. Passengers used to queue to sail with Captain Ilbery, whatever ship he captained."

And, as if to reaffirm her faith in her sailor-husband, she never applied to the courts to have him presumed dead, as so many others did. "Douglas Fairlie wasn't dead when the *Waratah* went down," she stated flatly. I used to visit her among the noble oaks of Stellenbosch, where she had a small house in classic Old Dutch style. She had settled in South Africa after the *Waratah* tragedy. In her will she had left me some priceless *Waratah* documents.

A few hours before, I had been excited, taut, eager for a voyage which I boasted inwardly to my own scientific ego could be a little Challenger expedition. My route lay first down the coast along the line of the largely unexplored terraces and seabed contours of the Agulhas Bank. Then my mission would take on a different form altogether—the study of wind, weather, and the uprising of great bodies of water in the cold seas to the south of Bouvet, towards the ice shelf itself.

Now, what an unknown girl thought, on seeing my cabin, predominated: to her it was beyond ordinary credence that anyone, isolated as I was in the trackless wastes of the South Atlantic, should for his sole relaxation content himself, as I did, with half a dozen books on Antarctic meteorology and the obscure rewards to be won from a wind gauge. It was not enough, she had reasoned. There must be more to me somewhere: she had gone to the photograph of the *Waratah* and the airliner to find it.

"A ship fine on the starboard bow, sir!"

Smit broke into my thoughts, but the sideburned Fourie, who perhaps sensed my wish to be alone, simply gestured out to starboard and ahead from the dimness of the wheelhouse. I saw them too—the lift of the supertanker's masthead lights in the swell. To port, we had picked up Slangkop light—a ship had died here a few days after the

Waratah, in the next great gale of the 1909 winter. Perhaps Smit, too, detected my mood, for neither of them spoke. "Everything well on board"—why did it keep coming back so compulsively since our meeting in the cabin? Those were *Waratah*'s last words to the world!

She held up a mirror to me: I was nearly thirty, but last year, one whole year, had been lost among the great seas of the Southern Ocean. Was she trying to tell me, by calling my cabin a cell, that life was passing me by? Yet life had been good—until the Viscount crash. Now it came to me for the first time that Dad had been barely a year or two older than I when the Second World War had broken out; he had flown with the first wartime squadrons of the South African Air Force against the enemy in Africa. What had he done before that? I simply did not know. Flying had seemed to be his whole life; I had never thought of him as other than a flyer. He had ended the war as a colonel, and it was he who had led the daring bomber raids against the Rumanian oilfields and Warsaw. He was old for a pilot when he died in the Viscount. It was to be one of his last flights before retiring as a civil pilot, which he had become after the war. My mother Anne Fairlie never recovered from the shock of the disaster and died a year later. It meant the end of a gracious home at Rondebosch, not far from the stately Groote Schuur, donated by Cecil Rhodes to be the official residence of prime ministers. My mother was ailing when the inquiry had questioned her about my father's health, and afterwards she never discussed the crash again except, like Granny Fairlie, to assert: "Bruce Fairlie didn't die at the controls. He was alive after the plane hit the sea."

Jubela came through to take the wheel and the midnight watch. The Cape Point light (Drake's "fairest Cape") stood out clear, but in the rain I could not distinguish the neighboring twin peaks, Maclear and Vasco da Gama. I kept well clear of the land with soundings going, for the Cape is the graveyard of careless skippers. Eastward bound as we were, Cape Point is the last of the three great lights of the Peninsula; now, in saying goodbye to it, I realized that I was saying goodbye to the person who had stepped so accidentally, yet so forcefully, into my thoughts. Would we—could we—meet again after that first revealing, penetrating encounter? I did not make up my mind, then: Agulhas, Danger Point, Quoin Point all lay ahead in the darkness and the rain, and she was behind now.

Jubela did not give me his usual greeting in Zulu, adding his deferential "Kosaan—little chief". Instead, he said quietly, "Umdhlebe." By that single word it was clear that he had read my preoccupation. With her?—I rationalized it, not her, but myself. Jubela was a witchdoctor's son; I never found out what brought him to the sea. His home was somewhere in the hot Tongaland sand forest where the Pongola River finds its normal channel too small to flex its flood muscles in and spills into a series of extensive, shallow flood pans. The Downs of Gold, the earliest Portuguese explorers called Jubela's land, looking optimistically at it with eyes seared by the sun of crossing half the world on their way to reach India. With that sixth sense the witchdoctor or *sangoma* inherits—psychological insight, one could call it—Jubela called me by the strange name he reserved for rare occasions.

Perhaps seven or eight months before, the weather ship had been taking it green as she plugged her way into the teeth of a gale far to the south of the Cape. The seas had been breaking heavily and lifelines were rigged. Jubela had been at the wheel, but I was anxious for the safety of our precious scientific apparatus, and I sent him aft to check whether our makeshift balloon-filling hut was standing up to the seas breaking aboard. He did not return. It was impossible in the darkness to see what had happened, but he had been washed overboard. Feldman, my No. 1, was regretful but adamant. To turn back to search the sea, he argued, would endanger not only the delicate apparatus, but most likely the safety of the ship herself; the chances of finding Jubela after nearly half an hour were remote.

Nonetheless, I went back, taking the wheel myself and picking a way as gently as I could amongst the hammer-blow seas. It was I who had spotted him, too, black like a seal against a breaking line of white. *Walvis Bay* could not go too close for fear of crushing him to death; we trained the upper deck spotlight on him, hoping not to lose him in the wild welter of water.

I went over the side with a lifebelt and line attached to drag us back, should I find him. Jubela saw me and swam. He came planing down a roller to the lifebelt, his seaboots tied round his neck. He always looked like a Spaniard, more so that the fine line of his teeth showed in the white spotlight. He made no attempt to grab the lifebelt, but he trod water, as if to get his balance. Then he reached forward with his right hand and took my right hand powerfully round the thumb and shook it once, dropped it, and reached again, his palm across my palm, both our elbows bent. He said nothing during this traditional gesture of comradeship gleaned from the bush and practiced upon the great waters: there was no smile, no thank you, only a strange, long, compelling stare.

They pulled us aboard.

I found a bottle of rum and two mugs in the wardroom. The cold of the Antarctic sea seemed to paralyze our throats.

Jubela stopped me as I raised my mug to his. His joking light-heartedness was back. A Tonga loves to make fun of himself, more than of anyone else. His seaboots still hung round his neck.

"I knew you would come back to find me," he laughed. "I knew it would take too much for you to explain to the government why the seaboots were gone. So I just tied them round my neck and swam. I was right. You came, Kosaan."

I grasped the mug with both hands to stop the rum slopping. I knew the rules of Jubela's game of banter.

"There was no other reason," I grinned back. "It would have meant too much paper work for me if you had been lost. The boots are worth far more than the man."

"I will hang these boots in my hut when I am old, Kosaan."

"Then what will I say in my report, Jubela? One pair of seaboots lost—as souvenirs?"

He put his mug down and took my hand and arm again in that strange double handshake. His hands were colder than mine, but still he did not drink the warming rum. The Spanish grin was gone.

"There is a tree of ours which commands respect," he said. "It commands respect, and this is due to you, Kosaan, the captain. It is different from all other trees, with strange big grey leaves, like the claws of an ostrich. It is a strange tree, because it weeps big drops like a woman's tears; it is lonely, because men avoid it, for they say it has the smell of death about it. The name is Umdhlebe."

He picked up his mug of rum and drank it off without stopping.

"I thank you, Umdhlebe."

The Cape Point light started to drop astern. Jubela at the wheel balanced himself as *Walvis Bay* gave a quick little duck-tail shake. At Cape Point the long levels of the Atlantic fall into step with the quick strides of the Indian Ocean, and *Walvis Bay* fell into step too, like the little thoroughbred she was.

Strange. Alone. Weeps. The smell of death about it. She had underlined the loneliness of the weather-watch patrol, but had not derided it, or held out the joys of the land to me. I had replied, "it suits me," and she had accepted that, but it still wasn't the answer. I had said I did not grieve for the *Waratah* grandfather I had never met; I knew the hazards of a pilot as I knew the hazards of the sea, and my father had survived more than his fair share of flak, bullets and war. Why should I weep inwardly, she had asked herself, why should I grieve? Why should Jubela have said, the smell of death? He could not read and the pictures of the *Waratah* and *Gemsbok* meant nothing to him—I doubt whether he had been more than once or twice in my cabin anyway. Was it possible to detect through me on an extra-sensory level the deaths of 211 people in the ship and forty-seven in the airliner? The moment had passed ever to question Jubela; I knew that if I did he would laugh and deny that he had said anything of the kind. Yet tonight, when she had been the agent in provoking this tumult of introspection, he had called me Umdhlebe.

A gust of wind—they call it a willy-waw—broke from behind Cape Point and slapped *Walvis Bay* astern; the squall and the rain obscured the last light.

The darkness of the night was my answer.

Two days later, I held *Walvis Bay* twelve miles offshore going north to Durban. It was a beautiful day and the great forests of the Transkei were clear to see on the cliffs and hills rising up from the coastline. A soft northeasterly breeze had no winter chill in it, and a quiet sea made no test of the weather ship's strong flared bow.

It had come to me, that night off Cape Point, that it would be a golden opportunity to pass up the coastline to Durban near East London on a course as near as I could steer to *Waratah*'s own, and perhaps form some sort of reconstruction of the disaster. Why? The only answer I could have given then, before the chain of events unfolded itself, was—*her*. Perhaps on my protracted return to Cape

Town I would be able to tell her something first-hand about the area which had swallowed up a ship and an airliner without trace, and take up, so to speak, where we had left off. I had sailed the route before the *Gemsbok* crash and knew the coast reasonably well. Was I merely building another façade by retracing *Waratah*'s course, like the one she had penetrated in order to see what lay behind? Or was I trying to create an easy excuse for seeing her again?

I plotted my course on the new chart she had brought me: here, under my keel now, somewhere between East London and the mouth of the Bashee River, more than 250 people had gone to a mysterious death sixty years apart in two vastly different craft. Could the two calamities be equated? More to keep myself occupied with the enigma than hoping for any real clue from it, I checked and rechecked the position of every headland, each river mouth up the coast—Nahoon Point, Gonubie Point, Kwelegha, Cintsa, Kefani, Haga Haga, Great Kei, Qolora, Kobonqaba, Nxaxo, Qora, Shixini—every one to the Bashee Mouth, until I felt repelled by the crop of outlandish names. Every position was right, every description faultless. The area was well frequented—*Walvis Bay* passed five ships going and three coming, including two big tankers. Through my binoculars I examined the shoreline and investigated every splendid headland. The bland sea smiled back with Oriental impenetrability. At length, off the Bashee Mouth itself where *Waratah* was last sighted, I could find no excitement. It was a calm, uncomplicated, beautiful day. It held no mysteries, no deaths. It was a passageway of ships on their lawful business, and ashore the holidaymakers and fishermen went about their holiday occasions.

Off Port St John's, where *Waratah* exchanged her last signals with *Clan Macintyre*, the ship which will always be associated with her name, it was the same. It was warmer there under the faint northeaster, and a friendly ski-boat from the shore circled *Walvis Bay*. I closed to the exact position where the ships had been off the magnificent Gates of Port St John's, but it was so prosaic that I found my attention wandering from what I had set out to do at the sight of the splendid 1200-foot cliffs topped by forests.

It was a day to offset the wild nights of the Southern Ocean.

Or did the very loveliness of the day, in its beguilement, shut fast

the tragedy which lurked beneath its easy waters?
    Accused, or witness, the sea?
    It smiled back now, bland and beautiful.

CHAPTER 3

"*Waratah*"

Alistair shied his empty beer can in a shallow trajectory towards the bulkhead. It made an adroit cannon off the steel beam immediately below the photograph and clattered unerringly into my wastepaper basket to the one side. He must have seen my face darken at his clowning—he was not to know that she had stood just there, treading gently and wonderingly into a mystery which had been woven into the fabric of a man she had just met—for he leapt out of his chair with schoolboyish zest, made an airplane shape of his hands, and zoomed them over the receptacle where the can still vibrated.

"Bombs away! Right in target area!"

His light-heartedness was irresistible. "That's where the Buck boys' training begins—in the stern classroom of the mess," he went on. "If you can hit a thing with a beer can, you can hit it with a bomb, says teacher. So..."

I grinned, "Have another can...a full one."

He nodded, and I slipped down to the tiny "wardroom" for a fresh supply.

Alistair was standing with arms akimbo surveying my cabin when I returned.

"For crying out loud!" he said. "This cabin of yours smells like...like..."

"Formalin," I supplied, handing him a beer to open. "Used to preserve fish and marine organisms. Plankton and such-like."

He grimaced. "It's almost enough to put a man off his beer.

33

Mortuary. Dead bodies. That's what it reminds me of. How you can live your life in this boat beats me, but when you add what you've taken aboard now..." He jerked off the lid of his beer, but this time he did not make an Aunt Sally of my photograph. He placed the empty carefully on the steel floor among the clutter of things in the cabin. He studiously avoided any mention of the *Waratah*, and I was grateful for it. He began to talk quickly, as if he feared I might bring it up.

"What the hell's all this stuff for anyway, Ian?" he demanded. "I thought you were coming to Durban to have some special met gear installed? These aren't weather instruments."

He took off his Air Force tunic, threw it across the table which had held the second chart (the one I could not explain to her that night of sailing) and sprawled with a sigh again in my armchair.

"Unfriendly, inhospitable," he grinned. "Only one chair. No creature comforts. In fact, what joy you extract from this sort of game is beyond my guess."

"It has its rewards."

It must have sounded ponderous, stuffy, for he glanced at me narrowly and then exclaimed boisterously:

"What about a little pubcrawl tonight, boy? Beat up the town, you and I. It's a good spot, Durban. We could..."

I liked Alistair, but there were too many undercurrents since Cape Town to surrender to his light-hearted mood.

"I sail tomorrow," I cried off. "No dice, I'm afraid."

He looked at me searchingly. "I guess, if you hadn't been sailing, there'd have been some other equally good reason. You're growing old, boy, and the grass is growing under your feet. Sorry, I forgot, there's no grass where you graze in the South Atlantic. You've changed since I last saw you, Ian, and that's only a few months back." He kicked at a length of rope on the floor. "Even to a dumb flyer like me, you can't pass this off as met gear."

I picked up the offending nylon rope. It had a wire core anchored round a thimble. I played with a loose plug-and-socket connection.

"It is and it isn't," I replied. "Once we get well south of the Cape, *Walvis Bay* will be in an area where there are all sorts of exciting and little-understood interchanges of warm tropical water with cold Antarctic streams. For a long time there has been need for an intensive study and we're going to try out a new technique for measuring sea surface temperatures. It's called a trailing thermistor, if you want to know."

Alistair eyed me quizzically. I wondered if Bruce Fairlie had been like that when he flew his crazy bombers, or was it Douglas Fairlie who had bequeathed Alistair the air of confident nonchalance which once might have graced the high controversial promenade deck of the *Waratah*? Those were the Edwardian days when captains still wore top hats, and officers fraternizing with attractive lady passengers was permitted only in so far as it promoted the interests of the Blue Anchor Line. Would Alistair mature from the unshakeable confidence of the jet fighter-bomber pilot to... I remembered then that she had spoken of Collingwood. The average age of Nelson's men at Trafalgar was twenty-two; and the Battle of Britain had been won by boys. Alistair was twenty-one.

"When the Buccaneers were ordered to come down to Durban for maneuvers, I expected to find my distinguished elder and scientific brother quietly fiddling over barometers and suchlike," went on Alistair. "After all, you said you were making this special cruise to gather met information which apparently no one else can get, it's so bloody remote. Fair enough, but you've been here ten days now, and I'll bet you haven't even been ashore for a run. You should look on me as a heaven-sent piece of luck."

"Not your sort of run, Alistair," I grinned back. "Backwards and forwards to the Institute..."

"Sounds slightly sinister to me," he rejoined. "I always felt you needed your head read."

"Institute for Marine Research. Down by the beachfront."

"You mean the aquarium?"

"The aquarium is only the shop window for the public," I replied. "The science lies behind. When the Institute heard I was in port, they asked me to carry out some deep-sea scientific studies for them—in addition to the investigations I've already been scheduled to do for my own people. After all, it isn't every day that a scientist gets the opportunity of taking observations in an area where no observations have been taken before..."

"Here we go," sighed Alistair. "Give me another beer, Ian, while you go off on your hobbyhorse. No wonder they all love you and clutter up your ship, even your own cabin. You're the country's No. 1 scientific sucker. Just say the words, where no research and observations have been carried out before, and you're sold on it. Ask you to examine the sex life of plankton in the Roaring Forties and you'd do it too."

Alistair was as uncomplicated as a summer high pressure system. And as warming too. Like astronauts, Buccaneer pilots must not be bedeviled by imagination.

I caught his bantering mood. "There's a sea worm called a Bonollia. She fixes what sex her young are going to be."

Alistair held up a hand in feigned protest. "No more without more alcohol."

"I'll get another from the wardroom."

"That's the place which is one spit long each way?"

"It is."

He took imaginary aim across my cabin. "This place is only half a spit. Easy to see why you don't keep your liquor here. If I were cooped up for weeks on end like you in this scientific bed-sitter, I'd reach for the nearest bottle. Wise man, to put temptation far away in the wardroom."

Before I could go, Feldman, the ship's first officer, knocked and said, "Can you come on deck, sir? We're having a bit of trouble with that crane-like thing."

"Coming, Alistair?"

He nodded. "Might as well see the worst."

Two dockyard men were trying to weld and bolt to the maindeck port rail the ungainly collection of pipes and pulleys called a Van Veen grab. It looked like a strange triangle forming an outboard derrick from the ship's side. At its extremity was a small bucket-like grab, worked by pulleys and chains from the deck.

"Looks like a steam shovel born prematurely," commented Alistair.

The two workmen relaxed. Alistair had that effect. I had pushed them pretty hard for the past few days.

"It keeps snapping shut," explained one of the workmen, "As soon as we start getting the rest properly into position, the bucket gets itself in the way. Can't you fix it somehow?"

I clambered out on the rail and adjusted the trip chain mechanism of the steel jaws (designed to bring mud samples from the ocean floor), so that it could not run free as it had been doing. This was to be one of my prime instruments for tests along the line of the Agulhas Bank, the oil-bearing continental shelf which envelops the tip of southern Africa. Since the Americans had found that it was uneconomic to exploit offshore oil when the depths exceed 300 feet, *Walvis Bay*'s mission was to proceed along the line of this depth and make preliminary samplings. Before striking south to Bouvet and beyond, I had been commissioned to deliver these samples to one of the big rigs already operating farther round the coast, from where they would be flown by helicopter to land research stations to establish whether more detailed seismic refraction and gravimetric investigation were justified. My route at first down the coast would seldom be more than twelve miles offshore, along the 300-foot line.

Alistair said, "You've already got one of these grabs on the other side of the ship—what do you want two for?

A slightly less complicated array of pipes, pulleys and wires hung from the starboard rail.

"The other's a gravity corer," I explained. "That thing like a mortar bomb hanging on the end is for penetrating the sea-bottom itself..."

Feldman interrupted. "It's all right off the coast, sir, but won't all this top-hamper make her a little unstable when we hit the Westerlies?"

I kept my reservations to myself. "Together they're lighter than the harpoon gun in the bows which we scrapped," I replied. "That kept her head down too much. I got rid of it to reduce her overall weight above the waterline and give her more buoyancy for'ard. In any event, the Van Veen grab will come into its own again once we start investigating the two seamounts beyond Bouvet."

"You can always cut all this adrift if you get into trouble," remarked Alistair.

The two workmen laughed. Feldman looked mildly shocked.

"At a guess I'd say the scientific equipment *Walvis Bay* is carrying is worth more than the ship herself," I said. "The type of apparatus we've aboard for observing the new weather satellite has never been taken to sea before, and we'll have to treat it like Dresden china. We spent our days in the Southern Ocean having litters of kittens over the radar scanner, which also wasn't designed to take the sort of beating the Southern Ocean hands out. These grabs and corers in themselves are worth thousands. You'd better come below and have your beer before you put more ideas into the crew."

Alistair sprawled himself again in my chair. "I reckon I'm in the wrong game. Fancy just cruising around taking a few barometer readings or plucking bits of mud from the sea-bottom! A few weather buoys would put you chaps out of business."

Alistair's jibes were sour. I remembered *her* admiration for my way-out job. It came home to me then that I would be away from her for two months at least. How trite then would sound my account of my sterile reconnaissance of the Bashee and the *Waratah*'s graveyard!

"My mission isn't the kind of scientific ivory tower you seem to think," I retorted. "What I find could determine the whole course of the offshore oil-drilling program. I've got to drive a cross-section investigation through three of the mightiest current systems in the world—the Agulhas, the West Wind Drift and the Benguela—and each one is going to throw its particular brand of toughness at my ship..."

"Boy, there's no doubt you're sold!"

"Listen," I said. "I see the storms born in the Southern Ocean. You couldn't fly your Buccaneer without the information I send back."

"You're so involved, you don't see the sea for the plankton," Alistair mocked. "Come and do a pubcrawl with me. Get it out of your system."

He didn't wait for my "no" but stood up and went to the two photographs on the bulkhead. She had also stood there and looked.

"You want to get rid of these!" he said. "Why don't you hang up a picture of *Touleier* coming in to win? Haven't you got a girl to remember down there in your God-forsaken Antarctic? Why fiddle around with these old dead 'uns?"

I have a picture of a girl standing there, I thought to myself, I shall always remember her.

"They're a reminder," I replied. "They're history; reality. I haven't your Air Force attitude. If I saw my best pal crash in flames, I wouldn't go and buy a beer in the mess for him as you do. You don't admit the brutal facts. I do."

"Some buy it, some don't," he said. "It's your skill, and what's not written—your luck. You can't escape it."

"Is that why the Viscount went into the drink?"

"Listen, Ian, you belong to the sea. As your brother, I can tell you to stick there. You don't know flying men. Dad was a flyer. He knew the risks—he'd been through them all. War. Peace. One night three years ago, flying a straight-forward run with nothing but a bit of wind, he bought it. That's the way it happens in the air. I don't believe he had a heart attack at the controls. Don't try and work it all into a neat pattern, or whatever you're trying to tell me. We don't, and we are the blokes who fly. Dad was old for a pilot, but he was still good. But the air doesn't want old men. You've heard of the Old Man of the Sea, but wouldn't it be bloody silly to say, the Old Man of the Air? Why, then, hang up this picture of the Old Ship of the Sea? No one will ever know what happened to the *Waratah*. They've all tried for sixty years; you'll beat your brains out against the wall if you go on. Leave it the way it is. Same with the Viscount. Take down these damn things and let's have something else in their place."

Alistair's appraisal was like a bucket of cold water. It could not, however, have been hers, I told myself quickly, for there had been that immediate rapport between us over the very object Alistair derided so.

I grinned. "That's quite a speech for you. Have another beer."

"Sorry I blew my top," he apologized. "Yes, I will. But you—somehow you seem to have got yourself in a corner and all this chatter about weather and oceans seems to be only a way of keeping you there."

Alistair's outburst showed me how deeply the *Waratah* had eaten into me. The red light was showing, clear. If I did not beat the *Waratah*, the *Waratah* would beat me.

I went for more beer. Alistair was facing the *Waratah* photograph when I returned.

"I feel like shaking this can and squirting it all over it," he said angrily.

39

I didn't want to sharpen the mental image Alistair seemed to have of me over the ship, so I said with studied casualness, "I came past the place where she sank on my way here."

I misjudged how deeply he felt about my involvement in the mystery.

"Why?" he demanded. "Why? Why? Why? You can't..." he fumbled for words "...make the sea give up its dead. Why try and make it? Take a look at it clinically, brutally. What would you actually find if by some chance you happened on the remains of the *Waratah* or the *Gemsbok*? A lot of stripped skeletons—what the sharks left, and it wouldn't be a pretty sight. Think of it like that. Leave it alone. Don't go messing around!"

Something, somewhere, was beginning to take shape in my mind, Seen as Alistair saw it, my preoccupation with the *Waratah* was sheer morbidity; with her...

"There was less than nothing all the way up the Pondoland coast. Just a calm sea, a couple of tankers. Nothing more," I replied.

Alistair clasped the beer mug in his strong, square hands. His words came tumbling out. "It took about a million Rand to train me as a Buccaneer pilot. That's what they say in the Air Force, anyway. A whole round million. What is this ship of yours worth—fifty, maybe a hundred thousand? I'm worth ten times as much at least, without my plane, which is worth another million. The money's there, that's what I'm saying. If they'd really wanted to, they could have spent ten times the value of your ship looking for the *Gemsbok* or the *Waratah*. But they didn't want to, once the immediate search was over. Why should *you*? What do you think you can achieve in a shoestring little outfit where all the latest electronic devices failed? They had the Navy and everything from Search and Rescue out looking after Dad's plane went in. They found nothing. Sweet nothing."

I think it was Alistair's bandying of those enormous figures which triggered to a conscious purpose the idea which was starting to form in my mind. I had heard the oilmen toss such figures around in describing their floating platforms in the same way a Hollywood producer boasts about his multi-million-dollar super colossal film. I had used the argument myself in persuading obtuse officials about the need for the weather ship...oil! My function at sea was to protect the floating oil rigs in advance by acute observation of sea and weather in the Southern Ocean, and soon those rigs would be moving round the coast to drill off Pondoland. The mere fact that part of my mission after leaving Durban was to sample the ocean bottom all the way down the Agulhas Bank off Pondoland showed how little was known about it. What better key to their safety than a series of sterile tabulations, day after day, week after week, would be—specific knowledge of what had sunk the *Waratah*! If I could find out what extraordinary conjunction of sea, gale and ocean-bottom contour had sent a brand-new 10,000-ton liner to the bottom without trace, it could provide a triumphant shortcut to knowledge for the oil rigs' safety and at the same time lay the mystery which had tantalized three continents for over half a century! I knew that a front was approaching the Cape, but its severity was completely unknown, since my own weather ship was not on station to forecast. Within forty-eight hours I would be at sea in the area where the *Waratah* had vanished, and what looked to be a promising similarity of weather—although it was impossible to judge at this stage more than vaguely—would hit the Pondoland coast, the Bashee Mouth at the same time...

Alistair was eyeing me curiously, "Look," he said impatiently, "if you were in my squadron I'd ground you for a psycho check. Every time the *Waratah* is mentioned..."

I decided to drop it. But I could not forget her, standing by those self-same photographs.

"Forget it," I grinned. "You send me your pin-ups and whatever else you think fit for my mental health, and I'll promise you I'll hang 'em up. But you still haven't told me what really brings you to Durban beyond that wonderful cover-up phrase—maneuvers."

Alistair seemed relieved. "Very hush-hush." He grinned a little. "Bet you have only the fishes to confide in, anyway. My squadron is to make a surprise test of the air defenses of every big port along the coast to see how alert they are to an attack from the sea. Russian penetration into the Indian Ocean and all that, you know. The Buccaneer is primarily a carrier aircraft, and it's built to fly under the conventional radar screens. So we're going to operate out to sea, as if the attack was carrier-based, and then come in low. See if Durban, Port Elizabeth and East London are awake to a surprise attack."

"East London?"

Alistair eyed me sharply. "What about East London?"

"Is that your particular target?"

"Oddly enough, it is. How did you guess?"

I could have said, Bruce Fairlie and his airliner. Douglas Fairlie and his *Waratah*—the Red Rose of the Sea, he had called her affectionately, since she was named after the national emblem of New South Wales, the waratah flower—that is why I knew. I deliberately shook the shadows out of my mind. I had made my decision. The *Waratah* and her fate would serve me, serve the oil rigs. I would break her hold on me by wringing from the sea the secret of her fate...

I laughed. "Good. Because that's just where I shall be, round about the same time."

"What do you mean?"

"I sail tomorrow; you're due at East London the night after. I'll loaf a bit down the coast doing a little sea-bottom sampling so that I can be off East London when you come in for the attack. You can wave me goodbye for my voyage."

Alistair got up and slapped me affectionately. "Dammit, that's just what I will do. Beat up this bloody little tin can before it gets beaten up by the sea! You've got some odd ideas at times, Ian, but I like the idea of this one! Let's make this a nice friendly, brotherly meeting."

"It'll be dark..." I began.

Alistair laughed, "I'll give you my ETA for the attack, and you can be in position between the Bashee Mouth and East London. You can put on the ship's lights, and I'll risk the plane's when I spot *Walvis Bay*. Then we'll know it's each other, huh?"

"I'll tell you what," I added, "I'll have all the lights on and in addition the floodlight aft near the radiosonde hut. Then you won't mistake *Walvis Bay* for any other shipping—and there's plenty up and down the coast."

"I'll come in for the attack at zero feet over the sea,"

Alistair went on excitedly, like a schoolboy out on a lark. "That's what my height has to be so that the radar won't pick me up. "I'll come in from the northeast, and we'll be far enough out to sea so that the defenses won't see 'em. You can also serve a useful function by providing me with a datum point for the attack—"I'll know exactly where I am when I pass over you. My instruments are set on the sea, you understand, so as to keep as low as possible."

Alistair's warmth and easy, extrovert manner turned us into a couple of boys plotting details of a raid into an apple orchard. We threw at one another speeds, positions, plots, times.

"Nothing like a spot of Fairlie attack co-operation, eh?" grinned Alistair.

I was glad I had suggested the rendezvous. I was getting as big a kick out of it as Alistair. The *Waratah* and the impending storm seemed very far away.

Alistair turned to go. He jammed on his cap at a rakish angle, and then strutted mockingly back to the photograph of the *Waratah*.

He threw a sham salute and made a noise with his lips like a beer can hissing.

"Hail and farewell, you bloody Red Rose of the Sea," he jibed.

CHAPTER 4

"A ship without a soul."

The words took on in my brain the rhythmic thump, break and swish of the seas as they crashed against the bow of *Walvis Bay*, not coming aboard yet, but with a strange quality of menace—of growing menace—as they raced in from the southwest. I had cut the sea-bottom sampling operation an hour previously because of the increasing motion of the ship, and I didn't like the color of the sky in the same quarter. Nor did I like the unnaturally high barometer. Usually, a southwesterly buster is preceded by a high barometer, then suddenly it goes down like a lift and, almost without warning, a gale is plucking like a thousand devils at one's ship and the sea. It was after midday and my rendezvous with Alistair was still a good six hours away; there would be no official weather warning to shipping (if it was to come) for another hour yet. As I stood on the bridge trying to size up the coming blow, the counter-combination of sea-strike and screw-thrust took on a beat which found expression in the words—as one frames phrases to the rhythm of a train's wheels—that turned round in my mind.

"A ship—without—a soul."

Those were the words of some forgotten shipmaster, a phlegmatic, matter-of-fact man of the sea and of action, not given to extrasensory things, when he first saw the *Waratah* on her maiden voyage in Australia. His own ship had been lying alongside a wharf in Melbourne and the brand-new *Waratah* had berthed alongside. In the tradition of the sea, and with some curiosity for the crack new ship of

44

the Blue Anchor Line, he had gone to pay his respects to Captain Ilbery. Standing by the wharf, looking at the new liner, this captain had suddenly found himself awed. There was something about the new vessel which lay beyond his extensive knowledge of the sea and ships.

"A ship—without—a soul."

Now, off the Pondoland coast, the words the captain had uttered to himself as he waited to go aboard the *Waratah* for a friendly noonday drink and chat thumped in my head to the measure of the gathering storm. I had sailed from Durban as I had arranged so light-heartedly with Alistair—as the *Waratah* had sailed—the previous evening. On her last fateful departure from Durban the passengers had entertained their friends aboard, the band had played, the ribbons had flown, and the farewells had been said—the last farewells in and to this world. By contrast, *Walvis Bay* had had only the Director of the Marine Institute to wave her goodbye, and she had slipped a hawser or two and slid silently out to sea. I had travelled at reduced speed down the coast, using the bottom-sampler as a pretext, in order to rendezvous, in the early evening about seven o'clock, with Alistair's Buccaneer between the Bashee Mouth and East London.

What would the weather do?

I handed the bridge over to young Smit and went to my cabin, which was also the chartroom. Pinned to my table was not the chart she had been at such pains to bring me, but my own, with its complex lines and figures. For a moment I stood looking at them; within hours, would that ominous sea and sky in the southwest put them to a fiery test?

During the long watches when the weather ship had been on station in the Southern Ocean, I had plotted, on the basis of all the information I could gather, the exact course of the *Waratah* after she left Durban on that winter's evening of late July 1909. Side by side with her course, I had traced the nearly coincidental course of the *Clan Macintyre*, the last ship to speak to the *Waratah* a few hours before she vanished. Gridded above the two main courses I had added the tracks of the three British cruisers which had searched for her in the days immediately after her disappearance, and had struck far southeastwards of the Cape in a competent square search on the assumption that she had broken down and been carried away towards Antarctica by the great Agulhas Current. Naval ratings had manned special crow's nests by day, and by night searchlights had swept the seas for the missing liner. I had also added the position of a liner called the *Guelph* off East London. On the night of the *Waratah*'s disappearance this ship had received a garbled Morse lamp message which ended with the letters "t-a-h". The identity of the ship which sent the message—known to be a big, fully-lighted liner on correct course for Cape Town—was never established. I had filled in, too, the track of the special search ship *Sabine*, a merchantman captained by a Royal Navy officer, which, after the fruitless search by the three cruisers, made a 14,000-mile, 88-day voyage through the seas and islands of Antarctica. She found—nothing. Fifteen steamers and two windjammers had been at sea between Durban and Cape Town when the *Waratah* vanished; their contribution to the mystery I had added in graphic form—courses, wind, storm. My father's projected track as he had flown southwards from Durban over the sea towards East London, ending at the approaches to the port, was precisely drawn in.

It was not so much upon the ships that I concentrated now. I had taken to the Southern Ocean with me in *Walvis Bay* volume after volume of weather statistics dating back to the beginning of the records, which was after the *Waratah* had vanished. I resuscitated from oblivion every winter storm of consequence for half a century. They, too, were set off in graphic form on my chart, and each had its own separate color.

Of the storm in which the *Waratah* had disappeared there were only limited meteorological records. Yet I had painstakingly gathered information from the logs of as many ships in Cape waters at the time of the disaster as I could still obtain. I had also unearthed a copy of the official Board of Trade inquiry into the loss of the *Waratah*, and from micro-film records I had the day-to-day newspaper reports of witnesses at the hearing.

The inquiry itself had been singularly barren of specific information on the storm; it had concluded vaguely that it had been one "of exceptional violence".

It was small wonder when Tafline came to my cabin that she should marvel that a man could spend months at sea with his only apparent companions some sterile books on meteorology; in actuality, the sifting and correlating of this huge burden of obscure, forgotten, time-sunk data had passed away my months on the weather station only too quickly. How could I explain this when she saw my *Waratah* chart with its "lines and figures"; how could I explain it all to a girl whose name I then did not even know?

Dominating all the other storms was the one in which the *Waratah* had vanished; I outlined it in black.

Now, because of what was happening up on deck, that black-circled storm was being wrenched out of the sphere of academic doldrums to find expression in the wild waters and insane wind which would surely come. How much could I deduce from it? The official forecast I had heard earlier had spoken of a southwesterly gale off the southern Cape coast, but in winter one can count on four or five of them a month. There was no hint of anything exceptional in this one—yet.

I held myself back deliberately for a moment on the threshold of plunging into deductions from that funeral-lettered *Waratah* storm. She had known none of this when she had stood by the cabinet where I had carefully stowed away all my facts about the *Waratah*—statistics, photostats, microfilms, comments, legend, a model of the ship even. Yet with some curious perception she had gone to my photograph of the *Waratah*. Why? Forces? Ultra-sensitivity to the pent-up transmissions of my own mind? She had called it grief, mistakenly, but still she had been aware of something pressing...

About a year before, when searching ashore for *Waratah* information, I had come across a folded sheet of notepaper in an archive. It was a lover's note, written that last sailing day from the *Waratah*. The very sheet of notepaper came from the ornate lounge of the *Waratah* herself. As I opened the note, my awareness of what I have come to call "forces" was overwhelming. I *knew* what that workaday shipmaster meant when he said the *Waratah* had no soul. The note was signed with endearments, "forever and ever". There were no proper names. What pair of lovers, I asked myself, had the *Waratah* separated, "forever and ever"? That old captain had seen the *Waratah* herself, not merely a sheet of notepaper, to reinforce the sort of imponderable emotions I felt at the sight and touch of the note. So strong had been his feeling that he had called his quartermaster and asked him what he thought of the *Waratah*. Quartermasters, especially those of half a century ago, were a breed of men not given greatly to flights of fancy. They had come up in the hard school of sail; they were tough; the sea was their life.

Looking at the pride of the Blue Anchor Line, the quartermaster replied quickly and simply, "I wouldn't sail in her for ten times my pay."

Smit knocked at the door with three radio signals. He came in, glancing inquisitively at my chart. As a yachtsman, he had that indefinable feeling for sea and weather which the plain man of steam lacks.

"In for a blow, sir?"

My assessment would depend on the signals he brought. If they fitted the template of *Waratah* weather which lay plotted in front of me...

I shrugged before I read them.

Smit said, "I was round this way once in early winter, and it was bad enough then, especially in a small boat. I thought my last moment had come at the sight of some of those seas."

"It's a question of what happens to an ordinary-looking gale once it rounds the ankle of the coast," I said. I grinned as he peeped shyly at the lines and whorls of my old storm fronts.

"Doesn't seem to be any very unusual yet," he replied. "Gale warning, Force 8—40 knots."

I knew exactly what it all looked like—on paper. I had been through it all a hundred times. But it was the clincher, those unread, apocalyptic messages Smit had brought and which I played with, which would provide the key, the dovetailing pattern, if it existed: I had sailed from Durban on what was a typical, mild winter's evening (warm enough to swim in the afternoon), no threat on the barometer, and scarcely a wind or sea worth speaking about. So had *Waratah*. I had resurrected from oblivion the port captain's weather report of July 26th, 1909:

5 p.m. barometer 28.860; thermometer 74; light northeast wind; harbor entrance, smooth; light northeasterly sea.

My own log read:

5 p.m. barometer 28.862; thermometer 73; light northeast wind; harbor entrance, smooth; light northeasterly sea.

Nothing could be more identical.

From the mustiness of old records I had found the log of the lighthouse keeper of Cape Hermes telling of the weather that last fateful morning when, in sight of his light off Port St John's, *Waratah* and *Clan Macintyre* had exchanged their last signals, "Hazy but fine," the keeper had reported.

A little while before *Walvis Bay* had steamed slowly past Cape Hermes. "Hazy but fine," I had logged.

Before coming below, I had requested from East London, Port Elizabeth and Cape St Francis, the projecting "ankle" of coast near Port Elizabeth, their sea and weather conditions that morning. These were what Smit had given me.

I would have liked to have shared with Smit the secrets of my heavily-scored chart, but there was too much at stake.

"I'll join you on the bridge in a few minutes," I told him. He looked disappointed and a little surprised that I had not yet read the radio signals.

Of the weather the day before the *Waratah* had vanished, I had annotated the chart:

Port Elizabeth—light westerly wind, smooth sea.

I unfolded my radio signal. It said:

Port Elizabeth—light westerly wind, smooth sea.

I ran my finger down to the crucial Cape St Francis.

Cape St. Francis—gentle northeast wind, smooth sea.

My signal read:

Cape St. Francis—gentle northeast wind, smooth sea.

Last was East London, nearest port to where the *Waratah* disappeared:

East London—gentle westerly wind, smooth sea.

There was scarcely any need for me to read the third radio signal:

East London—gentle westerly wind, smooth sea.

That was *Waratah* weather coming up from the southwest to meet *Walvis Bay*!

I knew what I had to do.

I went quickly on to the bridge. The sky to the southwest was a diseased cobalt. The sea had a peculiar sheen, like a "wet look" shoe.

"Course, southwest, true," I ordered Smit. I rang the engine-room telegraph. "Revolutions for thirteen knots."

Waratah had been twelve miles offshore in her last fateful hours; I would hold *Walvis Bay* twelve miles likewise; *Waratah* had been afloat at this point, and she had passed *Clan Macintyre* at thirteen knots, overhauling her and crossing her bows from the starboard, or landward, side. I would hold *Waratah*'s course from now until...until...I paused. Only the *Waratah* gale could tell me that.

I made a quick calculation. At her *Waratah* speed—I could hear the quickened thump of the screws under my feet now—the *Walvis Bay* would be almost exactly at my rendezvous point with Alistair at seven o'clock.

"I want you to make everything secure," I ordered Smit. "Lash down the radar sweep. I want a half-hourly report on the satellite gyro tracker. Rig lifelines along the foredeck and aft so that we can check the radiosonde hut. All unnecessary gear off the decks."

"Aye, aye, sir!" Smit grinned. "Coming up big, sir?"

"Mighty big, as I read the Indian signs," I replied. I was a little anxious about the delicate satellite observing gear. It had never been used at sea before, and my two technicians aboard had undergone a special course on its intricacies. The basic principle was a platform which was stabilized by a master gyroscope, which held it pointed at a constant angle at the weather satellite as it made its daily pass across the heavens.

"Double-lash the boats," I went on. "Also, bring up a couple of heavy tarpaulins from below in case of emergencies. Tell the cook to get a hand to help him, prepare hard-weather cold rations for the crew. I want hot soup and coffee for the night in the big vacuum flasks. Okay?"

I picked up the speaking-tube to the engine-room. "Nick? Can you rig an emergency battery circuit to the gyro platform?"

I heard the engineer's whistle of surprise. "What are you expecting, skipper—a visit from the *Flying Dutchman*?"

I was to remember his remark, later.

"You and the boffins worked it out in Durban in case we ran into trouble in the Southern Ocean, remember?"

"This isn't the Southern Ocean," he replied with a laugh. "I'm still thinking of those bikinis on the beach yesterday."

"You'll want more than a bikini before tonight's out," I retorted. "It's coming up rough. Real..." I choked back the word *Waratah...* "Cape of Storms stuff. From the southwest."

"Will do," replied the engineer cheerfully. "But the big problem remains—battery acid, if she starts to buck about."

I stopped Smit leaving the bridge. "Take a special look at the Van Veen grab," I told him. "It's awkward to secure, hanging outboard like that. I don't want the chains flailing around in the darkness."

"Aye, aye, sir. I'll get the bo'sun on to it first before the sea comes up."

Mine was a tough, well-tried Southern Ocean crew. But the stay in Cape Town, and the soft-weather delights of Durban at the height of the winter season, had taken the edge off them. I always had a sneaking sympathy with Odysseus trying to drive his languor-laden crew. *Waratah* weather wouldn't be the rearing, mile-long swells of the Southern Ocean they were used to; it would be a brutal tossing of short, quick blows and forty-foot waves, a savage, give-no-quarter infight. It had driven back the search tugs which had gone to look for the lost liner; it had hammered one of the 2200-ton cruisers for nine days until her hull was so strained that they had had to dry-dock her. Naval divers had had to work on the second cruiser for eight days before she dared put to sea again.

The string of orders and need for action to snug down the ship had taken my mind from the problem which now loomed. Smit brought it home like a dollop coming over the side.

"Feldman will be coming on duty soon, sir. You'll be able to give him your signals for the Weather Bureau."

Feldman telescoped the duties of radio operator with first officer. Smit could help out with incoming signals, but was incapable of transmitting.

My preoccupation with the *Waratah* had driven momentarily from my mind that other track which ended where hers did in a circled question-mark south of the Bashee—*Gemsbok*!

Gemsbok had flown on a *Waratah* night; tonight a *Waratah* night was lying in wait for the Buccaneer!

51

My next order froze. How could I stop Alistair flying tonight? Even the most guarded message would somehow betray that we had some sort of tryst—the pilot of a crack squadron using a crack plane for some private arrangement with the trusted skipper of an experimental weather ship whose success depended largely on his judgment and seamanship? Beating up shipping in Buccaneers is a court-martial offence: when I had reminded Alistair of it, he had laughed and said: "I don't see brother Ian peaching on me, do you? Who's to know anyway in the dark?" We had left it at that.

Send a slightly overstated on-the-spot weather report to the Bureau hoping that they would supply it to the Air Force who in turn would call off the maneuver? My mind, jeered at me even as I composed it—how would you get away with that one? "On the basis of my observations of a storm sixty years ago...!" What else was I basing my assumptions on? Not the tight interwoven system of highly scientific observations from a score of professional stations in this year of grace, transmitted at the speed of light to the central Bureau in Pretoria, digested by computer, and fed by skilled professional weathermen every few hours to hundreds of ships round the coast, scores of jetliners over the land, and squadrons of faster-than-sound military aircraft at a dozen bases. I felt the first tingle of doubt when I turned the spotlight on myself. If I dressed up the message in professional code, someone might see through it and say, Fairlie's been too long in the Southern Ocean, he's losing his nerve. He's lived with these gales so long they're starting to get under his skin.

Signal the Air Force? Even if I knew their wavelength, such a by-passing my own people would invite a rocket which might mean my getting no nearer Antarctica than the next port...

Say even the Weather Bureau were to accept my assessment of the impending gale—against all the skill and advice of their other weather stations—what would their reaction be? *Walvis Bay* carried a load of scientific equipment whose delicacy had caused a hundred headaches ashore and afloat. The Weather Bureau would play it safe. Get out of the storm area, it would say with complete justification. If there's any risk to the equipment in making the nearest port, turn back to Durban. You can still be there, safe in port, ahead of the storm. If you can't risk that gear in a winter's gale off the Cape, then there's no point in trying it in the Roaring Forties.

They wouldn't appreciate the finer points of difference between the ocean swells of deep waters and the sort of seas I knew spelled *Waratah* weather.

My glance at my watch was more instinctive than anything else. It may even been subconscious, the rendezvous time.

It gave me reason to beg Smit's question. I needed time. I must not miss the once-in-a-lifetime opportunity which offered to try and solve the *Waratah* mystery.

"The shipping forecast is due in ten minutes," I said.

"Bring me up one of the transistor portables from the wardroom. Come and hear yourself what the Weather Bureau thinks of it."

"Good—I mean, very well, sir." I liked Smit's unquestioning enthusiasm which burst through his veneer of formality as soon as he came under pressure.

I took another long look at the southwest. That curious sky and blanched sea still told me—*Waratah*. If it was, or if it wasn't—like a martyr on a gridiron, whichever way I turned I would get myself burned.

The Weather Bureau turned the spit again with its lunchtime forecast.

Smit came racing up the companionway just as the bland tones of the woman announcer, sitting in her soundproof box 600 miles away inland, said, "There *is* a gale warning. We repeat, there is a *gale* warning."

Smit grimaced derisively as she shifted the emphasis from one word to another with professional satisfaction.

"A strong southwesterly wind between East London and Durban will reach thirty to forty knots in the south of the area."

Forty knots! Smit glanced sideways at me. I could sense his letdown. Here I had been virtually ordering the crew to panic stations with threats of a Force 10/65 m.p.h. gale while the Weather Bureau—the people who had access to all the information and mutations from their weather stations—came up with a piddling little thirty-forty-knot blow which would do little more than wet the weather ship's decks. My letdown was the kicker to years of patient, often heart-breaking, research and compilation into which I had thrown all my spare time in the Southern Ocean. Had I, as Alistair had said and *she* made implicit merely by her lovely presence, been simply wasting my time in a self-made statistical funkhole while life rushed by a thousand miles across an ocean waste?

My bitterness rounded on young Smit. "Switch off that damn thing," I said harshly.

"Aye, aye, sir," he said, scared. "Orders for the ship, sir...?"

"My orders stand," I snapped. "Look at that sea, you fool. And that sky, Can't you...*see*?"

"No, I mean, yes, sir. Snug the ship down, sir. Grabs to be secured. Emergency..." he forced himself to say the word "...gale rations from the galley. Galley fire to be doused by 1800 hours. Crew to stand by..."

"Don't go on like a bloody parrot," I snarled.

He stopped at the bridge ladder. "In case...in case...you have to leave the bridge, sir, what course, speed?"

The way he was repeating everything made it all sound doubly ludicrous; now he was trying to use a euphemism to try and say that if my non-existent gale washed me from the bridge...

"You heard—as before," I retorted. "Course, southwest, true, speed thirteen knots. No reduction or change of course without my express permission."

"Aye, aye, sir." Smit fled down the ladder.

By mid-afternoon the old shipmaster's words had begun not to sound but to thunder in my mind—"a ship—without—a soul". They took on the rhythmic thump, rip and rend of the seas which now smashed against the bow of the *Walvis Bay*, throwing themselves in spouting cascades of broken water and tails of spray high over the platform where the harpoon gun had stood, and then spreading themselves feet deep across the decks like ragged, too-eager fingers searching again and again for a weak winch, a fatigued hatchcover, or a loosened stanchion to pluck away over the side. *Walvis Bay* knew how to toss them clear, and she was still fighting well within herself; nonetheless, I could hear her strain in the shuddering vibration of the hull and propellers. I had stood and watched with a kind of morose satisfaction at the rapid build-up of the sea and the gale until young Smit, oilskins streaming, reported to me before going off duty.

"Handing over, sir."

I nodded.

"Shouldn't...er...it's getting a bit wet up here, sir. Can't I bring you your oilskins...?"

I regretted my curtness earlier. "Yes, thank you."

He grinned and said boyishly, "Looks as if you're right and they're wrong, sir."

There were too many things on my mind to accept the compliment. I was far too unsure, too. I checked my briefness and said:

"See what the wind gauge says when you go to my cabin."

He returned and helped me into my waterproofing. "Only thirty-eight knots, sir." He sounded disappointed.

I grinned at him now. "So who's right is anyone's guess."

"When it gets worse—I mean, if it gets worse, sir, don't hesitate..." He stopped at the presumption.

"I'll call you all right if it really blows."

"Thanks awfully—I mean, very good, sir."

In his haste, he nearly bumped into Feldman. Feldman was slightly older than I, an unemotional, rather wooden first officer with a shock of black hair and a full face. He had none of Smit's volatile enthusiasm—the enthusiasm of a man of sail, I told myself. Feldman was reliable, providing the decisions were made for him. He spoke slowly, deliberately, and was, on occasion, almost pernickety.

He greeted me briefly. He held on against the bucking of the ship and took a long look to the southwest, and then westwards towards the hazed shoreline. Jubela had been at the wheel for a few minutes before Feldman's arrival—morose, silent, withdrawn. There had been no conversation between us before Feldman came, except helm orders.

Feldman finished his long scrutiny and then said slowly, as if afraid almost to voice his thoughts, "Shouldn't we reduce speed a little, sir? She seems to be taking a lot of water. There's the gyro gear..."

My surprise at Feldman's querying a decision of mine shook me for a moment out of my *Waratah* train of thought. Never in a year at sea had he done anything but follow my orders. He did not look at me but, as if to reinforce his views, he seemed intent on examining the wind-torn sky southwestwards.

Feldman was right: the hull of the weather ship was straining and thumping in the mounting seas. It was not the elated drum of the waves one hears when a racing yacht is running at her maximum speed, or the exhilarating crunch as she planes down one roller and up the hill of the next, but the head-on slug of evenly-matched boxers, the savage softening-up in-fighting to produce the final knockdown. During the past hour I had watched critically the build-up of the sea. No need now to refer to those innumerable painstaking computations. The reality before my eyes brought every fact to mind with startling clarity. My guess was that it had not reached its maximum yet, whatever the Weather Bureau might say. Nor had the wind. Where *Walvis Bay* was now, the *Waratah* had been forging ahead at thirteen knots. So, whatever *Walvis Bay* suffered, she must hold *Waratah*'s speed.

Walvis Bay's course—*Waratah*'s course—was about twelve miles offshore, and this corresponds roughly with the maximum southward flow of the Agulhas Current. This is a river of warm tropical seawater (known as the Mozambique Current north of Lourenço Marques) which touches a surface speed of five knots hereabouts, although divers have reported much higher underwater speeds. What drew my attention now—I could see by the jerky boil of the water between the ship and the land—was that a powerful counter-current was in the preliminary stages of building up, the sure herald (in my view) of a severe southwesterly buster. Despite what the official forecast said, I felt sure that this counter-current, hammering against the mighty Agulhas Current striking south, would create a maelstrom of a sea before the night was out. This was the way it had been with the *Waratah*. I had the *Clan Macintyre*'s own log to back me, and this is the way it had been with her. She had been only a little way behind the *Waratah*, and had barely escaped disaster herself. The main instrument in the provocation of these great natural forces was the southwesterly gale, which would move up its own massed battalions of sea to reinforce the counter-current against the dominant Agulhas flow. What would transpire, only the night would show. And I intended to be in a ringside seat with *Walvis Bay* to see.

56

I knew Feldman's devotion to officialdom.

"It looks worse than it really is," I jollied him. "The wind hasn't reached forty knots yet. The Weather Bureau says there's nothing more than an ordinary blow to it."

He looked relieved, although still dubious at what lay before his own eyes.

"I've just checked the wind," I went on, "A mere thirty-eight knots."

What I did not say, was that I considered Smit's reading of a little while back already out of date. I guessed it at forty-five knots now—and increasing.

Alistair! My foreboding at the thought of the Viscount's course running dead as it did on my chart jerked me back to an objective assessment of the whole situation. Say the wind was gusting forty-five knots now—what was that, in Alistair's own words, to a machine capable of the speed of sound? Was I not projecting all my *Waratah* fears and shadows and my own experience as a sailor into a quite different medium without due justification? The night the Viscount had vanished, land stations noted a speed of fifty knots. That was enough to inconvenience, but not threaten, a machine backed by thousands of horsepower. Was I not thinking in sea, rather than air, terms? At the moment there was no way I could see of warning off Alistair, anyway.

Feldman said, after another long look at the southwest, "I've never seen a sky quite like that. But the weather people must know. They've got all the information which we haven't..."

By late afternoon, even Feldman's faith had evaporated. He answered in monosyllables only as the weather became wilder, until I could stand his moroseness no longer.

"I'm going up aloft to take a look round," I said.

It was simply to get away from him; the bridge of the converted whaler was, in fact, the highest point of the ship after we had dismantled the special whaling lookout on the crow's nest at the time of her original conversion.

I made my way to the scrap of deck high up aft near the radio hut.

The bridge, which was enclosed, gave only a forward sight of the sea; hanging on to a funnel stay-wire, I had an all-round view. I was taken aback at the wildness of the scene. I was aware that this type of storm developed rapidly, and that its storm center moved equally quickly, but it was nevertheless startling to see it happening before my very eyes. To the southwest, towards East London, the sky was a curious purple-black over the land, and night-black out to sea. It was like looking from a spaceship at the dividing line between night and day on earth. The dying sun was able to create a lightness over the land, but the sea-black was relentless, ominous. Between *Walvis Bay* and the great blackness was a kind of no-man's land of wind-torn sky and cloud flying at impossible speeds; these were the outriders of the main army of the storm, the light armor probing with quick thrusts the *Waratah*'s battlefield of death. All round *Walvis Bay* the seas leaned to a plume of spindrift; they were not so high as steep, a sure sign that the general engagement with the Agulhas Current still lay ahead; the counter-current was still testing the enemy's defenses.

Involuntarily, I looked astern. I found myself reading the situation by hindsight. Sailors of the caliber of Douglas Fairlie and Captain Ilbery were not afraid of a storm, and the *Waratah* was a new ship, stout, fast, well-found. In the immediate uproar after her disappearance, sailors had no difficulty in believing that Captain Ilbery would have pushed her through the storm. Both men had served in clippers whose captains rejoiced in nothing less than a full gale, men who knew how to pile on canvas to the royals and to use to the full the great westerly winds of the Roaring Forties. They were iron men who battened down their hatches because their decks would run awash for days under the press of sail; they were cruel, proud time-makers who armed their officers with pistols with orders to shoot down any terrified seaman who tried to let fly a halyard.

There was not the least anxiety in the *Waratah*'s last messages to the *Clan Macintyre*. She had not even reduced speed. This evening's sea would have looked just as wild from the bridge of the *Waratah*, and she had been nearly twenty times the size of my game little whaler.

A short while before arriving at her present position, the *Walvis Bay* had passed a curious natural arch of rock known as The Hole-in-the-Wall which rises sheer out of the coast. The massive, soaring slab is pierced by an archway: the low sun broke through the gloom of the land and backdrop of great forests and for a moment the arch appeared like a bright nature-made headlight shining from the black land. One of the stories scouted after the *Waratah* had disappeared was that she had been sucked into a blowhole similar to The Hole-in-the-Wall and drawn down, by the strong inshore counter-current, into a vast undersea (or underland) cavern. A companion theory was that, under the extremes of gale and sea, a natural vortex had formed in the sea, and into this the liner had been sucked.

How much, I asked myself hanging there and seeing the storm forces unleashing themselves—the same question I had asked Alistair—did we really know about the ocean's secrets? I ran my mind now over my own scanty knowledge of the ocean floor beneath *Walvis Bay*'s keel. Round the coastline of South Africa runs a narrow continental shelf known as the Agulhas Bank, oil-bearing, elusive. It drops away in successive shallow terraces into very deep water. With something of a shock, I realized that the course I was holding was roughly the line of the final terrace of the Agulhas Bank before it fell away into abysmal depths. Meaningful? Meaningless?

The oil rigs, having drilled unsuccessfully elsewhere, were now planning to move operations to the Pondoland coast. Was enough known about the area to dismiss wholly the theory of an undersea cavern, or a vortex? Why had nothing happened to the thousands of other ships which had used this same route? Would—whatever it was—lie in wait for one of the giant oil rigs and strike it down as it had struck down the *Waratah*? The most far-fetched speculation was no more absurd than the plain historical fact that a 10,000-ton liner, classed AI at Lloyd's, and commanded by one of the ablest sailors of the day, had vanished utterly, without trace, within sight of the land, in broad daylight, somewhere where I was now.

What had destroyed the ship had been something terrible and swift, something the skilled sailor could not calculate or foresee.

The two banks of blackness ahead of *Walvis Bay* began to merge; the darkness grew.

I hung on to the lifelines I had ordered earlier in the afternoon to be rigged as *Walvis Bay* went deep through a huge wave—not a roller, but a short, high, spume-tipped load of water. Her hull trembled, and the screw chewed air and thin water with the same kind of brash rattle that a car makes when the clutch is thrown out and the engine continues at speed. It went against all my seaman's instincts to push the game whaler like this—but I had to know, and this was *Waratah* weather. *Walvis Bay* dipped her entire starboard side under, and I ducked gratefully behind the solid bridge and forward superstructure which occupied most of her whole width of beam and was designed specifically to break the force of such as this as they swept aft.

Streaming water, I regained the bridge.

Taylor, one of the two technicians aboard whose function was to care for the scientific apparatus, had turned green.

"The gyro doesn't know its arse from its elbow, with this bucking," he said, hastily averting his eyes from a rearing oncoming sea. "Nor do I, for that matter."

"What's the trouble?" I asked. "It was supposed to hold the platform steady in Southern Ocean seas."

"This isn't the Southern Ocean," he retorted, gesturing half behind him as if the sight of the seas were too much for his stomach. "It's different. It's this bucking and lurching that it can't take. Overcompensates. The platform rocks around like...like..." he motioned to the sea. "Now she's overheating. If she burns out..."

"Switch the damn thing off, then," I snapped.

"Can't—the rest position was designed for rest, not for...for...this, No one thought to have any securing bolts. If we switch it off, it'll rock itself to pieces. Can't you do something about this bucking?"

It was my turn to gesture towards the sea. I didn't say, if I'm right it will get a lot worse before the night is out. If the gyro went, the whole purpose of tracking the new satellite would go overboard. Yet here was an opportunity which in the long run might prove far more valuable in saving rigs worth millions of pounds than not taking a chance with the gyro.

I said, "Go and have a chat with Nick Scannel. He's the engineer, maybe he can suggest some way of securing it."

Miller, the other technician, came on to the bridge. He eyed me balefully. "Have you told him?" he asked Taylor.

Taylor did not seem to trust himself to reply. He nodded.

"Gyro's getting hot," said Miller.

"See Scannel and get on with it," I said.

"Perhaps if I puke over it, it'll cool down," coughed Taylor. He vanished hastily.

Feldman stood by during the conversation, silent, lips pursed. Was I, I asked myself quickly, succumbing to the mysterious forces of that soulless ship, dead for over sixty years in her grave, by pushing *Walvis Bay* down the same Pondoland coast, at the same season of the year, into the same sort of storm, on her same track, at her same speed? With that question, the cold thought swept over my mind, cold now as the sting of the cold rain mixed with bursting spray on my face: am I treading on *Waratah*'s grave at this moment? I made a quick calculation: no. Although I could not see the land well enough to be sure, *Walvis Bay* was still approaching, on a line out to sea, the mouth of the Bashee River. *Waratah* had been twelve miles out to sea; I held *Walvis Bay* twelve miles offshore likewise. *Waratah* had still been afloat at this point, and the *Clan Macintyre*, although eight or ten miles astern of her, had her still in sight. *Waratah* was by now on the port bow of the *Clan Macintyre*, having crossed shortly before from the landward side. *Waratah* had been doing thirteen knots, and the sea had been smashing into her, rising progressively on the southwesterly gale, as it was doing now.

Feldman said cautiously, "If we reduced speed a little, sir, it might help the gyro."

Everyone wanted speed reduced—the ship, the men, the gyro!

I controlled my reply and said evenly, "She's making the best heading under the circumstances—she's taking the run of the sea dead ahead. If I reduced speed, it would make the motion worse, not better."

I knew what I was saying was merely a half-truth, begging the question.

Before he could start to argue, I followed it up. "No further word from the Weather Bureau?"

"No, sir. Next forecast is not for another couple of hours."

"Good, Then we can take it things are not really too bad, eh?"

I was using sophistry, not seamanship. Feldman was unconvinced. He gestured to starboard, landwards.

Three flashes.

"Bashee Mouth," he reported formally. He seemed to be wanting to say something more, but he went on, irrelevantly, as if to force conversation, "Light's situated on the northeastern side of the river."

We had opened the gate of the *Waratah*'s tomb.

The enclosed bridge gave a sense of security compared with the exposed wildness of the upper deck.

I played along with Feldman. "How's the wind?"

"Force 8, gusting harder than that, though. Over fifty knots."

Force 8. The threshold of a real buster—with worse to come. It was still not the gale "of exceptional violence" which had crippled other ships at sea the day the *Waratah* had disappeared. Had she not quite plainly rolled over and sunk? It was the complete answer— except that it begged one inescapable fact: not one body, not one shred of evidence of wreckage, had ever been found of the *Waratah*. If she had turned turtle, there was the *Clan Macintyre* to find wreckage coming from behind; steaming towards her was another liner, the *Guelph*. All the search ships had found not one plank.

I told Feldman, "I'm going to my cabin for a moment."

I wanted to check that chart in the actual presence of a big storm to see if I could not uncover some new factor, some practical aspect perhaps, which had escaped my academic investigations.

I did not go to the chart, however. I stood for a moment undecided at the same doorway she had stepped through. And it was she, Tafline, who occupied my thoughts at that moment of crucial decision for the ship. I went across and stared at the old photograph as she had done. It meant nothing. It was—simply a photograph. It was the thought of the slim, lovely presence that held me. Was her hair dark or light? Neither. It came to me now—it was the indefinable color the fronds of kelp have on a clear day in the Southern Ocean as they grace an iceberg, neither dark nor light, yet with some unique quality of vibrancy they take from the refracted light which changes magically as the ice lifts and falls—three qualities of light, one from the sea, one from the ice, one from the sky.

I stood, and looked as she had, at the Viscount.

Bruce Fairlie the pilot had not been afraid of storms. Why should he be? His machine was powered by thousands of horsepower, it had every latest radio and radar device. His last signal to the land had shown no concern for the weather. He had reported simply that he was flying low over the sea in strong wind and rain and would be coming in to land in a few minutes at East London airport... I shrugged off my thoughts impatiently. I had worked all this out before. All it added up to was that the airliner had been over the sea, low, south of the Bashee Mouth,

Bruce Fairlie had also opened the graveyard gate.

It had closed forever behind him.

No wreckage, no bodies, had ever been found. Not a plank.

I went to the chart now. On it, *Waratah*'s track ended a little to the south of where *Walvis Bay* pitched and rolled. The terminal point was approximate, since she may not have vanished immediately the *Clan Macintyre* lost sight of her. Alistair intended to come in to attack East London on a course converging with mine—and the *Waratah*'s, He said he would be so low that there would be no chance of the radar defenses picking him up. His Buccaneer would be flying at more than twice the speed of the lost airliner. Would that ensure his safety— would he fly tonight? It seemed that whatever had struck down the *Waratah* and the *Gemsbok* took no account of speed, if one considered the discrepancy between them.

Where lay the common factor?

I saw.

Southwest.

The run of the sea was southwest.

The gale was southwest.

Waratah's course was southwest.

Gemsbok's course was southwest.

The Buccaneer's course was southwest.

Walvis Bay's course was southwest.

The course was death.

CHAPTER 5

"It's the whip after the lurch," protested Taylor. "It's like a sjambok being cracked. It's shaking the guts out of all the equipment."

"It's only a matter of time before the spindle of the radar antenna goes," added Miller.

Feldman glanced nervously half-over his shoulder. "One big sea will carry away the radiosonde hut."

The two technicians were defiant; they were civilians and could say their say to me; Feldman, without usurping authority, could give them his backing. Fear has many faces, and Feldman's was ugly to me.

I tried to keep tempers smooth.

"Take a look at the problem from my point of view," I said. "You want me to do something about it. If I turn the ship beam-on to the sea, what do you think will happen? It's bloody dangerous anyway, but how do you think she'll roll then? Twice what she's doing now. The best way to face a storm like this is bows-on. That's the way I'm doing it."

The Bashee light was dropping out of sight astern. Grey and uneasy, the coast lay crouched in a haze of spray, the high shoulders of the black promontories braced against the storm. Very soon it would be completely dark.

Feldman said, "We've seen a lot of rough weather in the Southern Ocean. But look at this sea—I've never seen anything like it. Down south they come as long rollers, and there's a breathing space in between. I've never seen *Walvis Bay* taking it green the way she is

64

now."

"The gyro would be quite happy like that," Taylor went on. "That's what it was designed for. It's in the specification..."

"Blast your specifications," I retorted impatiently. "I can't specify the sort of sea one gets."

"All we're asking is for you to give us a sporting chance," muttered Miller. "Here you are bashing the ship with everything full on..."

Feldman saw his chance. He said tentatively, "You haven't reduced speed. She'd ride easier if you did."

"I'm the captain, and I make the decisions around here," I snapped.

"Even a captain can be wrong sometimes," replied Miller truculently. "We're telling you plainly and simply that if you don't do something quick, you won't have any apparatus left in a couple of hours."

Taylor was more conciliatory. "Couldn't we make a plan..."

I loathed myself for pulling my rank, but I simply could not attempt to explain. How could I say that I was deliberately trailing my coat, for greater ends even than the valuable instruments which were the true heart of the weather ship? Every suggestion the three men were making was in accord with common sense and sound seamanship. I was driving the ship unnecessarily, risking valuable equipment, property, and maybe even lives.

I tried to bluster my way out. "Would you like me to put in to East London then and signal the Bureau that the gear's a failure even at the start, and you can't cope?"

"You'd think it was *our* gear and that you were only the driver," snapped back Miller. "You're in this just as much as we are, if not more, don't forget."

My nerves and temper were stretched. The bridge clock showed 5:30. Perhaps, I thought with a sense of relief which was overwhelming, the Air Force won't fly tonight anyway. However, did they—or the Weather Bureau—really know how out at sea it was working up into something really dirty? Freed of the awful responsibility of Alistair (the *Gemsbok*'s identical course seemed burned into my brain), I alone could test what there was to test about the *Waratah*, but I would have to be very sure that the end would justify the means—in other words, the pitiless hammering which was being handed out, with my full concurrence, to the scientific gear. Would it, like my coastwise trip, be meaningless? If I accepted the futility of what I was doing, I would reduce speed right away and cosset the apparatus, perhaps even take her out into deep water, where the wave effects were bound to be less than in the shallow waters of the Agulhas Bank. I crushed down the idea. I had decided to follow the *Waratah*'s course at the *Waratah*'s speed to smoke out what had sunk her, and stop it doing the same to the great oil rigs. I had that rendezvous with Alistair; if I were not there, I told myself, perhaps my very absence might drive him into the arms of the *Waratah* danger if he started to look for *Walvis Bay* in the wild seas...

I bit back my reply to Miller. "What did Scannel say?" I temporized.

"He's got so many of his own problems, he hasn't been able to spare time for ours," retorted Miller sullenly.

I picked up the engine-room voicepipe. "Nick? I've got a crisis on my hands. The satellite observing gear and the radar antenna are shaking themselves to pieces..."

The sea's thump in the engine-room below the waterline came through clearly on the instrument. It was like a rubber truncheon being beaten against a steel drum.

"I'll be right up," said Scannel briefly. I wished I had a first officer of the caliber of my engineer.

Scannel took a brief look round when he arrived on the bridge. "Is that what's making all the racket?" He gestured to the sea.

Feldman muttered, half to himself, "It would be less with less speed on her..."

Scannel snorted. "Listen, chum, my engines are good for sixteen knots, gale or no gale."

I grinned at the engineer. It was comforting to have some backing.

"The gyro is overcompensating and heating up..." Miller and Taylor went into a string of technicalities.

"Okay, okay," replied Scannel. "Let's go and have a look. I have an idea..." He glanced derisively at Feldman's back where he stood peering through the bridge screen windows. "You won't be wanting any more speed for the next half-hour or so, will you, skipper? I'm going with these boys."

He grinned and winked. One could almost see the wince pass up Feldman's back.

I didn't want to have to bluff and fence with Feldman once the others had gone.

I said, "Please make a round of the ship, No. 3, and check all lashings. Double-check the radiosonde hut. Smit rigged some extra stays to prevent any movement."

Feldman eyed me oddly. For a moment he glanced uneasily through the bridge windows as if to say something, but then stopped himself.

"Aye, aye, sir."

He left without speaking. Jubela and I had the bridge to ourselves, Living close to anyone in a small ship at sea throws a heavy psychological burden on one; with Feldman, the burden was double.

Walvis Bay gave a series of three heavy crashes, slewed slightly to starboard and then, under the weight of water, listed sharply over towards the land.

Jubela grunted. The wheel whipped and spun.

"Hold her!"

It was involuntary from me; Jubela needed no coaching in wheel orders.

He said, "It is as bad already as the night you came back for me—Umdhlebe."

Twice on this short voyage he had called me that. Twice, since I had met Tafline.

I was tempted to tell Jubela then about the *Waratah* and the lost airliner. Should the skipper confide to the seaman? I think Jubela would have understood. We talked the same language, he and I.

I began lightly, an appeal to the sense of fun which lies so close beneath every Tonga's skin.

"Those boots of yours are so worn now they're not worth coming back for anymore," I laughed. "Look, it's only a few miles to the shore. I'd really let you swim this time."

But Jubela did not respond. He gazed stonily ahead, pretending he could see through the streaming water which deluged the bridge windows.

A curious tense silence came between us.

What strange prescience had choked the Tonga's usual ebullience to sullen refusal to talk? Were we indeed in the presence of that ill-omened, fated ship? Was the influence clearer to Jubela with his highly-developed intuitive faculty?

For the next half-hour *Walvis Bay* labored and plunged. Jubela and I said nothing.

Feldman came back, nodded, clasped his hands behind his back, standing correctly where a first officer should stand in a storm. He gave no report of the ship, and I asked for none. The silence became tighter.

The radio warning buzzer went. Since there was no full-time radio operator, the device signaled the bridge when a message was due; if on watch, Feldman would answer.

Feldman nodded again perfunctorily and went.

Even before he handed me the signal on his return, I could tell by the smug, tight purse of his lips that it was of moment, and that I wouldn't like it.

> From Weather Bureau and C-in-C South African Navy, Simonstown. Advise storm of unusual intensity south Port St John's and Bashee Mouth towards East London and approaches. Anticipated Force 10 gale, southwest, 60 m.p.h. All shipping northbound from Port Elizabeth to Durban is hereby ordered to seek shelter at nearest port; all southbound shipping from Durban is ordered to make for open sea and deep water clear of Agulhas Bank at best possible speed.

I looked up from my first reading of the message, carefully avoiding Feldman's gaze. I saw the light reflect the veneer of sweat on Jubela's neck as he spun the wheel to maintain *Walvis Bay*'s course. He had discarded his leather jacket and there were patches of wetness on his shirt.

I read it again.

When *Waratah*'s secret lay perhaps within my grasp an hour or two away, I was ordered to get right out of the area as quickly as I could. It wasn't only advice the signal offered: the fact that the C-in-C was included meant business.

"Acknowledge, sir?"

I hesitated. If I said I had received it, they could pin me down later...

I pointed to the superscription. "It's not addressed specifically to *Walvis Bay*. It's a general warning..."

"And order," added Feldman.

"...to all shipping. There's no reason why we should acknowledge."

"We're a weather ship, and we belong to them," went on Feldman, eyeing me. "The Bureau would probably appreciate an on-the-spot appraisal from their own people. It could be extremely valuable."

"They took the decision without asking us," I replied. "If we're as valuable as you say, they'd have signaled us before sending out that general warning."

Feldman was silent for a moment. Then he gestured to the signal in my hand and said, "What new course and speed, sir?"

I took the decision which had been crystallizing in my mind from the moment the warning message came in, the decision which was to have such momentous consequences for her life, for someone whom I had met for only a few minutes, whose name I did not know.

I said harshly, "Course, southwest true. Hold her that way."

I stepped over quickly to the voicepipe. "Nick? Revolutions for thirteen knots. Hold her that way."

"I wasn't thinking of doing anything else," said the surprised engineer. He had heard the tone in my voice. "Anything wrong up there, skipper? That gyro's not gone, is it—I fixed it with an improvised spring to hold the platform down against the roll..."

"No, Nick, nothing wrong," I replied. He was the man I wanted with me tonight, not this lily-livered civil servant behind me, Smit, too, I could count on—already my mind was on what lay ahead.

I turned to challenge Feldman. He indicated the signal.

"Would you mind signing that, sir?"

I scrawled my signature at the bottom. "You've left the 'h' out of Agulhas," I said sarcastically.

"It's very difficult to write plainly with this sea running," he answered. Feldman had cleared his yardarm all right. My signature on the message told me what his attitude would be if he were questioned afterwards.

He took the paper from me. "No reply then, sir?" He was being meticulously correct. I could imagine him going to his cabin and logging our conversation, word for word, just to keep the record straight.

"No, Number One, thank you. Nothing at present."

I could detect Jubela's puzzled expression at my change of tone. Feldman must have no more ammunition than he already had.

The sea would give the answer tonight.

Walvis Bay crashed towards the heart of the storm.

I kept her remorselessly at thirteen knots.

The bridge remained tense. None of us spoke.

The tumult inside me grew. Would Alistair come? Would the Air Force risk flying? The warning sent out by the Bureau contained no mention of aircraft. Were the commercial jets flying, or grounded? My guess was that conditions were reasonable over the land; the sea held the key to the weather tonight. Had it not been for Feldman's attitude I would have used the ship's radio to listen in on the passenger jets' frequency to lay the ache in my mind; if I tried it now, it would be another black mark against my name.

Only the event would tell. I must be at the rendezvous in case Alistair came.

Somehow, too, I must warn off the Buccaneer. How? An ordinary signal lamp would be useless. A pilot approaching at nearly the speed of sound would not be able to read it, even if I could train it on a plane travelling so fast and keep it aimed. He would be past before the shutter had clattered out more than a letter or two.

A distress rocket? *Walvis Bay* carried some big four-inchers which would light the whole sea in red. But could a rocket get into the air quick enough to intercept that speeding jet? Say it rose a mere 100 feet before exploding—how long did that take? How close would the jet be before I spotted it? The Buccaneer might leave the thing half a mile behind by the time it became effective.

I had a Very pistol that fired a red flare from a cartridge. It would be quick enough, but would a thin red streamer be sufficient in itself to scare off the confident Alistair? He might think it merely an addition to the brotherly greeting...

I knew!

When we had taken over the weather ship she had been fitted out as a whaler. She had been bought complete, ready for sea, I had found myself in possession of a miscellaneous collection of equipment, some of which I had decided might come in useful.

In the hold were six big whale-marker canister flares.

Catchers signaled the position of their prey at night with them to mothership helicopters. They were fired electrically.

Alistair might realize when he saw such a dramatic flare that something was seriously amiss. It would stop his onrush towards—what?

Yet—one fired on board would be a danger. The flaming burst could well set the ship alight...the radiosonde balloon platform! We had deliberately isolated it from possible entanglements to give the weather balloons free ascent. It was the ideal flare launching pad!

"Number One! I want the bo'sun and three good men up here—at the double!"

Feldman looked startled, but he jumped at my tone.

"Fourie!" I told the inquiring bo'sun who stood with his team in streaming oilskins. "I want one of those whale-marker canister flares from No. 1 hold, Get it up aloft and lash it to the radiosonde platform..."

"What...!" exploded Feldman behind me. I ignored him. I could not trust myself in front of the crew.

Fourie grinned. "'Guy Fawkes' night, sir? Remember when we tried out the first one down south—a real tit of an explosion..."

The men were grinning too.

"Don't blow yourself up on the way," I responded. "Take it easy and hang on to the bloody thing—all of you. The ship's bouncing like a drunken impala in these seas. That detonator..."

Fourie threw a shabby little salute. "Not to worry, sir. She's as good as fixed."

The team made off.

Six-thirty.

Half an hour to the rendezvous!

The sea had built up terrifyingly. The wind simply tore the water up. All the devils of the deep were unleashed in the darkness. It was this malignant quality of the sea, something I had never witnessed even during the worst storms in the Southern Ocean, which awed the three of us on the bridge into a still more frigid silence: even through the icy, pouring rain the frost-white of tormented water would show when *Walvis Bay* rose to the top of a wave, before making a slewing, sickening descent into the trough. She seemed more under water than afloat; yet, as far as I could judge, we had so far lost only a few stanchions and some loose gear which had not been securely lashed. I had had no further damage reports from the two technicians, Miller and Taylor; perhaps Nick Scannel's ingenuity had saved the delicate apparatus. The flimsy radiosonde hut abaft the funnel was still standing, mainly, I think, because we were taking the run of the sea slightly on the starboard bow and the heavy bridge structure formed a protection against the hundreds of tons of water which continually swept the whaler.

The battle was on in deadly earnest.

After sunset, I had had a curious, mainly instinctive feeling that *Walvis Bay* had been actually travelling faster over the ground than the thirteen knots I had ordered. I had nothing specific to account for this feeling. Any land observations were out of the question: the strip of maelstrom between *Walvis Bay* and the land held up an impenetrable curtain of darkness, rain and driving spray. The Agulhas Current was credited with a five-knot maximum, but I had felt earlier that it was pushing southwards faster than that, battling the counter-current and the gale, bearing *Walvis Bay* along with it, and masking my dead-reckoning still further.

Walvis Bay gave three short staggering leaps across three white-tops and then, like a man losing his balance after a frantic attempt to keep his feet, collided with her starboard side into a fourth, huge roller. I felt the shuddering wince of metal high up aft. The vibration rippled through the superstructure. I could see only sea through the bridge windows.

Feldman turned to me, his face mottled with fear. There was no need to voice his unspoken question. Miller or Taylor would be here soon enough to tell us.

It was Miller. "The radar antenna's gone!" His voice had a hysterical edge. "We hit something..."

"Something hit us," I retorted. "It was the sea—just plain sea. Pull yourself together, man! Where is Taylor?"

Miller took a grip of himself, but he could not look beyond the bridge windows.

"Lying on the floor—out," he said. "I think he needs a doctor..."

"He doesn't," I snapped. "Try him with a shot of rum from the wardroom locker." I wanted Feldman out of the way too, If the two men's hysteria got loose among the others, it could mean the end of the ship.

"See to it," I yelled to Feldman above the noise of the gale. "Take a look at the wind gauge as you come back."

Feldman was back sooner than I thought. The bridge smelt of rum. He had interpreted my orders liberally.

"Force 10—gusting 65 miles an hour," he reported.

A whole gale, that rare animal, a whole, whole gale!

Now there was a new alignment of sea and gale, by contrast to what I had felt before: the wind was able, by its power alone, to hold back the progress of the weather ship, unlike her previous forward rush under the current's impulse. The powerful bridge and enclosed forward superstructure became a metal sail held up against the wind. As she reared to the crests I could feel the gale take hold and thrust the small ship bodily backwards and sideways; Jubela's shirt was soaked, despite the iciness outside, as he tried to hold her on course. It was impossible to see the length of the foredeck because of the rain and breaking seas. Had another ship loomed up ahead, we could not have seen it in time to avoid a collision. I comforted myself that all shipping had cleared out of the area by now. The run of the sea had changed, too: it struck strongly from the southwest into the teeth of the master Agulhas stream, breaking up its customary southwards flow into a tumult of jerking seas which became progressively higher and steeper. Judging by the ship's motion, it seemed likely that she was actually standing still in her progress over the ground, despite the unreduced engine speed.

I checked the clock.

Six-forty-five.

Barely fifteen minutes to the rendezvous!

The quarter of an hour was about the limit I could go on flogging *Walvis Bay*. I would have to slacken speed soon; at any moment I expected to hear that the complicated satellite observing gear had gone. It was not the gear alone: the very fabric of the ship was under pressure. On occasion I wondered whether she would dive headlong into the next wave and never come up again. She was not riding and throwing her head clear any more, but ducking into the sea with a tiring action, a growing unwillingness to rise.

I did not hate the southwest wind that night. Not as I do now. Nor did I hate the southwesterly run of the sea. I did not fear when the wind gusted over sixty knots. At that time they had still not touched her, Tafline. I was seeing them for the first time as nakedly and unfettered as *Waratah* had seen them for the last time. I was a sailor at sea that night, and she was safely ashore in Cape Town; we had not, she and I, joined our forces to challenge the scend of the sea. I was seeing professionally, detachedly, how much strain a hull, two engines and a crew could stand in the face of the worst storm I had ever encountered. I was pushing all to the limit, but I knew there was a limit, and that it was in sight. Douglas Fairlie and Captain Ilbery would also have judged what the limits were—or did they ever have the opportunity to do so? That is what I had to find out tonight.

Now, as I think of it, the southwest wind carries its message of fear and I cringe away from it because of her, and my heart misgives me when the wind scale rises. I fear because of what it did to her, and the cold terror comes to me, as did the ice then on the driving rain.

That night, however, I was sure, confident: I had weighed the opposing forces, so I thought, and although the margin was small, there was still a margin.

I ordered Feldman, "Put on the upper deck floodlight. I also want every light in the ship switched on."

He gaped incredulously, simply repeating my order without inflexion in his voice. "Put on the upper deck floodlight. All lights in the ship to be switched on—aye, aye, sir."

There was a kind of cold automatism in my actions. I even debated quickly whether I should not fire a second flare. It would be madness to fly over the sea...

I knew he would come.

I had no real idea of *Walvis Bay*'s position. My dead reckoning was pure guesswork. On the chart it looked businesslike, but I myself considered that we had been driven much farther south than it indicated and that the whaler was now somewhere between the Clan Lindsay Rocks and Cape Morgan, a treacherous headland whose shallow waters stretch out to sea for about half the distance—five miles—*Walvis Bay* was supposed to be from the coastline. It was impossible to compute how near or far we were from land.

I had to inject some morale into the jellying Feldman. He might do anything with the ship while I went up aloft to signal Alistair.

"No. 1," I said, trying to keep the contempt out of my voice. "You've been wondering why I have pushed the ship on a night like this, and why I disregarded the storm warning."

He simply gazed owlishly at me.

I had to make the escapade look good, on the surface at any rate. My results would have to justify this lie—later.

"I have sealed orders, which I am permitted to reveal at 1845 hours," I said. I almost laughed at my own pompousness. I sounded like Feldman himself.

"The Buccaneer squadron is due to make mock attacks tonight on the main South African ports. My brother will lead the attack on East London shortly after seven this evening..." Feldman was taken aback. I could almost see the slow tumblers clicking into place in his brain.

"Alistair and I discussed the possibility of a storm when he came aboard in Durban. We—that is, the authorities, my brother and myself—arranged that this ship would be used as a datum point for the East London attack. I had to go have her in position by seven o'clock, whatever the conditions. It's nearly that now. My brother will pick up the ship on his approach run. Hence the lights. Because of the storm, I decided on the canister flare, just to make sure he spotted us."

Jubela grunted as though the wheel were hurting him.

I added quickly, "The Buccaneer will be flying very low, very fast. He intends to come in under the radar defenses."

Feldman glanced at the clock. Five-to-seven.

"I'll get the lights on right away, sir."

I breathed a sigh of relief. At least, he was acting now like a seaman and a man. The lie had been necessary, I told myself, to get him back on his feet.

Feldman returned. "All lights on, sir. Upper deck floodlight on. Flare plunger ready."

My anxiety slipped out before I could check myself. "I want you to keep a tight eye on the plane, once he's passed over."

Feldman had regained his poise and correctness. "If he comes from any quarter but ahead, I won't see him from the bridge, sir. Especially in this."

Two minutes to seven!

Hurry!

"Come up aloft with me," I said. "Let's move!"

It was impossible to keep one's feet on the cramped section of deck near the radiosonde hut—miraculously still standing—without hanging on. The orange canister flare, the size of a football, was still firmly in position. Firing wires led back to the hut. The wind had taken on a solid roar: speech was out of the question. We could not hear the remains of the radar sweep bashing itself to fragments directly above our heads. The whaler was completely awash and it was easy to see the reason for her lethargy: she could not shake off one wave's burden before the next overtook her.

I needed both my hands free to fire the flare. I gestured to Feldman. He grabbed a bight of rope to lash me to the lifelines. A lurch brought us crashing together shoulder to shoulder, throwing us to the deck. I managed, somehow, to keep the firing plunger from smashing on the metal deck. I pulled myself upright and splayed myself against the wall of the hut, clasping the plunger against my chest.

It was Feldman who saw the Buccaneer first.

"There she is!"

His words were blown away by the wind, but his gesture was plain. I thought for a moment it was a ship, but Feldman was right. The lights were coming in fast, winking and blinking under the plane's belly and atop the high tail which is such a distinguishing feature of the Buccaneer.

It was Alistair all right.

I jammed down the firing pin.

The ship, the mast, the funnel, the sea—even, it seemed, the pencil-like shafts of rain—stood out in soft rose, not red. The giant Roman candle effect appeared to color the swirl of low-flying cloud. With a silence that was uncanny, the aircraft hurtled at the ship, so low that as it swept overhead the streaming wet fuselage was suffused in rose light, through which I caught a glimpse of the blinking red aircraft light and the five-pointed symbol of the South African Air Force, representing the five bastions of the Cape of Good Hope Castle. The Buccaneer was certainly living up to its reputation as the lowest-flying strike aircraft in the world. The high tail flashed past.

Feldman was excited, grinning. He shoved his mouth close to my ear. "She's going to turn...coming back...look..."

His words and the storm were drowned momentarily by a shattering roar. The noise of a jet engine, when a plane is travelling as fast as Alistair was, seems to be slightly behind it. The thin metal wall of the radiosonde hut vibrated like an eardrum.

Half-dazzled by the flare, I saw the flashing lights tilt slightly as the Buccaneer began to bank to port. Alistair, having located and identified *Walvis Bay*, was about to make a wide circle and come round for a second beat-up of the ship. My danger message had got across!

How long were the plane's lights visible at its speed and our reduced range of vision—five seconds? Ten seconds? Less?

We could still see them winking.

Then they went out, as if they had been switched off.

CHAPTER 6

Feldman, looking strangely large in the unreal light, turned to me, gesturing and grinning that the incident was over. At least he seemed to have snapped out of his previous attitude. He made a wide sweep of his free arm, hanging on with the other, as if to indicate that he had expected Alistair to have completed his circuit and come back over *Walvis Bay*. Then he grinned again and shrugged his shoulders, surprised that he had not done so.

I still faced the direction in which the Buccaneer had disappeared. The flare burned lower.

With the same sort of slow shock that one feels in the presence of an inescapable, evil reality—I felt now as I did once when I came face-to-face with a black mamba rearing man-high on a forest path in Natal—I knew I would never see Alistair alive again.

The Buccaneer's lights had winked his last farewell to me; I had watched him go to his death. How or why, I did not know, but the instinctive realization was there, as surely as the moment Tafline stepped under the photograph of the *Waratah*, she became part of its tragedy. In the numbness of that moment on the icy sea-and-rain-drenched deck, I turned to the recollection of her in my cabin. I, in reconstructing the *Waratah*'s night of doom, had brought doom to my brother, and added yet another victim to her charnel-house. The power of the seas was puny alongside that other force, which stood with its headman's axe dripping and bloody in the night.

Feldman was shaking me and shouting. I could not hear what he was saying. A whole hill of water had fallen on top of the gallant little weather ship as I stood numb. The flare was out. Even on the upper deck, I was waist-deep in water, and the lifeline dragged at my oilskins. The floodlight still threw its bright clinical white light over the scene: even high up the ship seemed deep in water, scarcely with the strength to ride above the waves. The screws had a newer, higher note when next they broke clear—soon they would tear themselves out of their bearings. One more wave like that at present speed and *Walvis Bay* would dive down and never come up again.

I yelled back at Feldman and indicated the bridge. His schoolboy grin was gone; he was grey, afraid again. I, too, was afraid. My earlier cool, detached assessment of force and counter-force was gone: all at once I was fighting something bigger. I could not put a name to the sinister force. I must throw everything into saving the whaler. Her speed was madness. I had held on to it for too long.

We groped and scrambled our way along the lifelines to regain the bridge.

Jubela was quicksilvered in sweat. He gave one quick look at my face. He did not speak.

I grabbed the engine-room telegraph.

"Half speed ahead!"

Feldman's relief was overwhelming.

If I was to save *Walvis Bay*, I must break off the *Waratah*'s course. The very strength of the sea and the gale forced the logic of a southwesterly course upon me. That course common to all the tragedies—southwest! It drummed through and through my mind. That is the way death lay, whatever the other dictates might be, however telling they might sound.

I must break for the open seal!

The risk of turning away from meeting the seas head-on was great, but the whaler's low freeboard and streamlined superstructure gave her a sporting chance. She had, moreover, that splendid flared bow designed specially to cope with the huge Antarctic seas.

For one moment I hung on my decision.

Bashee!

What did it imply? *Waratah* had vanished—south of the Bashee. *Walvis Bay*'s position, although highly uncertain, was certain in one respect only—she was south of the Bashee. Death had come to my father and brother—south of the Bashee. What did it mean?

I rejected the doubt sabotaging the precious moments.

"Bring her round! Gently, Jubela, if you value your life! Course—south, if you can. Watch it, for God's sake and ours! Choose your moment!"

Jubela nodded helplessly at the bridge windows. Through them, one could not see even the foredeck.

A racing driver, they say, steers by the seat of his pants. Yachting is like racing, but one steers by the soles of one's feet. The master helmsmen of Captain Ilbery's day of sail preferred to stand barefooted at the wheel—without a sou'wester if they could—so that they could feel the motion of the ship under their feet and the way of the wind on the nape of their necks. When a yacht is being hard pushed, one can detect the slight movement of the deck seams; these things are still more meaningful than all the instruments invented.

Walvis Bay was riding easier now that the way was off her, but I felt sure that we were being pushed backwards by the storm.

"Now!"

But Jubela shook his head, poised slightly on the balls of his feet.

The radio warning buzzed. Before Feldman could go, it buzzed peremptorily a second time. I jerked my head for him to go. All my attention was on the ship.

The sea poured over the bow and sluiced down the deck. As she rose, the wind threw it bodily against the bridge structure and the rain added its quota of icy wetness.

She sank in the trough and started to roll to starboard. Jubela flicked the wheel to port, eased it back, and flicked it again to meet it head-on as the next roller hit her. Water poured over the ship again, but this time the direction was slightly more on the bow.

Walvis Bay had gained a few precious points of the compass towards safety.

Again, Jubela waited.

I went forward to the compass. South-southwest. That was better! *Walvis Bay* seemed to be regaining her resilience too. There was a faint improvement in her motion, although she rolled more heavily now that her bow was away from the eye of the gale.

Feldman came back.

"Urgent signal to you from Weather Bureau, sir."

I took the paper and turned from the compass. I started towards the port bridge windows, the way I was trying to edge her seawards, My attention was on the ship. I tried to penetrate the driving water. My eyes dropped to the signal.

> Urgent. Weather Bureau to *Walvis Bay*. Report your position immediately...

The deck canted forward.

Walvis Bay dropped her bows like a stone.

Until now, she had been a ship laboring and fighting. Now she was out of control.

I was thrown off my feet into the corner of the bridge. I had been too late in my turn-away! The name burned in my brain—*Waratah*!

Walvis Bay was making her final dive to her death!

As I sprawled, I had a momentary glimpse of Jubela throwing up his right hand to protect his face, as if warding off a blow. With the other, he still held the wheel. There was an awful sensation of the ship falling literally forward and downward.

There was a tremendous crash, and the bridge windows splintered in, as if by bomb-blast. The lights went. I heard a heavy thud inside the bridge itself, and Feldman screamed as if in pain. Water—hundreds of tons of sea—came pouring into the shattered bridge.

Still the ship nose-dived at that impossible angle.

Waratah!

I was picked up by the wall of water and carried headlong aft as it swept through the open door at the rear of the bridge, down the companionway into my cabin. I clutched at something metal and hung on against the rush of water. As the rudder lost its power to control her, so the seas took command. Now, as *Walvis Bay* dived, I could feel a frightening loss of control; she was also slewing sideways as she dived. With the weight of water pressing her down thundering into her, she would be on her side soon.

I hauled myself into a crouching position and threw my body forward to where I knew the wheel must be. The steep forward angle helped me, but the water catapulting through the broken windows hit me in the chest like a blow.

The jar of the spinning wheel which I grabbed was almost as great as the water crashing in. Mine were instinctive movements; there was no time to think or reason. All I knew was that I must hold her, try and bring her head round.

The deck levelled under my feet.

Still the water poured in.

For one irrational moment I thought the whaler was floating level under water, and that she would quickly fill and go to the bottom on an even keel. Strange, too, the wild motion of the past hours had eased. She rode, not easily, but dead...

Feldman screamed from the other side of the bridge. I started to turn a split second from my fight with the wheel.

I stopped, transfixed.

Dead ahead, through the gaping windows, loomed something big and black, right in the whaler's path.

I spun the wheel to port, giving her the full weight of water and all the strength of the gale to try and bring her head clear.

Then I saw nothing.

Water burst through the bridge openings and the ship lay over again, tiredly, heavily. The sea tried to pluck my hands from the wheel. Yet I sensed that her head had fallen off the wind and the bow seemed to be sheering away from the danger—whatever it was— quicker than I could have hoped.

I felt, but did not see, the next sea. This time, would the game little ship roll over on her side? Or would there be a sickening crash and rending of metal which meant that she had gone bows-on into the obstacle in her path? I felt the roll begin to port—I detected that easier motion somewhere—and I waited, cowering, for the next hill of water to crown that which now pinned her down.

Walvis Bay rolled farther.

The sea held back its fatal punch.

Hundreds of tons of water cleared themselves off the decks in that life-giving roll; somewhere aft I heard, above the gale, the tearing of metal.

Feldman screamed again in agony behind me, and some heavy object rolled, bumped and thumped.

Walvis Bay came upright.

Still the sea did not strike.

Why?

I was flabbergasted at the relative calmness of the sea. The gale still brought the icy rain and spray in bucketfuls through the gaps and *Walvis Bay* rose tiredly at first—as if herself cringing from that final crushing weight of water—and then more optimistically. Then she was on an even keel, sharp, back on her feet, fighting. She completed that long purgative roll to starboard and I caught the glimmer of clear deck below me.

Where was that thing in our path? Whatever it was there was no sign of it now.

Walvis Bay rose confidently to the next wave.

She had won through.

The bridge was a shambles. It was still a foot deep in water, which I could hear thundering into the bowels of the ship. There was broken glass everywhere. I tried to see our course, but the compass had been stove in.

Something heavy bumped behind me. I risked a glance to see what it was. The barrel of the heavy winch below the bridge, which in her whaling days had been used to secure whales after harpooning, had been torn free by that crazed dive of hers and pitched bodily through the front of the bridge. Had I not moved away from the compass when I did, it might have killed me. Feldman had not been so lucky: the flying winch had struck him a glancing blow, breaking his left shoulder and pinning him against the deck until *Walvis Bay*'s life-giving roll had freed him. He was lying amidst the glass and water, groaning, his right hand at his damaged left shoulder. Jubela, spitting seawater, was half on his feet, cut and bleeding about the head.

The engine-room voice-pipe shrilled incessantly. At least something was working! Scannel was not a man to get rattled easily, but there was an overtone of fear in his voice.

"What are you trying to do to us, skipper? I thought this was a whaler, not a submarine..."

I explained quickly, at the same time leaning forward to try and assess the damage on the deck below me.

"Get four men on to the foredeck, quickly!" I told him. "Lash a tarpaulin over the deck where the winch was..."

"Was?"

"It looped the loop and left a hole in the deck you could drive a car through. Caught Feldman up here," I got out hastily. "Get the men up quick, before another sea puts paid to us."

"There's enough of the ocean down here already," growled Scannel. "She's half full of water."

"Pumps...?"

"I've got them going full blast. I don't know for sure, but perhaps we're holding our own. Lot still coming down from your part of the world."

I quickly sketched what had happened to the bridge. My cabin and the wardroom were probably flooded too.

"What's that noise?" I asked.

There seemed to be a jarring thumping coming from outside the hull. The whole ship reverberated with it. I had new anxieties forward of the hole in the deck.

"The foremast has come adrift," I told Scannel further. "Get another team up and frap the stays before it goes over the side altogether. Seems to have a couple of feet of play from here."

Amidst the stream of orders, I still had room for puzzlement. There remained that curious lack of punch about the sea. The waves looked the same, the wind looked the same, but nonetheless they seemed to lack the power to break and destroy.

"It's not the mast making that racket," Scannel retorted grimly. "Something's hammering the hull from the outside."

His voice was drowned by a vibrating crash which I felt on the bridge. The enclosed space of the engine room magnified it like a sounding-board.

I heard Scannel shouting orders below, above the crash and bump of something heavy against the port quarter. At the same time, *Walvis Bay* started to slew against the power of the rudder. I corrected her quickly. I guessed what had happened. For some reason or other, one screw was out of action.

"Port screw," Scannel confirmed. "Bit into something solid. Either badly chipped or smashed. Can't tell."

"Rock...?"

"No, something's beating the hell out of the hull. Reckon it's one of those fancy crane things we took aboard in Durban."

The Van Veen grab with its chain-controlled bucket—like a small steam shovel, Alistair had said—was housed on the port rail.

"Can you be spared from the engine-room for five minutes?" I whipped out. "I'll get aft there to the grab. See you there."

"Aye aye."

Smit was gaping at the wreck of the bridge. "She's chasing her tail—one prop's out," I told him. Jubela, on his feet now, still looked stunned.

"Try and hold her steady," I went on. "No course. Anything—just keep the water out of her while we make some jury repairs."

"Came past the gyro gear on my way here," replied Smit. "It's gone for a Burton..."

"It'll keep," I snapped back. "It's the ship now above anything."

I knelt and examined Feldman cursorily. His face was strained, white, terrified. He looked fearfully at the heavy winch barrel on the gratings.

"Don't let it come at me again," he mouthed. "Keep it away, for Christ's sake. Not again."

I waited until it rolled towards us, then I guided it with my foot towards the doorway. It skidded and jammed itself across the lintel.

Scannel was waiting for me at the stern with a torch. *Walvis Bay* still rolled heavily in the seas, but nothing like the previous quantity of water was coming aboard. Scannel's light showed what was left of the Van Veen grab. It had been welded as a triangle of steel bars: one upright from the rail, one at the top jutting out horizontally, and a double support running upward and outward to form the third leg of the triangle. There were big block-and-pulleys at the top and at the extremity from which the bucket grab was suspended on chains. The two projecting bars had been twisted and buckled out of recognition by the sea and now trailed in the water. These had fouled the screw.

Walvis Bay dipped for a lee roll and then started to come back.

"Nick! Duck! Watch out!"

A shower of sparks arced round towards us from the direction of the stern. The bucket grab, snapping and gaping with the ship's movement, swung round from the remnants of its support, crashing and banging the steel deck straight towards the engineer. If those clamping jaws fastened on an arm, they would bite it off like a mechanical shark.

Scannel threw himself on the deck and the torch went out. There was a crash and a clatter, another shower of sparks, and then the wild thing was past.

I leapt to Scannel's side. The grab revolved out over the stern again; in a moment it would crash back in a malicious, deadly circle.

My grip slipped on his wet leather lumber-jacket which he had thrown over his dungarees, but I scrabbled and snatched him to the safety of the lifelines, out of reach of the swinging grab. Scannel was shaking from cold and fright.

"We've got to get that thing secured before we can attempt anything else," I said quickly.

"Aye," replied Scannel. "It could have taken my head off—thanks."

Again the whaler rolled. We cowered back, waiting for the clatter and the sparks to go past.

"Now!"

We raced for the rail. I reached out with a securing rope for the chains at the top of the grab, but the ship heeled and it slipped from my grasp.

"Get back!"

We dodged to safety while the grab made another spark-trailing orbit.

"Next round, hang on to my legs—it's just out of reach," I told Scannel.

We waited our moment and sprinted to the rail. Had the supporting bars been in place, I could have used them to hold on and secure the grab with my free hand, but they were adrift, crashing and banging against the ship's stern-plates.

Scannel took me round the waist as if in a rugby tackle. At the top of the pendulum swing of the bucket, I whipped the rope's end through the chains at the top. I tugged it fast. It took only a moment then to bring the grab itself inboard and lash it firmly to the shattered remains of its base structure.

Scannel flashed his light over the wreckage. "You'll have to hang on to me this time," he remarked grimly. "Hell, what a shambles! This will need an oxy-acetylene cutter."

The sea came over and drenched us.

"Can you keep the flame burning?" I asked anxiously.

"Got to," he jerked out. "If those cables or chains wrap themselves round the screw..." he gestured.

"One's already out of action," I said.

"I don't know how bad it is—I stopped her before it could do itself more damage," he replied. He took a hard, long look at me. "I guess you'll want everything she has, to get through the night?"

"Yes, Nick. We're in trouble. Big trouble. But one dud screw or not, if another sizzler like that big wave hits us, we've had it. Just say your prayers—if there's time. She's got a hole in the foredeck the size of Table Mountain. No tarpaulin is going to be worth a damn in another sea like that."

Scannel's eyes were sizing up the job professionally as he spoke. "It wasn't like any wave I've ever encountered. The engine-room floor suddenly nose-dived. It was like putting her head down an escalator."

I found my hands shaking on the lifelines, reaction to the dive like a near-miss car smash. Deliberately, consciously, I crushed all thought of the *Waratah* out of my mind. I must not be hamstrung in coping with our mortal peril by shadows from the past.

"Put that light on the gravity corer on the other rail," I told Scannel. "Maybe we'll have to cut that one away too. Not such heavy gear as this one, though."

Scannel laughed mirthlessly. "Take a look." Across the wet deck, only a few stumps of metal showed where the gravity corer had been.

"The sea's done that job pretty well for us, but for this we'll want an oxy-acetylene cutter—le Roux can help. He's a good boy. Won't panic."

"I'll wait," I said briefly. "Feldman's injured. Smit's trying to sort things out on the bridge."

I tried to get my bearings as Scannel staggered off along the bucking lifeline. On the exposed deck the gale was penetrating, Arctic. *Walvis Bay* rolled heavily, but still the seas were not sweeping the decks as they had done before the great wave. Something seemed to be taming them. The crests still broke aboard, but *Walvis Bay*, with all the weight of water inside her, was riding them, not plunging headlong.

The fear rose in my throat at the thought of the black shape into which *Walvis Bay* had so nearly plunged. I took a grip of my nerves and edged over to the windward side of the deck, trying to pierce the darkness, trying to bring to rational, everyday terms the thing I thought I had seen. The gale still tore its Force 10 swathe from the southwest. Tears streamed down my face as I held my eyes into it to make sure it held the same quarter. *Walvis Bay* was edging slowly towards the deep sea—towards safety. Had the savagery of the seas lessened, I asked myself, because there was already deeper water under her? Had we side-stepped some diabolical sea-bottom contour which lashed the waves to such madness?

I wiped the spray and the rain from my eyes with the back of my hand and tried again to find the black mass which had stood in our path. For perhaps half a minute I could see before the iciness brought a fresh gush of tears. Nothing. Could I find the place again? The compass was hopelessly wrecked; more than before, even, my dead reckoning was pure guesswork. We could be five miles in any direction. I turned my face from the scalpel of wind and spray. Had it simply been a trick of the light which had made a big sea loom to take shape like...I dared not bring the thought out from shadows as Avernal as the darkness around the battling ship.

I heard Scannel shouting to me from the other side of the deck, near the grab. I made my way back cautiously. He and young le Roux were sitting astride a heavy gas cylinder. If that broke free, I thought quickly, it could be as big a menace as the swinging grab had been. A crushing impact against a broken-off stanchion could explode the high-compression gas inside...

Scannel had not forgotten to bring a strong light as well as a rope.

"Get a turn round her," he panted. "Can't work if this thing's going to go wild."

I wormed a noose over the steel neck of the bottle, round a couple of severed stanchions, and then back over the smooth cylinder barrel.

"Every time that spar dogs into the ship, I die a little," Scannel remarked. "It's bad enough here, but you want to hear it below in the engine-room. I'll bet there are some holes punched in her plates already."

He worked deftly as he spoke, trying to ignite the torch. Le Roux and I huddled close to form a windbreak. The cutter suddenly burst into bright flame, hissing and spitting in the rain and spray.

"I'll go for the big boy first," said the engineer. He looked apprehensively at the grab I had made fast. "I'd really like to ditch that to begin with, but if I cut it loose it may only get fouled up with the clutter under the stern. Then we double our problem."

Holding the spitting, blue-tongued flame in his left hand, he steadied himself against the buckled rail with his right. He strained to see where to begin.

"Bring the light closer, skipper," he called. "This will be trickier even than I thought."

I shone the beam on the twisted mass. The main three-inch heavy tube was so contorted that it seemed impossible that the sea could have wrought it. Strong, flexible steel cable, used for lowering the grab hundreds of fathoms deep to the ocean floor, was snarled about it like a knotted ball of wool. The winching device which was integral to it had been unseated from its bolt and seemed inextricably mixed up with the lower portions of the crane. No part of it would ever be fit for use again.

The three of us ducked as a wave crest toppled over the rail on the lee roll; again, I was surprised at the sea's lack of viciousness. The waves were no smaller, but they seemed to be pawing at the ship now rather than punching.

When the water cleared, Scannel hung over the rail. "I'm going over head-first, skipper," he told me calmly. "You'll have to hang on to my legs while I work. Piet, boy, get yourself alongside the skipper. When you see a wave coming, shout. I'll hand you the torch. Shove it above your head—keep it out of the water—do anything, but keep it alight."

"You'll get drowned, Nick," I objected. "This is a modern variation on keel-hauling a man."

Scannel brushed aside my anxiety. "If you yell in good time, I'll take a long breath. Getting wet doesn't matter. We can't play musical chairs with each wave, back and forth to the deck and over the side again each time. Every time that wreckage bashes her, our chances of seeing tomorrow get slimmer."

"Right," I replied. "But don't object if I recommend you for the George Cross or whatever they offer engineers in tight spots."

Scannel already had his flashlight on the heaving water, judging his moment to go overside. The water looked murky, oily, almost as if someone had drawn a thin sheet of plastic over its surface.

"Here we go!"

Scannel stuck the cutting torch, where the metal joins the rubber tubes from the cylinder, between his teeth and plunged himself full-length over the rail; I held his lower legs and feet, and young le Roux craned over to snatch the vital light from being doused.

Had it been a matter of cutting away the gravity corer on the other side of the stern, our task would have been far easier. There was a great deal more water coming aboard on the lee roll (where we were) than on the weather roll opposite. The cold, too, made movements stiff and hands clumsy; I worked my jaws to keep my face from freezing.

Scannel called to le Roux to open the gas cock. The whole scene flared into unnatural, incandescent brightness as flame bit into metal, throwing up showers of blue-white sparks.

In that sudden brightness, I spotted the next wave.

"Nick! The torch—quick!"

The engineer was almost through the thick pipe. Despite my warning, he went on cutting, using every last second. The sea started its upward heave. The seared metal support broke and swung, bringing with it a flurry of flaring steel which exploded in a sizzling cascade over Scannel's neck and chest.

The wave broke.

I had a momentary glimpse of his agonized face: he swiveled sideways and upwards and thrust the torch clear of the water into le Roux's grip; he rammed it high above his head.

The rail dipped under. Water engulfed us.

It cleared. I reached forward and dragged Scannel bodily back on to the deck. His left shoulder was a polka-dot of burn-holes. He would carry those scars for the rest of his life.

He managed to speak. "Let me get back—give me the torch! I'll have her completely free this time..."

"Nick—no—"

He shook his head, as if not trusting himself to speak through the pain. He gestured for me to take his legs. He snatched the torch from le Roux and dived, so it seemed, headlong over the side once more.

Again the bright light lit the scene unnaturally white. Then, miraculously soon, Scannel signaled to be pulled back.

"There's only the cable left, and that's nothing," he said quietly.

"Here it comes!"

We ducked for another sea, but le Roux hung on, standing upright.

"Good boy!" exclaimed Scannel after the roller had passed, "Now for the cable."

Skillfully and quickly he sent the flame through the tangle of wire and chains. The wind drowned its splash.

Scannel grimaced in agony.

"Nick," I said urgently, "I'll come below to the engine room and fix you up, We've got to get something on those burns right away..."

"I did," he winced lopsidedly. "Seawater. Try it some time. The hot so hot and the cold so cold. No, skipper, someone else can patch me up—you're needed to save the ship, not play nursemaid to me."

He was right. *Walvis Bay* now had a sporting chance. It was up to me to exploit what Scannel had achieved.

"Okay," I answered, "but, Nick, that doesn't mean "I don't appreciate..."

The pain and reaction were hitting him. "Save the speech for a calm sea," he said.

"Can we risk that screw?" I asked.

"We'll try, anyway, and see what happens." He snapped out the torch, "I'll get on the bridge blower as soon as I can. Pumps, too. We've had a lucky break from the calmer seas. Just depends whether that tarpaulin holds over the hole in the deck..."

I groped my way along the lifelines to the foredeck below the bridge. The men were putting the final touches to sealing the ragged hole where previously the winch had stood. Ends of the double tarpaulin still flapped and snapped, but my team was on top. Apart from another mammoth wave, it would keep out enough sea to enable the pumps to cope with what did make its way below.

I headed for the bridge.

Smit had rigged a couple of storm lanterns overhead and both he and Jubela were heavily oil-skinned against the driving rain. He had cleared away some of the glass and seen Feldman below to the wardroom. He had also found a small boat's compass somewhere and had taped it over the smashed binnacle.

"Do you think we'll make it, sir?" Smit was more excited than fearful.

I dodged a straight answer. "How's she steering?"

"It would be a big help if we could get the port screw working."

Walvis Bay's head seemed to be pointing somewhere east of south, but the tiny compass made it difficult to tell with any degree of accuracy.

"We'll try," I replied. "There may be a chunk out of it, Scannel thinks, but we still could get by if the shaft's not messed up."

"Better than nothing at all, sir."

I picked up the voice-pipe. "Nick? Can we risk that port screw yet?"

The engineer's voice was tight with reaction. "Aye. But we'll have to cut speed on the starboard prop first. Quarter-speed to start with. Maybe we can work up a bit more later, if the other can take it."

Jubela gestured to me as I spoke.

I, too, felt the change of motion. *Walvis Bay* rose sharply to the next sea, quite unlike her longer, lazier motion a little while before. The white crest crashed aboard and sluiced to port, with the earlier characteristic deep lee roll. She lifted her bows well, but I could detect the inhibiting weight of water inside her.

I nodded to Jubela. "Nick," I went on. "The sea's beginning to hit her again. I don't know why, but it is. How soon can you pump the water out of her? I need all the buoyancy I can find."

"Couple of hours," he answered. "Depends on how much comes via the tarpaulin. Skipper—here comes your port screw."

There was a squeal of agonized metal and a heavy, thumping vibration. It struck right through the hull to the bridge. The voice-pipe dropped with a crash the other end and Scannel yelled orders to stop the engine. The shattering noise stopped.

Scannel came on the voice-pipe.

"That's the sort of scream you should have let out just now if you weren't such a bloody spartan," I told the engineer.

The engineer was in no mood to respond. I knew how much that damaged prop hurt him.

"She's bad, skipper—very bad," he said. "The shaft must be bent—what else, only a dockyard could know."

I made my decision. "Nick," I said, "I'm going to heave to. The sea's gone back to what it was before the big 'un hit us. I can't hold her all night with the engines like this. See if you can coax that starboard prop into giving me just enough to help hold her head into the run of the sea. I'll stream a sea anchor and a drum of oil. The oil will soften the waves and keep them off the decks, maybe."

CHAPTER 7

I fought, hour by hour, for the life of the ship through the long night that followed. What I did not know was that the news of the storm I was challenging had brought as great a storm, emotionally, to Tafline in Cape Town. Her storm, like mine, held its secrets: when the shockwaves of her long night were over, she admitted consciously that she was in love.

It began, she told me afterwards, like mine, with the Buccaneer. She heard the radio announcement that a Buccaneer had gone missing on a training flight. Aboard *Walvis Bay*, all radios were dead. The main set was out because the radio hut had been smashed. All portable sets had been flooded and their batteries swamped. Until daylight it was impossible to find new ones in the 'tween-decks shambles.

She had frozen at the Buccaneer announcement. She saw intuitively behind the standard, cautious, well-used phrases: she guessed it was Alistair.

A second radio bulletin later increased her own tumult. It described the severity of the great storm I was riding out, hanging between life and death at the end of a wood-and-canvas sea anchor and a drum of oil. We had knocked holes in the drum before getting it overboard to let the oil seep out and try and soften the waves from swamping the laboring weather ship. Nonetheless, all night they broke through the shattered bridge; they cascaded through the hole in the deck; again and again we replaced the torn canvas. Our hands were numbed by the cold. Our nails were ripped. Our flesh bled. The tarpaulin reared, whipped, lashed, like a maniac. Strong men wept and cursed the southwest wind. Again and again it tore away their puny efforts to save themselves.

Then the Weather Bureau stated: "Radio contact with the weather ship *Walvis Bay* in the storm area has been lost."

At that, she had known the answer: *Waratah*!

She had made a long-distance telephone call from Cape Town to the Port Met. Office in Durban. Where, she asked, had I last been heard of? The weatherman told her more than he normally would a stranger. There must have been something in what she said which made him guess how close, how newly close, she was to me. He did not tell her, though, that the Air Force had confided that they held out little hope for the Buccaneer. The search would be their main concern now.

It would have comforted me, that night, to have known of her anxiety, but I did not. All I had was the decision-tapping attrition of icy gale and sea on a mind growing more and more numb as the hammer-blows followed one another unabated. When a pump burned out in some desperate hour of the night, I thought the storm had won. Scannel, disregarding the burns which had turned his upper chest into a Martian red surface of craters and blisters, calmly stripped it down with the unruffled patience and steady hand of a Grand Prix mechanic who sees the race roar past while his driver loses precious race-winning seconds. The pump drew again, and once again we sucked out the life-inhibiting load of water.

The first stunning wave had pitched the steel cabinet with all my *Waratah* material across the cabin on to my bunk. Hurrying below to visit the injured Feldman, I stopped at the sight of it. Like the peace at the heart of every cyclone, the outside roar ceased to exist for me, and telepathically she was there in that moment of exclusion.

I did not try and move the cabinet; maybe it was safer on the bunk than on the floor, where the water from the bridge still sloshed past on its way to the depths of the ship. Beyond a wetting, the documents were in reasonable shape—another chapter of the same story was being written at that moment up above in wind, wave and water! Likewise, my marked chart escaped only with a drenching.

Automatically, I looked at the photograph of the *Waratah*.

Something had been hurled across the cabin; its glass was cracked clean across.

The ship's wind direction and velocity gauge on the top deck had been wrecked; the cabin repeater pointed statically, ironically— southwest. The books she had taken from my shelf lay in a pulpy mess on the floor.

Where, Tafline had asked, had contact with me been lost? Bashee, the weatherman replied. South of the Bashee. There had been no need for her to hear any more then.

She had thanked him mechanically, put down the telephone, and gone over to the window of her flat. The Mouillé Point lighthouse nearby always used to flick an arrow of light against the flat wall, and she screwed up her eyes against it now. She loved the lighthouse as her Welsh grandfather had loved the one he had tended. Tafline—the Welsh ancestry had given her that soft name, and somehow the sixth sense of the Celt enabled her to identify herself so closely with the mysterious fate of the old ship. She loved the sea too, a derivative from Viking blood on her father's side. The Olens had come from Sweden to South Africa sixty years before and had pioneered a Scandinavian settlement in the Transvaal. It was this seafaring streak which let her understand, with almost Arab fatalism, the ocean drama being played out of which I was part. Below her window in the light winter rain car headlights made a home-going procession. She watched. She did not weep; she did not do any more than make that one telephone call. The cinemagoers, the diners, the dancers, would sleep tonight, but she would not.

There was a last news bulletin that night. The Buccaneer, *Walvis Bay* and the great storm took top place. Growing concern, said the radio, was being felt for the safety of the ship and the jet. Despite repeated attempts to make contact with the weather ship, there had been no response.

Feldman lay half-conscious in the wardroom, mumbling, only half-aware of his surroundings. We strapped him to the bunk to protect his damaged side from the ship's lurches. He was our only operator; even if we had had a spare, the radio hut was gone.

Finally, she heard the radio appeal to all ships to be on the alert for traces of the weather ship and to go to her assistance if spotted. The storm warning and order was repeated. Three Navy frigates had been ordered to the Pondoland coast, and Maritime Command was to fly rescue sorties at daylight, if the storm would permit.

Traces? she asked herself in agony. Had there been some further information behind the news bulletins which already presupposed the loss of the weather ship? For a moment she was tempted to telephone again, but she resisted it. She made some tea, put out the light, and let the recurring lighthouse flash be a pulsating, calculable goad across her face all through the long night. When it became colder, she fetched a rug and put it over her knees and pulled on the thick yachting sweater with its strange shoulder design, the one she had worn when she came aboard my ship in harbor. She remembered that too.

She sat and waited, because in her heart she knew, like the other Fairlie women who had waited, the one for the *Waratah* and the other for the airliner, that the man she loved was not dead.

When the light came, the lighthouse's scalpel no longer cut into her eyes, and she slept in the chair.

When the light came to my eyes, a bright imperative flash cut across the waves under the grey cloud scud. I could not see the signaling ship itself in that wild sea, but that quick, professional clatter of the shutter told me it was a warship.

What ship is that?

"Get me a torch—a lamp—anything that signals," I ordered Smit.

He went below to look. The warship was coming up fast; I began to make out her guns and radar through the water she was throwing over herself. For a moment the sailor in me paused to admire the splendid sight, but my pleasure was rapidly overshadowed by the fact that the warship represented, in the most tangible form, the authority I had defied. A string of explanations raced through my mind, for daylight had shown what a beating the staunch little whaler had taken. The flimsy radiosonde hut had been flattened to the deck; its companion, the radio hut, was still standing drunkenly, one side crumpled and askew. The fragments of the radar antenna, the high direction-finder forward of the funnel and the small stern mast were wrapped together in an inextricable embrace with stanchions and bridge plating which had been torn away. The catwalk for'ard to the bows from the starboard side of the bridge to the harpoon gun platform was bent to the deck in an untidy V. Two heavy steel supports with which it was normally attached to the starboard rail had been snapped off. We had managed to save the stocky foremast from going overboard by frapping the stays, but nevertheless it lay over drunkenly too; the metal outriggers which took the masthead lights seemed somehow to have woven themselves into the ratlines. Normally the harpoon gun was positioned between the flares of the bow, but I had had it removed in Durban, so that the break which it would have afforded to the head seas was missing. As a result, a solid body of water had smashed on to the foredeck, ripping from its foundations the big winch, which had been thrown upwards through the center of the bridge windows.

I had had no damage report from the two technicians in charge of the satellite observation apparatus, but Smit had told me enough to know that it would never work again. The hole in the deck had been our biggest anxiety during the night, but with daylight it was evident that the worst of the storm had spent itself, although the wind velocity was still, I estimated, Force 6 or 7, which meant it was blowing between 30 and 40 miles an hour. Far less water was coming aboard, and the pumps were managing. *Walvis Bay* was, however, a sorry sight, and I would have to answer for it.

The sharp bicker of light became more imperative.

"Identify yourself, please. Identify yourself. Why do you not reply to my radio?"

The warship—I could see now that she was a frigate—slowed and started to circle. It was not by coincidence that she was at sea, I told myself grimly. She was searching—for *Walvis Bay*.

Smit returned. He had unearthed a battered old signal lamp, but it worked.

"*Walvis Bay*," I spelt out to the warship.

Again the quick staccato of light. "Answer my radio signals—immediately."

Smit glanced sideways at me. This was certainly not the lost sheep and joyful shepherd approach.

"Cannot," I replied. "Radio washed away. Operator injured. Requires medical attention."

The frigate edged closer. Her captain must be taking a long look at what I had done to the weather ship. I felt naked under the silent scrutiny. Through my binoculars I read her name—SAS *Natal*.

Here it came. "What are you doing in the prohibited area?"

"Trying to keep afloat," I replied flippantly.

There was no humor in the Navy this morning, however. I could imagine what a shaking that lean hull had taken during the night with her captain under orders to look for me "at best possible speed."

The light said: "Repeat, what are you doing in the prohibited area? Did you not receive the storm warning?"

There was no use denying it; Feldman would see to that.

"I received the storm warning. My ship was damaged shortly afterwards. One prop is out. Unable to steam."

There was another long, uncomfortable pause.

"Base informed that you are safe," resumed the light. "A Shackleton from Maritime Command will be over soon as standby. Come aboard and report personally."

A tiny pulse of hope beat for a moment through my tiredness. Maybe they were out looking only for *Walvis Bay*, not for Alistair!

"Regret cannot comply," I replied. "Cannot leave my ship."

"Come aboard! That is an order, not a request!"

Smit had found a working portable radio. I, too, heard the announcement. It brought confirmation of the news I had dreaded all night: Alistair had indeed crashed. I was the one who had seen him go in; I must persuade the Navy that *Walvis Bay* was in no urgent need, that it was imperative that I should take the frigate to where the Buccaneer had crashed.

"Have you any casualties?" asked the warship. "I intend to sling a breeches buoy to you. A boat's too risky. Stand by. Skipper to precede casualties."

I picked up the voice-pipe to Scannel. "Nick, I'm transferring you to the frigate for those burns. Stand by, will you?"

There was a moment's silence, then the engineer's voice came through. "Boy, that will be the day! Do you think I'm leaving the ship stuck like this?"

"Listen, Nick..." I began, but all I got was a derisive laugh and the instrument went dead.

I signaled the warship. "My first officer has a badly crushed arm and shoulder. What about using a helicopter for him?"

"No question of it in this weather," answered the light.

"I'm coming close. I'll fire a line across you..."

I was given instructions how to secure the springs of the lifeline and told to keep the whaler at a fixed distance during Feldman's transfer—and my own. I hoped my exhausted crew could manage. Jubela was dead on his feet, and it was mainly upon his helmsmanship that success would depend. Smit went to help Feldman on deck.

The frigate drew in. The rise and fall of a solid object gave the seas a new and frightening proportion. The other vessel seemed to be lifting fully thirty feet above us and then falling deep below in the troughs. She was being beautifully handled.

"I'll come round into the wind," said the warship. "This will call for your full co-operation. Can you get rid of that sea anchor and make some speed?"

"I can manage a couple of knots on one screw."

"Ready, then?"

"Ready."

The frigate circled our stern and came up on the starboard side in order to give me a lee against the waves and the gale.

I did not hear the crack as she fired a line. Jubela compensated, but the shot went wide.

The frigate bucked wildly as she lost way, trying to accommodate herself to our limping pace. Again she fired the lifeline. This time it snaked across our deck and we made it fast. While we hauled in the main cable and secured it, *Natal* gave another magnificent demonstration of seamanship, holding a course parallel to ours at walking pace almost.

I climbed into the canvas "breeches" as I had been told, not raising my arms but letting myself hang limp to be hauled across.

Feldman, his face grey with pain, fear, and I think resentment at not going first, eyed me silently. I jammed my battered cap, whose crown had taken a beating from the lashing tarpaulin when it had blown off my head once, tight over my eyes.

I swung free of the weather ship. I had gone perhaps a quarter of the distance when suddenly the line sagged. I saw the white-topped sea below me rush up to meet my feet. The sickening drop brought back acutely *Walvis Bay*'s moment of life-and-death in the great wave. It was *Walvis Bay* now that edged away slightly, bringing the line taut, but not too taut; I blessed Jubela's judgment. As I reached the warship's side, a big four-engined Shackleton came over low, circling, watching.

I was hauled on to the deck.

Commander Lee-Aston did not waste any time. When I saw his stubble-blackened face and red-rimmed eyes, I wondered how my own must look. A patina of dried salt lay across his shoulders like snow. His oilskin crackled like mine.

He nodded briefly and led me below. What was obviously a conference cabin had been cleared, as if for action. Piles of chairs lay lashed against the steel walls, with carpets, pictures, and smaller furniture.

Lee-Aston sat himself on the corner of the long table. "We must talk fast," he said, "That line between the ships is damn dicey. Where's your log?"

"You didn't ask..."

"When were you damaged?"

"Shortly after seven."

"Where—position?"

"Not a clue."

"I see. But you were in the prohibited area."

"You make it sound like the diamond fields."

Lee-Aston's voice was tired, edged. "Just answer my questions. I've had a rough night. The guts have been shaken out of my ship and the whole forepeak section is badly strained."

"I..." I checked what I wanted to say about *Walvis Bay*'s ordeal. The less said, the better.

"What time did you receive the Navy's get-out signal?"

"A little after six."

"Yet—an hour later, when you could have been safe in deep water you were, where? How far? Why?"

My mind balked. There were too many things I could not answer.

"All this questioning—I don't know whether it's your function or not. I certainly will get all I can face from a lot of other people when I get ashore..."

Lee-Aston looked at me bleakly. He didn't drop his probing, judicial air. "I think we should get the division of authority clear before I proceed. Your Weather Bureau is without law enforcement authority. At sea, they call in the Navy. Within territorial waters, the Navy's word is law. So I call upon you to explain—and it seems there is a considerable amount to explain. The Navy's authority ends ashore. Along the coastline, the Railways and Harbors Police, not the police, exercise authority. If something like wreckage is involved, I hand over to them..."

"Listen," I said, trying to overcome his cool self-assurance, "at the moment both of us are sailors, up against the sea. We can discuss later whose authority I fall under. But now—if you will cast off that lifeline to my weather ship, I'll take you to where the Buccaneer went in."

"You'll—what?"

"I saw the Buccaneer go down, and I know just about where it was. Young Smit can take charge of *Walvis Bay*. She won't sink—not yet, anyway. Let's get back to the crash area—fast."

Lee-Aston slid off the edge of the table and simply stared at me. There was a small tic in one of his red-rimmed eyes.

"I saw the Buccaneer go in," I repeated. Careful, I told myself, don't implicate Alistair. Low-flying is strictly against orders. Shooting up shipping is a cardinal offence. Lee-Aston wasn't Feldman, he wouldn't swallow that datum-point yarn.

Lee-Aston was incredulous. "It is nearly twelve hours since the first signal came in that the Buccaneer was missing! You say you saw him crash, and you made no attempt to go to his rescue or report it? What did you think it was—a dolphin?"

"No," I said. "It was my brother."

Lee-Aston broke the ensuing silence. It was the only time he became animated during the interview. "Then think, man—your position! South of the Bashee doesn't mean a thing! You've got to pinpoint the place!"

I was too exhausted to be anything but on the defensive. "My ship was damaged before I could report or go to his rescue..." I started to say. I pulled myself up. My story could wait. I dug a spur into my jaded brain. I must try and give Lee-Aston positions and plots for the search, then perhaps I could return in the frigate... Where, I asked myself under the captain's cool scrutiny, where exactly had I seen Alistair go down? I had held the *Waratah*'s course but after that— what? I had no idea where the frigate had found us. We could have drifted twenty miles in the night, and even farther, out to sea. I had also to take into account that extraordinary feeling of standing still while *Walvis Bay*'s engines pounded at thirteen knots...

I came out with figures, positions, estimates. When I had finished, Lee-Aston did not answer, but picked up a telephone. "Lieutenant, come down here, will you? I want you to see Captain Fairlie safely to his ship."

The agony of Alistair and the agony of the night flooded back. I grabbed Lee-Aston's salt-caked jacket. "I've got to find him...!"

He eased himself free of my grip, unruffled at my outburst. He was as detached, as professional, as a surgeon at an operation.

"I was given a job, and I've done only half of it by finding *Walvis Bay*. She's a dockyard job. The other half is to get her safely to port." He shrugged. "Your position figures—the Navy and the Air Force are working on the Buccaneer's projected crash area. That's at least forty miles to the north of where you say."

Exhaustion slipped the halter on my words.

"Nonsense! It was right in the *Waratah* area, not to the north..."

My words froze under his cool appraisal.

"Ah, *Waratah* Fairlie, the *Waratah* man!"

I dropped my eyes, fumbling for a reply.

He went on slowly, levelly. "I've heard of your interest in the *Waratah*. So has the C-in-C."

Feldman, the bastard! I thought. During those long months I had worked at sea on my computations, he had probably been quietly talking about my preoccupation with *Waratah*. In a small ship like

Walvis Bay there can be no secrets. Only he could have gabbed about my extracurricular activities to people in the Weather Bureau— possibly in an attempt to discredit me and try and get the command for himself.

The abyss gaped in front of me. Watch and wait is all I could do.

Tafline, too, watched and waited by the radio. She had shared her anxiety with Mr. Hoskins. Not even in the final days of *Touleier's* race, he had confided to her, had he felt such concern as now: the yacht had deliberately kept radio silence to fox her rivals. A loner if ever there was one, Mr. Hoskins had said—and she gleaned something more about me from his warm affection—but now there is something more than that. Hard to put your finger on, but he's changed. Somewhere deep inside him he's got a problem and he's trying to thrash the sea to work it out...

"Have you ever been on board his ship?" she asked.

"No", replied Mr. Hoskins, surprised. "Did you see anything...?"

Yes, she thought to herself. I did. I saw the photograph of the *Waratah.*

But to Mr. Hoskins she said, "No, nothing. It was just an impression. It's all so stark, so clinical, so functional. All the man is kept out of sight."

Mr. Hoskins had smiled. And she smiled too, but she did not say that she had sat up all night.

Mr. Hoskins said, "He was never the same after his father's airliner crashed. Almost in the same place as..."

She said, not thinking, "As his brother crashed."

Mr. Hoskins said, "How do you know that? The radio didn't say so."

"No," she replied, "but it is."

Mr. Hoskins put down his work and said, "If you know that, wouldn't you rather go home and listen?"

Then the radio broke in and gave a news flash. *Walvis Bay* was making for port. "No," she said, "but I'd like to go out and send a telegram."

* * *

I caught a glimpse of *Walvis Bay* through the frigate's porthole. I had turned from Lee-Aston's stare, trying to muster an answer. The weather ship rolled comfortably, almost, taking aboard only an occasional dollop. The thought goaded me at the sight—the thing which had nearly destroyed us during the night was slipping away with the realignment of the violent elements, master-current, counter-current, gale. I *had* to persuade Lee-Aston!

I went for the truth. I said slowly, "I defied the Navy order. I admit that. I risked my ship; I admit that. You were out in the storm last night, and you saw what it was like. I had to find out every detail of it. Sixty years ago a fine liner went to the bottom in exactly the same sort of storm. The fundamental purpose of this weather ship of mine is the protection of oil rigs. In knowing why the *Waratah* sank, I can best ensure the safety of the oil rigs when they start to drill off Pondoland."

Lee-Aston remained remote, unmoved. "Maybe—maybe not. Fortunately I am not called upon to judge your motives. I am only a naval officer, doing his duty." He gestured to the lieutenant who had come to the door.

"Lieutenant, see Captain Fairlie back to his ship. Cast off the line. Get a tow aboard the weather ship."

"You...are...not...going...for...the...Buccaneer...?"

"Captain Fairlie, my orders were to find you. I have. If *Walvis Bay* was a navigational hazard, my orders were to sink her by gunfire. If she was afloat, I was to take her in tow to Cape Town. The search for the Buccaneer is being well cared for, I assure you. Unlike you, I obey orders. Now please get back to your ship and make fast the tow."

"You can't..." I expostulated.

"Subordination to orders is the heart of the Navy," he replied. "It has also been recommended, in another context, as a true philosophy of acceptance in life. I commend it to you. I shall let the C-in-C have a full report of our conversation. He is acting on behalf of the Weather Bureau since it concerns the sea and ships. Now, may I wish you good morning?"

I went.

The tow was secure, and I was pulling off my boots on my damp bunk before trying to snatch some exhausted sleep. Smit and I had heaved the cabinet off the bunk. The wetness and chaos made the place doubly depressing. There was wreckage everywhere.

Smit knocked at the door and handed me a paper.

"Signal from the frigate, sir. To be passed on to you personally."

I unfolded the slip and read the relayed telegram.

Until we see each other, please keep away from the *Waratah*, Tafline.

Tafline!
So that was her name.
So she knew.
So did the Navy.
So did the Weather Bureau.

CHAPTER 8

"Captain Fairlie will report to the C-in-C, Simonstown, at 10 sharp tomorrow."

The frigate's snapping signal lamp had come to symbolize my rejection by the Navy and Weather Bureau during the past four days of the tow. Orders from the warship to the laboring weather ship had been restricted to what was strictly necessary. Their brevity indicated Lee-Aston's intention to demonstrate his basic philosophy of subordination. He had passed on equally brief messages from the Weather Bureau. They had to do with towing, getting the ship safely to port and docking. There was no word of sympathy for my casualties, not a hint of appreciation for what my crew or I had gone through to save the ship.

I had forced Nick Scannel to go aboard the frigate to have his burns treated by the ship's doctor.

He reported back, grim-faced.

"They're building up the case against you, skipper," he told me. "Ably assisted by that rat Feldman."

"Case, Nick?"

"I'm damned if I go aboard again," he burst out, "burns or no burns. Wanted me to make a statement about the other night. What were you up to? What was behind the meeting between your brother and yourself? What—" he shrugged angrily, and then winced from the pain.

"What did you say, Nick?"

"'I take orders,' I told that iceberg frigate captain." He grinned

107

mirthlessly. "'I was in the engine-room. You don't see or hear anything down there, except what comes down the voicepipe. Unlike some of the arse-licking sons-of-bitches who frequent bridges.'"

I could not help laughing at Scannel's vehemence.

"It's bad enough, without taking cracks as well," I said.

Scannel mimicked the cold preciseness of the Navy captain.

"'I would have you know, Mr. Scannel, that Mr. Feldman has been of the greatest assistance to us in our preliminary investigations.'"

"I'll bet he has," I said. "If he sucks up and gets the command of *Walvis Bay*, you'll find yourself with a weather ship and no crew."

"'May I remind you, Mr. Scannel, the *Walvis Bay* is not a naval unit. We are acting at the request of the Weather Bureau. I am simply collating facts for my superiors.'"

"'And you can go and stick your collation right up the frigate's condenser pipe,' I told him, and walked out.'"

"Thanks, Nick," I replied.

The engineer stared hard at me and said. "You're going to fight them, aren't you, skipper?"

I avoided his eyes. I did not reply.

"You've got something to fight them with, haven't you, man?"

"Yes and no, Nick," I answered slowly. "I don't know whether it'll do any good anyway."

"There's not a man of us in the crew who holds the other night against you, skipper. I'd like you to know that. We've all watched you for a whole year slave your guts out to make this ship something really special." He became almost pleading. "You wouldn't have thrown it all away for the sake of nothing, would you? You found something which will get you off the hook, didn't you, skipper?"

"Yes and no, Nick."

He came and crashed his big hand on my shoulder.

"Don't keep saying, thanks Nick. Yes and no, Nick. Get your head up, boy!"

Now the tow was virtually at an end. *Walvis Bay* lay wallowing under Tafline's lighthouse at the approaches to Table Bay harbor. The frigate had cut her speed to barely steerage way in order to hand us over to the care of a port tug. I had hoped to make Cape Town at dawn, but the crippled whaler had labored so after rounding Cape Point, the extreme tip of the Peninsula, that it was mid-morning before we made port. A thin, wintry rain on a nor'wester added to our difficulties, and visibility was poor, I was already bracing myself against the publicity which would attend the battered ships' arrival; except for our small portable, we had been without news from the outside world during the slow plug round the southern tip of the continent.

The warship's light blinked.

"Acknowledge C-in-C's order forthwith."

"Acknowledged."

"Cast off the tow."

The warship gathered way and swung in a wide arc seawards, heading back round the Peninsula to the big base at Simonstown. No goodbye. No good luck. None of the usual courtesies of the sea.

The docks were cheerless when we tied up. The men who threw the securing hawsers were only too glad to get back to their shelter rather than pause and gape at the damage. Either the weather or some other scoop had mercifully kept the press away.

"Finished with engines," I rang down.

It was a pure formality, since we had merely used the auxiliaries during the tow. The ship had an end-of-school-term air; I had been ordered to send the crew ashore while the dockyard took over *Walvis Bay*.

And Tafline?

Where, I asked myself again and again during the long slog of the tow, where did she come in? I did not—dared not—reply to her telegram. What construction had the probing Lee-Aston put on her words in the first place when he relayed it to me? Would she misconstrue my silence as resentment at her unfortunate interference? I wondered, as the low blur of the mountainous Cape coast slid by, I wondered many things. I had no answers. I did not know of her night's vigil.

The gangplank went down, and the first men hurried ashore, laughing and joking. The cranes, the concrete quays, the dripping black tarpaulins over the railway trucks and the shrouds of steam above the shunting locomotives were as a desert to me through the weather ship's gaping, glassless bridge windows. I went below to my cabin, down the short companionway, still bent from the impact of the winch barrel. Unshaven, weary from nursing the whaler all night round the Cape of Storms, and exhausted by the tumult within me, I did not bother to take off my oilskins but stood looking disconsolately at the cabin.

Where would I begin? I would have to prepare a detailed report for submission to the C-in-C, and then amplify it verbally when I was interviewed by him. By bringing in the Navy and the C-in-C, the Weather Bureau gave the whole affair a quasi-court-martial aspect which did not appeal to me. I could see why, when ships and the sea were in question, of which the Bureau had no real knowledge, but it started things off on the wrong foot as far as I was concerned. I would far rather have explained to the people I knew in the Bureau, and who knew me.

Soon, too, there would be the official inquiry, to be held in public as they always are, into the loss of the Buccaneer, and I would have to appear as a key witness. My heart sank at the thought of still further painstaking, carefully considered reports, and consultations with lawyers, no doubt. I turned to the tiny chart table, thinking to make a start by rolling up the annotated chart.

Then she stood in the doorway.

She stood and simply looked at me. I looked back, not speaking either.

She just walked past me and went to the photograph of the *Waratah* with its broken glass.

In all the time I knew her, she always curbed her emotions, but now her voice was unsteady.

She said, "It had even to throw something at the picture of itself, didn't it?"

"Yes."

She was very quiet. I know now that the way she stumbled over the quotation, looking at the *Waratah*, that there was no gainsaying the still, soft call. "Built in the eclipse, and rigged 'mid curses dark."

She faced the other photograph, of the airliner, perhaps so that I could not see her face.

"He's dead, isn't he?"

"Yes. I saw him go in."

"You saw him go in! The papers didn't say that."

I told her briefly of our rendezvous, the beat-up of the weather ship by the Buccaneer, the way Alistair's lights vanished.

"Mock attacks on shipping are strictly forbidden in flight orders," I added. "Alistair knew that. Discipline is razor-edged in the Buccaneers. He simply laughed it off when I raised it..."

She came and stood by me at the chart. She had never been as close to me as this. The line of her profile was exquisite against the chart's parchment. The tell-tale question mark with its circle at the end of the plot near the Bashee Mouth told her everything.

"There? *Waratah*?"

"*Waratah*—there," I replied.

"Was it your idea, or Alistair's, or both?"

It was the only time she hurt me. I did not know that the detachment almost in the curt query meant that she had clamped on the rebellious emotions which, when she saw me, threatened to run riot.

I replied slowly. "Almost the last words Alistair said to me about the *Waratah* were that if he had me in his squadron, he'd ground me and send me to a psychologist."

She pretended to be studying the chart. I thought the way her lips moved meant that she was repeating the plot to herself. She could not trust herself to speak.

I waited, and she waited in her own unique fashion, shaping things her way. She wanted to give me the comfort I needed, soothe the rawness of having killed my own brother, and the censure of the authorities. How then did she manage to square that with the cyclone of feeling within her heart?

I had to lean down to hear her murmur. "It reached out for you, too, that night—remember that. And I bless it while I hate it, whatever it might be, that it missed."

She looked up from the chart and I saw her eyes, and the double pain was gone. Currents greater than Agulhas were carrying us along; our incomplete words were the snow-plumes blown from the iceberg while the great mass of it remains out of sight, inarticulate, known but only hinted at.

"I came to the cabin that night," I said, "I—remembered."

"I...I...watched a lighthouse. I was—aware."

There were a thousand banalities which I might have resorted to, but each one would have denied her, Tafline. She pretended to be studying that circle on the chart ringing the question-mark whose name was *Waratah*; she played unconsciously with the big navigational dividers with her left hand. Her hair was short and soft, and I could see the white skin in the nape of her neck as she bent forward.

I said, picking my words in order to navigate my tumultuous inward current. "*Walvis Bay* did not catch it immediately. Alistair's lights went out, all of a sudden. He had started to bank. I thought—Feldman did too—that he was coming back. The Air Force refused to believe that. Their plot put Alistair well to the north of where I last saw him. They said my positions were too uncertain to work on. They maintained that, because the weather was bad, he would have gone straight on to make his attack on East London, once he had identified the *Walvis Bay*."

She still played with my dividers and pencils.

"What about the low-flying?"

"I'll have to do my best at the inquiry. It'll be held in public, I should hate them to put his death down to negligence, or breach of discipline, or anything that he really wasn't."

"The search hasn't been called off yet, though they've found nothing," she replied. "You talk of an inquiry already." She looked up at me then. "You believe he's dead, don't you, Ian?"

"Yes. When his lights snapped off, that's when it happened. Don't ask me why, but it is so. If I had been a few miles further to the south, I might have seen what took him."

She made a quick gesture to take in the shattered photograph and the wrecked deck above our heads. She lifted a corner of the veil on her night of agony.

"If you had been to the south, it would have been Alistair and not you I would be talking to now—if ever I had got in touch with him,"

She drew an unconscious pattern with the V of the dividers: its apex settled on my circled question mark, and a pencil on either side completed the doodle. She had formed the letter "W".

She smiled a little crookedly. "It always comes up that way, doesn't it?"

"Yes," I answered. "It's been that way for a long time with me."

"I didn't know it could be so big," she murmured, and I had to crane my neck to hear her speak, as if to the chart. "A dead ship, ruling the living. Superimposed on everything one does, says, thinks. Reaching into recesses. Reaching into..." She did not go on. I longed to hear more, but there was her curb.

She gave a slight shake of the head as if to dispel her thoughts, and said levelly. "I want to know from you yourself what happened that night."

"The gale was working up to full strength," I said mechanically. "A full-blooded southwesterly buster. After Alistair vanished, I knew that *Walvis Bay* couldn't take much more at the *Waratah*'s speed..."

She glanced sharply at me for my reconstruction and her lips twitched, but she did not interrupt.

"Then, when the speed was off her, I sensed that something— don't ask me specifically what, because I've thought and thought about the answer and haven't got it—something maybe in the conjunction of the gale and the Agulhas Current, something maybe about the counter-current with the weight of that gale behind it, something maybe about an unexplained up-current caused by the sea-bottom contour thereabouts—*something* was different. Jubela sensed it too. It was what so bedeviled things later when they pressed me as to my exact position when I last saw Alistair. Frankly, I don't know. Not within miles."

"They found a lifejacket," she said. "The papers were full of it. Near Port St. John's."

I shrugged. "The drama was starting to get cold for the newspapers after a couple of days, I expect. I heard about it on the radio. It seems it was the sort of lifejacket ski-boaters wear."

She came close to me, searching my face. My pulse raced. The shadows were in her eyes.

"Why did they push you aside, Ian, the very man who saw the Buccaneer vanish? They had everything to gain from consulting you."

"I defied an explicit order from the Weather Bureau and the Navy to clear out of the storm area. I still have to answer for it. I smashed up a fine ship and thousands' worth of valuable equipment. They won't forgive me for that in a hurry. When I tried to explain my motives to the Navy...I am branded as unreliable, overwrought, a nut chasing a crazy notion. That is why they wouldn't listen to me about the search area, despite the fact that I made no secret of the fact that I wasn't sure of my position at the time."

"South of the Bashee?"

She let the words fall slowly, deliberately.

I nodded, and there was silence.

Then I said, "South of the Bashee! You'll find with this thing that the same words keep coming back, recurring like a symptom in a disease that mocks every change of treatment. Some have a rhythm, and seem to beat about in your brain. You claw for meaning, light, anything. Bashee—I don't know what it means. The experts say it is lost in time. Yet I beat against it!"

I pulled myself up. "*Walvis Bay* wasn't in danger immediately after the Buccaneer disappeared," I resumed. "At that stage she was taking a bad beating, but she wasn't damaged. Yet—there was something peculiar about those seas which I've tried again and again to define. It was the same for all of us."

"Us?"

"Four Fairlies," I replied. "Our gale was from the southwest. Our run of the sea was from the southwest. Our courses were all southwest. That is our one common factor. Two of us were flying at 300 to 600 miles an hour. Two of us were doing thirteen knots..."

"No!" she burst out. I was startled at her sudden outburst. "No! Not you—and the *Waratah*! You're here—alive, well, unhurt in the present. She's dead, gone, wrecked, in the past! No," she corrected herself, "it isn't like that at all, is it, Ian? The *Waratah* is here and alive, as much as you and me, isn't she?"

"Yes." Outwardly the answer was reserved; inwardly, my heart exulted. In that outburst I had seen in her things more precious for me than all that long-dead secret.

I therefore almost regretted that she controlled herself. "I'm sorry. The *Waratah* reached out for you, still another Fairlie. The fourth. Please show me every detail. I want to know."

I showed her on the chart. The nearness and warmth of her sent my blood tingling.

"I began to turn seawards, towards deeper water. Here, this little arrow shows it, the one I've drawn by the question mark. I thought that with more depth under her, she might ride more easily. She was pitching and rolling, taking a lot of water aboard. Then suddenly there was a great crash, the lights went, the bridge windows were stove in, and we all hit the deck. The ship dived like a mad thing, putting her head down like nothing I've ever known. I thought she would plunge clean to the bottom. I grabbed the wheel so she wouldn't broach to. Then I saw something...I...I..."

She was staring at me, startled, penetratingly.

"Why do you say it like that, Ian?"

I, in my own way like her, had to control my runaway emotions.

I picked my words.

"The mere fact that a great liner vanished in broad daylight on a short three-day passage, within sight of the coast, on a well-frequented sea route, makes it strange enough. But it becomes stranger still. One man projected the *Waratah* mystery into the fourth dimension."

She glanced at the cracked photograph and shivered. She waited for me to go on.

I rummaged in the cabinet and found what I wanted.

"There has never been anything like it in a sea tragedy, before or since," I said. "On her last voyage, between Australia and South Africa, the *Waratah* carried a passenger named Claude Sawyer. Three or four days out from Durban Sawyer dreamed a dream. Here are the exact words in which he described it to the official inquiry in London, which praised his integrity—and his courage.

"'I saw a man with a long sword in his left hand, holding a rag or cloth in his right hand, saturated in blood.

"'I saw the same dream twice again the same night, and the last time I looked so carefully that I could almost draw the design of the sword.'"

The only sound in the cabin was the distant clatter of loading cranes on the dockside.

She asked quietly. "How was Sawyer able to appear at the hearing? Did he disembark in Durban?"

"Yes. He was so shattered by his dream that he left the ship. But he was to be more shattered still. The day the *Waratah* disappeared, Sawyer was alone in a Durban hotel.

"'That night I had another dream. I saw the *Waratah* in big waves; one big wave went over her bows and pressed her down; she rolled over on her starboard side and disappeared.'"

She glanced uneasily at the *Waratah* photograph, as if to reassure herself that it was once 10,000 tons of real, tangible, steel.

Then she asked, "Did Sawyer say he spoke to the man with the sword and the blood-soaked cloth?"

"No, Sawyer never at any stage in the future varied his story or elaborated it, but the name which has become attached to the figure he saw is Vanderdecken."

"Vanderdecken?"

"Vanderdecken was a medieval Dutch sailor, the legend goes, who diced with the devil for his soul. He lost, and was condemned to sail perpetually round the Cape of Storms. Like Drake's Drum, in times of danger and calamity men claim to have seen the Flying Dutchman's ship. But no one has ever seen the person of the Flying Dutchman close to, like Sawyer."

"Do you believe it, Ian?"

She was grave, unhappy. I knew, in that moment, that like Vanderdecken I was dicing, but I was dicing for a heart.

I temporized.

"The star witness of the *Waratah* inquiry was the first officer of the *Clan Macintyre*, Phillips. He was specially commended for his evidence. He gave the world the last, most explicit, facts about the *Waratah* that we have. His bearing at the inquiry made him what is called the perfect witness.

"But there was something else, something which Phillips did not record until later."

I searched in the cabinet again and pulled out a photocopy document.

I quoted. "'During the evening of the second day I was on the bridge of the *Clan Macintyre*. I saw—or thought I saw—a curious thing.

"'Just as the angry light from the storm was fading from the wind-torn sky, to which great waves were leaping, I got a glimpse through the wrack of a small vessel far away to starboard, or landwards.

"'I rubbed my eyes and looked again, but the gloom and piling seas had hidden her, and I did not see her anymore. Yet I am absolutely positive she was not imaginary.

"'She was a weird, old-fashioned sailing ship, with a tremendous high bow and stern, squat and square, with three masts, the foremast raked forward and the mizzen raked back.

"'What made me feel colder than the icy rain and wind was that she was sailing *into the teeth of the wind*—a thing impossible!

"'Was she the *Flying Dutchman*, going to the *Waratah*'s funeral, or returning from it? I did not like the look of that ship in the distance, and had three cups of boiling cocoa to bring me back to the present.'"

She was silent, puzzled.

There was an imperative knock at the door.

The moment was past.

"Dockyard superintendent to see you, sir." It was Fourie, the bo'sun.

"On deck, sir." He grinned. "Can't believe his bleedin' eyes, begging your pardon, miss."

I saw the man examining the hole in the deck. I dodged and took her up to the crushed radio hut. After what I had just said, I owed it to her to show what the storm had done to my ship. Patches of rust had begun to appear on the jagged metal where the radiosonde hut had been, and along the buckled edges of the forward catwalk to the harpoon gun platform. During the first day of the tow we had planked a wooden patch over the gaping socket where the winch had been; now it looked more irregular and untidier in the rain coming in from the grey sea than it did when dry; the rain also emphasized the line of the buckled bow; it drifted in through the broken windows of the bridge.

She looked round intently, disbelievingly. She did not speak. Her only response was a quick jerky sigh, an intake of breath maybe, a smothered exclamation. Then—our lips were together and our bodies close and warm, as if of their own impulse they sought to burn out the icy desolation and terror of that night whose witness was before us. How long we stood in each other's arms I do not know.

It was Fourie and his sideburns who brought our surroundings back to us. He came carrying a battered umbrella with an air of diffident, apologetic gallantry. The deck, the docks and the rain came into focus again.

"Begging your pardon, sir," he said with a sidelong, half-reproachful glance at her damp hair. He held out the umbrella to her; abstractedly she took it and thanked him. He gave a half-amused salute with his fist and shambled away.

I groped for something ordinary to say. I nodded towards the dockyard man.

"When I hand over to him, I hand over my command. That is why I wanted to let you see the ship first."

Her eyes never left mine. She, too, was living on two levels.

"They're not—sacking you!"

"Not quite. On extended leave, pending repairs to the ship and investigations. It will take at least a month to get her shipshape again. My first run of the gauntlet is my interview tomorrow with the C-in-C..."

She laughed softly, and the drops showered through the leaky umbrella.

"Mr. Hoskins! There weren't any doubts before, as far as he was concerned, and there'll be fewer now!"

I was at a loss to follow, but she raced on. "Mr. Hoskins and I spent a lot of radio time over you, Ian Fairlie! I don't think he'll find it so strange when I ask for my holiday to coincide with your ship being repaired."

I held her round her slim waist, pressed hard against me, and we faced the city and the great mountain. A month! What would we find among those streets and houses, she and I, during those coming weeks which would be ours, inalienably ours, because it was we who would set our hearts' seal upon them?

I drew her round. Her eyes were alight. I looked into their depths.

She smiled. Her smiles seemed to start as light far back in her face and be the distillate of her quiet moments, a kind of gathering together of all the joy which had gone before, as if it were awaiting that one moment for expression.

I held her close.

CHAPTER 9

"Then give me the position, bearing, and depth of the wreck of the *Waratah*, and the nature of the phenomenon which sank her."

The C-in-C leaned sideways, flipped a switch on his intercom, and said crisply, "Watch that recorder, Perry. This is important."

The sulky hum of the tape-recording machine limped slightly on a warped cassette. There was no other sound in the big room. The officer was monitoring our conversation from the next room; the two of us were alone. For hours we had sat like that in his office at Simonstown, once the headquarters of the British South Atlantic Command. For over a century Simonstown was an enclave of the Royal Navy at the tip of the African continent, and the room was impregnated with that long occupancy. Under a huge painting of the sinking of the famous Birkenhead troopship off the Cape was a signed letter from the first German Kaiser eulogizing the men in her who had gone steadfastly and unflinchingly to their deaths. A faded print showed a steam-cum-sail warship attacking a land stockade. The title hit me—HMS *Hermes*!

Only yesterday, on the deck of my ship, everything had changed. One chapter had closed, another had opened. We should have been free to have taken the Mini and lost ourselves inland—away from the sea—somewhere among the vine-rich earth and purple mountains of the Cape; or gone laughing and skiing in the snow; to have drunk wine; simply to have been with one another. Mr. Hoskins had readily agreed to her leave and we found ourselves together, a little uncertain and greatly excited about our weeks ahead together. In that spirit I had brushed aside the significance of my appointment with the C-in-C; I'll be back in an hour, I told her, arranging to meet her nearby at an eccentric aunt's who kept a thirty-acre wild garden under the batteries of the naval base.

Now almost the whole day had passed. When I had first been shown in, the C-in-C had been curt.

"The Weather Bureau has requested me to conduct a one-man investigation on its behalf into the damage suffered by the *Walvis Bay* and the causes of it," he told me, "The Bureau itself has no experience of maritime matters." He stared at me penetratingly. "As well you know." He gave a throaty, mirthless chuckle. "They nearly lost the one ship they had. Both the Bureau and I felt it was logical for me to act, since the Navy has already been so closely implicated in this...uh...incident concerning your ship and the storm order. Kill two birds with one stone, so to speak."

I had decided the previous day, after Tafline had left me, that my best defense of my actions would be to make a clean breast of the whole *Waratah* saga and weather enigmas. I could justify my actions to a sailor, I reasoned, and the C-in-C was a sailor. He had boasted publicly of his descent from the Sea Beggars of William the Silent. The emotionless moon face and rather flabby eye-sockets gave no hint of the iron personality in whose hands lay the destiny of Britain's great trade and oil routes round the Cape. In line with my decision, I had brought with me for the interview a mass of *Waratah* documents, as well as a scale model of the liner I had originally begged from Lloyd's of London.

It was not, however, an interview but a trial.

For hours I had expounded, argued, reasoned, explained, sought to justify. I had shown him on the model a hundred technicalities which might have caused the liner's end. I had gone into every facet of the contradictory storm weather which the *Waratah* and the *Walvis Bay* had shared.

The C-in-C had been a good listener. He ordered mid-morning coffee; his only relaxation was to get up and speak to a budgie in a cage which repeated after him, "Don't talk about ships and shipping."

"Ten generations in his ancestry since the war," he had remarked with a ghost of a smile. "Still says the same damn thing."

It was the only warmth I saw.

The C-in-C had sent the officer who was in charge of the big tape-recorder into an anteroom, while he himself kept an eye on the revolving cassettes. I appreciated his gesture of privacy between us. Nonetheless, every word, every hesitation of mine, was remorselessly logged.

Now my throat constricted. Should I answer, south of the Bashee? I remembered Lee-Aston's reaction.

I wanted to get up and tear that grinding cassette from its socket. Its rhythm willed me to say, a ship without a soul!

I looked away, fiddling with my documents.

The C-in-C said in his deep bass. "I have three warships in the area. Lee-Aston's a good man. Has a great interest in these sort of things—weather, currents, seabeds. I sent him to the French inquiry when one of our subs on delivery nearly sank a Frenchman in a collision off Southern Spain. There are all sorts of tricky currents and sets where the Med meets the Atlantic."

Lee-Aston! I wish I had known. It would have made all the difference to my approach.

The C-in-C bridled in his chair. "Well, man?"

"I am uncertain what my position was at the time," I mumbled.

"Captain Fairlie, you have based your entire justification for your extraordinary actions on your need to find out where the *Waratah* sank, and what sank her. I ask you, where did she sink, and you say, I am uncertain of the position."

"That is correct."

"How far are you uncertain?"

"I was south of the Bashee. My dead reckoning became suspect once I became aware that although I was actually supposed to be doing thirteen knots, I felt I was in fact losing way over the ground."

"Captain Fairlie!" snapped the C-in-C. "No destroyer ever laid a smokescreen like you are trying to do. You have talked ceaselessly, articulately, for hours. At one straight question you dodge behind a screen of words and uncertainties."

"If I had found the *Waratah* I would have solved one of the greatest mysteries of the sea..." I stumbled on.

The C-in-C threw his big bulk back in the chair with a snort.

"But you chose to try, nevertheless, using a valuable ship and highly expensive scientific equipment. You defied orders to get out of the storm area. Why?"

"The oil rigs," I said helplessly. "I tried to tell you..."

"Again, nothing but a smokescreen of words!"

"My actions were inseparably connected with the safety of the oil rigs."

"You have spoken about what you call a *Waratah* storm which you say has special features which no other storm has. What are they?"

"The counter-current seems to take over..."

"Seems! Are you incapable of giving me a straight, factual reply, Captain Fairlie?"

I said, "It's the effect of all this—the build-up. I've never known a wave like that. She didn't rise. *Walvis Bay* put her head down, not up, as she would do normally..."

"Bah!" roared the big man. "There's not a man of us who has been to sea who hasn't seen a hell of a wave sometime. Now you want me to believe...what the devil do you want me to believe?"

I had come prepared to tell him everything. Now I could not. If what I had explained was so patently unacceptable, how much more would that other be?

The C-in-C snapped the intercom switch impatiently.

"Perry! Come and shut this blasted thing off, will you?"

We waited until he had gone again. We sat and faced one another.

Then the C-in-C said, "What I report to the Bureau may well rob you of your command—you know that, don't you?"

"Yes."

"They tell me you're a damn fine sailor. They've got nothing against you as a captain or a first-class weatherman except..."

"*Waratah*," I said.

"You've allowed something which hasn't any substance to eat into you, cloud your judgment—even risk your life and your ship." He stopped and added brutally, "Kill your own brother."

I was alone on that shattered bridge with the water pouring through, trying to swing her head clear of that dark sinister shape among the white waves.

I said, without heart, "There'll be a proper official inquiry into my brother's death."

"Then I feel sorry for you if you can't do better in public than you have with me in private," he replied tartly.

There was a pause. My mind shut fast on the *Waratah*. I had made up my mind. I wondered what Tafline had been doing during the hours I had been with the C-in-C.

"You're holding back on something, Fairlie," snapped the C-in-C. "I've a damn good mind to send a frigate or two to have a close look at the area."

"South of the Bashee!" I interjected ironically. "Listen!" he replied brusquely. "You can make up your mind which way it's to go. You can tell me confidentially, and then we'll set the recorder going and I'll ask you the right questions and you can give the replies, as if we had never discussed it meanwhile with the machine off. That'll let you out. Otherwise..." He shrugged.

I stood up. "Thanks for the chance. You're wasting your time if you think your ships will find anything where I failed. I've been there in daylight, too."

The C-in-C's rough surgery was gentle compared to the brutal cautery of the Buccaneer inquiry.

When the massive air-sea search failed to find Alistair or any trace of his plane, the inquiry was announced for ten days later. It seemed to me to be rushing things, but public interest remained at a high pitch and I suspected that the Air Force wanted to put itself in the clear as soon as possible. The hearing was scheduled to be in public, as is customary with all military and civilian crash investigations.

Smarting from the interview with the C-in-C, I wanted to get away inland with her, find solace, forget about the *Waratah*. But I had brought my cabinet from the ship and stored the documents in her flat. The model of the *Waratah* had intrigued her first. She had made me lift off the removable top to explain the interior, She expressed delight at the scale reproduction of the first-class music lounge with its tiny "minstrels' gallery" of carved wooden pillars in the center and heavy curtains gathered at each wooden corner supporting post; plush, comfortable settees with backs tuckered like a Tibetan anorak; concealed lighting (the *Waratah* was the first ship ever to try it); and, inevitably, some potted palms. Starting with the model, she had lost herself in the mass of documents, microfilms, newspapers, weather reports, and the full evidence of the Board of Trade inquiry in London, until the days slipped by and we still had not moved from Cape Town.

Both of us had been tense at the beginning of the Buccaneer inquiry. She had sat by me on a hard chair in the big Ministry of Transport conference room. It had low concrete beams and a rather battered dais at one end for the chairman and two assessors. The place smelt of stale smoke. The battery of pressmen used old tin lids on the battered tables to crush out their cigarettes. The presence of so many reporters reflected the intense public interest. The public galleries, too, were crowded. Witnesses, set apart to one side of the room, had to run the gauntlet of the public eye as they walked from their seats to a stand by the chairman's table. The down-at-heel air of the place seemed an unworthy funeral parlor for a creature as swift and noble as the Buccaneer.

I was called on the second day. She pressed my hand quickly as I rose and walked up to the stand. A ripple ran through the news section. They, like myself, had been lulled into a comfortable drowsiness by the previous day's flat monotone of technicalities, flying and meteorological. The hearing was taking shape as an open-and-shut case of an aircraft being lost in bad weather through nobody's fault.

That is the way I wanted it, too, for Alistair's sake.

Musgrave, a Supreme Court counsel who had made his name by specializing in aircraft matters and was often called in to serve on boards of inquiry, led me through my sighting of Alistair's Buccaneer coming towards *Walvis Bay*, his passing over the ship, his disappearance. I breathed a sigh of relief. No suggestion of low-flying! Only a casual, passing reference to our rendezvous. I glossed over the datum point story; no one probed it.

I waited to be told to stand down.

Musgrave said, "Thank you, Captain Fairlie."

I turned to go, but he said almost casually.

"Did you and your brother find the *Waratah*'s treasure, Captain Fairlie?"

A galvanic shockwave passed through the newsmen. Pencils were grabbed, unsmoked cigarettes forgotten. Men and women whispered to each other in the public galleries.

Bewildered, I looked across at Tafline. She was sitting very still and upright on her hard chair; I could see how white her knuckles had gone from clenching her gloves. Already some people were starting to crane forward to look at her—they had seen me come from her side.

"There was no treasure in the *Waratah*," I stated flatly.

"Which means, of course, that you found the ship which for sixty years has defied every effort to locate her?"

"I didn't say I found her," I was confused, rattled, off balance. "There was nothing in her manifests to show she carried bullion..."

"Bullion, Captain Fairlie? Who said anything about bullion?"

Already a newsman or two had broken from the table and were racing for the nearest telephone.

"Listen," I said desperately. "The *Waratah* was carrying a cargo of frozen meat from Australia, some ore, a couple of thousand tons of bunker coal, 279 tons of fresh water..."

Musgrave nodded, pleased. "Exactly. We take your word for it, Captain Fairlie." He slapped a pile of papers in front of him. "In fact, in going through every single detail in connection with the *Waratah*— even to such a minute fact as the amount of fresh water in her tanks— I think it is fair to say that there is no living person who knows as much about the *Waratah* as you do."

I cringed for the next blow.

"In fact, Captain Fairlie, if it wasn't treasure you were after, I cannot see any reasonable..." he emphasized the word "—person going to a hundredth of the trouble you have done: weather, metacentric heights, minute analysis of evidence..."

Feldman! The C-in-C, too, had sold me down the river! They had turned over everything I had said and collected to this sharp-tongued barrister who was in the process of making a Roman holiday out of me!

"I wasn't after treasure, nor was my brother," I flared. "I wanted to find out what sank the Waratah so that I could make sure it didn't

125

happen again."

"A very commendable sentiment," murmured Musgrave. "Yet, despite the fact that this was the very purpose for which the authorities sent your ship to sea, you saw fit not merely not to consult them about your...ah...proposed enterprise, but you acted in flat defiance of their order."

I could not reply.

Musgrave went on. "It seems, on looking at the case as an outsider, that there must have been some compelling reason why at least three members of the Fairlie family have chosen to risk death—endure death, even—for the sake of the *Waratah*." The bland tone vanished. "Tell the court, Captain Fairlie," he ordered.

"I've already told you—the safety of the oil rigs."

"Then," said Musgrave, "you can undoubtedly describe, on the basis of your near-miss with death, and your brother's death, what those conditions are?"

I said unhappily, "There are still certain imponderables which require elucidation."

Musgrave let the lightning rest on every syllable as he repeated my words. "There-are-still-certain-imponderables-which-require-elucidation."

The newsmen were grinning and scribbling. This was what they wanted.

Musgrave went on. "I put it to you, Captain Fairlie, that you used your brother and an aircraft, irreplaceable because of the arms embargo against this country, as a spotter for some nefarious enterprise which you will not disclose to the court, and in doing so caused his death. You also used a ship belonging to the state for the same purpose and caused tens of thousands of rands' worth of damage both to the vessel and her equipment. You have also destroyed the value of the weather watch in the Southern Ocean by breaking its continuity, so that the observations carried out during the past year will have to be scrapped, and the whole project begun again."

I looked desperately across at Tafline. Her eyes did not meet mine. She was taut, white-faced. Had the *Waratah* cost me her, too?

I did not know the answer to that when, raw and damaged, I returned to her flat after the inquiry. There was no doubt that in the

126

court's eyes the whole broadside of blame would be mine. She opened the door and went straight across to the window, not speaking. The dusk had come and the beam of light from the lighthouse flicked across her face and gave it a brightness which is with me still.

She still did not face me when she asked.

"That night when the big wave hit *Walvis Bay*—what did you see, Ian?"

"Dead ahead I saw a ship, an old-fashioned ship. She was heading into the wind."

She did not turn, and the light beam cut across her face. It came and went as she stood looking out.

I do not think either of us heard the telephone ring the first two or three times. Then she went slowly across to the instrument and spoke quietly. She said "thank you" mechanically and went back to the window.

She waited, then said, "That was Mr. Hoskins. The late papers are full of it. The Navy has found part of your father's airliner. It has got a message on it—for you.

"It is addressed from the *Waratah*."

CHAPTER 10

The ragged rectangle of aluminum, about the size of a bathmat, looked strangely dull against the polish of the colonel's wooden desk. The edges were scalloped as if they had been hacked off with some inadequate instrument. The metal, section of an aircraft fuselage, did not lie flat and streamlined but was buckled and uneven. Painted orange letters, discolored and faint but still readable, spelled "b-o-k". The upright stroke of the "b" was half obliterated by the torn edge. Fastened through the aluminum by its corroded strap was a gold wristwatch.

Tafline was with me at Railways and Harbors Police Headquarters the next morning. The day was bright and mild; we had lingered a little in the street before the building to admire the glorious proteas, the over-early yellow ixias and Tyrian purple babianas of the Malay women flower sellers. She was quiet and serious and refused flowers after we came out again.

She had been that way ever since I had told her about my sighting of the old-fashioned sailing ship in the path of *Walvis Bay*. She had not, as I feared, derided it; she simply did not refer to it again, but she had been abstracted from time to time during the evening.

Both our consternation and perplexity at Mr. Hoskins' news—I had gone out and bought newspapers with their screaming headlines—had been heightened by a second telephone call hard on the heels of his. The caller had been Colonel Joubert, head of the Railways and Harbors Police. He had first made sure it was Tafline he was speaking to, and then had requested—in a way which made it clear it was more a command than a request—that *both* of us should meet him the next day. Why Tafline? What had she to do with the finding of a section of fuselage purporting to have come from my father's airliner? How, I asked myself uneasily, did Colonel Joubert know in the first place to find me at her flat? It presupposed that the authorities had a close eye on me. The papers stated that the Navy had found the panel floating at sea when the last warship (unnamed) was returning to Simonstown after a stay on the coast more than a week after the search had finally been abandoned. At first, the floating panel was thought to have been part of the Buccaneer; when it was realized that it was not, it was turned over to the Railways Police as falling within their sphere of investigation.

By some tacit understanding, Tafline and I did not discuss the *Waratah* or the panel or the hundred questions which thronged our minds that evening after the two telephone calls. After supper, we had sat on the floor of her flat, in one another's arms, and, as the lighthouse flash came and went, she had told me of her night's vigil and the dawn of her love; she took the pain from my wounds; we lost ourselves in each other. I would wait with a kind of unbelieving impatience for the light flash to come and tell me that the lovely face was real, close to my face; when it was gone, the warmth of her lips against mine would underwrite the moment's vision with a searching tenderness.

Now, Colonel Joubert said tersely, "Usually the sort of thing we have to cope with is an old bottle with a tear-jerker message in it, supposed to have been set adrift in an emergency which existed only in the joker's imagination. This has an original slant to it."

He lit another cigarette off the one he was smoking and placed it, ash towards himself, on the desk's pock-burned inner camber.

A police major, sitting to one side of the colonel, said sarcastically, "At least your father doesn't claim to have met your grandfather aboard the *Waratah*."

The policemen looked as if they had listened to too many woes to accept anything at face value; several civilian aircraft experts, whose exact function I did not know, seemed strained.

"Not so fast," I started to say. "The only information I have is from the newspapers, but first I want to know why..."

"Why the *juffrou* has been brought into it?" The colonel swung back on his chair and blew a cloud of smoke towards the ceiling.

"She sent a very strange telegram to you."

"Strange? There was nothing strange about it!"

He picked out a photocopy from a file in front of him.

"'Until we see each other, please keep away from the *Waratah*. Tafline.'"

There was certainly nothing wrong with the Navy's staff work. First, the record of my interview with the C-in-C which had been turned over to Musgrave, and now a private telegram to me!

"In view of what is written on that panel, I want a lot of explanations..."

Tafline startled us. After the stiff, formal introductions she had been silent. Now she stood up, walked to the desk, and ran a finger over the twisted, sea-marked panel, as if to establish some contact. She might have been quite alone. She did not react to the colonel's demand. The circle of watching men was stilled; she was oblivious. What was she seeking from the panel which itself had been in the physical presence of the world's greatest sea mystery, probably even seen the corroded hulk of what had been Captain Ilbery's pride, the metal coffin which had broken so many hearts so long ago and tantalized so many minds since?

She took up the watch, too, and turned it round in her hands. Her unspeaking action seemed to have taken the initiative from the colonel and his peremptory demand about the telegram.

He reddened and snapped. "That watch and all the rest of it looks like something picked up from the films."

"It isn't a fantasy," Tafline said, not looking up. She turned the panel this way and that to catch the light.

"It is a will."

Addressing only me, she read out in her soft, clear voice:—

"'To my son Ian Fairlie I bequeath wreck *Waratah* south Bashee...'"

I gasped. "It's...it's...too fantastic! A will—written on a piece of metal! He bequeaths me the *Waratah*! How...where did he find her?"

My flow of words died at the colonel's cool, professional scrutiny. I felt he was logging every reaction of mine, almost every eye-blink.

"That is exactly what I want to know. That is why I asked you to come and explain. Both of you."

"I...I simply don't know! I've never heard of such a thing..."

"Nor have I," he retorted. "The more one goes into it, the more incredible it becomes. Not only the panel itself, but the circumstances surrounding it. All of which involve you."

I did not know what to reply.

Tafline came to the rescue. "There is more writing. But the wording becomes very indistinct. There are some figures, too. It looks like—no, I can't make it out."

One of the civilians, his plain clothes contrasting with the smart blue uniforms and white collars of the police, said. "We cleaned it up, in order to read it. Warren and I have been working most of the night on it. Eh, Warren?"

A heavy-eyed, bearded civilian nodded. "*Waratah* was plain enough. Aluminum, of course, doesn't rust in seawater."

Colonel Joubert said. "Please leave that alone, *juffrou*, and sit down again."

Tafline put it down gently. As she did so, she swung round and looked full at me. Gone was her earlier abstraction; her eyes were shining, as if she had come to some big decision. I was bewildered, the move was so deliberate.

The telephone rang and the colonel answered in Afrikaans, deferentially but firmly.

He put down the receiver. "Pretoria!" he exclaimed. "What am I doing about the *Waratah*? The powers in Pretoria want to know! What do the preliminary investigations show? The press wants to know—the whole world wants to know! Already this morning I've had four calls from London, one from Munich, and two from New York. You've got a lot of questions to answer, Captain Fairlie!"

I didn't care for his overbearing attitude. I gestured at the panel. "I've got a right to know first what all this is about."

"Tell him, major, you took the first call."

He said, "This panel was picked up about twelve miles offshore, north of East London, by the frigate *Natal*..."

Lee-Aston!

I broke in. "What was she doing *there*?"

The major looked surprised. The colonel leaned forward expectantly. I saw the flash of suspicion.

"Why?"

"Well...*Natal* towed me in to Cape Town. I thought the frigate was damaged. Her captain said he was going to Simonstown for repairs. The search area was to the north of the Bashee—Lee-Aston told me so himself."

"*Natal* was damaged," replied the major. "But Commander Lee-Aston joined the search in its final stages. However, when it was called off, the damage to *Natal* was found to be more extensive than was at first thought. *Natal* did not return to base. She stayed over at East London for more repairs. That took some time. She was on her way back when she spotted the panel..."

It slipped out before I could check myself. "But if she was making for Simonstown, she would not have been north of East London but south..."

Lee-Aston was not the cold, inflexible machine I had thought him to be after all. The main search having failed, he had gone straight to the area I had urged him to search! And he had found part of the *Gemsbok*!

Both the colonel and the major were staring at me.

Joubert said thoughtfully, "You're very clever about these things, Captain Fairlie."

The major resumed, not taking his eyes from my face. "Commander Lee-Aston first thought he had found part of the Buccaneer."

"Why didn't he say something!" I burst out.

"You've been a great deal in the news lately, Captain Fairlie," replied Joubert. "How the press must love you! One drama on top of another! Fortunately Commander Lee-Aston chose his duty above publicity. He kept his mouth shut until he reached Simonstown and the origin of the panel could be established."

There was an innuendo about the colonel's words which should have warned me.

He threw away his cigarette. "If you listen hard, you can hear the reporters grinding their teeth outside that door waiting to interview you. Howling, in fact. How did they know?"

He eyed me searchingly.

"Are you trying to imply...?"

"I am implying nothing, Captain Fairlie—at this stage. All I can say is that the way one drama is piling on after another..." He shrugged. "It gets like a drug, being in the headlines. There was a man I wanted once whom we chased all over the country. Every day he had the headlines. He got away. He was quite safe where he holed up. The papers cooled off. He couldn't bear it. So he arranged with the papers that he would give himself up at a particular spot and they'd be there—reporters, photographers, the lot. He was perfectly happy when we arrived to arrest him. He was back again on the front page. It is quite amazing how co-operative the press proves on these occasions..."

"To the other side," growled the major.

I looked from one to the other. They had not accused me of a put-up job with the press, but they were pretty close to the wind.

I bit back my reactions, "Is that panel really part of the *Gemsbok*?"

One of the civilians—Warren, the aircraft manufacturer's representative—said wearily from the depths of his shaggy beard, "That section of fuselage comes from a Viscount, you can take it from me. The rivet style and metallurgical content correspond with the *Gemsbok* mark. It is certainly not a Buccaneer."

Another civilian, a Transport Ministry Inspector of Crashes, was about to speak when the door was opened by a sergeant, who showed in an officer in Air Force uniform.

"Sorry, colonel."

"We hadn't gone far," said Joubert shortly. "This is Captain Fairlie,"

Major Bates's handshake was firm but uncommitted. "I saw your ship from my Shackleton the other day. My crew were laying bets how long you would stay afloat." He looked inquiringly at the metal panel, at the colonel, at Tafline. No one spoke. He found himself a chair in the silence.

The Inspector of Crashes broke the uncomfortable atmosphere.

"The style of stencil and type of paint is the same as we use for our Airways planes. No doubt. Of course, we haven't yet had time to make a full chemical analysis but it looks good at first glance."

Tafline broke in, "Those other words and scratches—they run into one another. What do they mean?"

"We've tried them and the figures also, but they look pretty hopeless," Warren replied. "Most of them are on top of each other. We could try some specialized photography and the handwriting experts, but I'm not very hopeful. It seems as if the man who wrote this was either dying or injured." He turned to me. "Sorry, I forgot for the moment it was your father. One becomes impersonal about these things."

"I don't accept that," snapped Joubert. "Anyone could have fabricated a thing like that. Who ever heard of a will being scratched on a chunk of metal by a pilot who died at the controls of a plane which vanished without trace?"

"I might agree with you, except that panel came from a Viscount," answered Warren. "No question about it."

"Is that all you can tell?"

Warren glanced at the Inspector of Crashes and grinned. "I said, we were busy on it all night. It tells a whole story."

The colonel flushed with annoyance when Tafline said quickly, "Such as?"

Some of the tiredness seemed to ease out of Warren as he warmed to his explanation. "One works backwards in these matters. The buckling of the panel forward where the *Gemsbok*'s name was shows that the force of the crash was underneath and upwards; in other words, the Viscount did not crash nose-first into some obstacle. It also shows that there was no explosion in the turbines on the port side, or else there would be blackening. We can pretty well rule out fire."

"The sea would put out a fire anyway." Joubert tried to halt Warren's exposition.

Warren ignored him. "The style of curvature of the buckling shows that the airliner went in at full power, hit something hard like the sea, bounced, and then hit something else with the starboard or opposite wing. That something did the real damage. Probably tore off the wing and killed most of the passengers."

"You can't possibly tell me you can find out all this from one piece of metal," objected Joubert.

The Inspector of Crashes rushed to the support of his technical colleague.

"We have a set number of things we look for in every crash."

"Listen..." exclaimed the red-faced colonel, but the Inspector and Warren continued to ignore him.

"There was no explosion in this case, or else the pilot couldn't have written the message."

"Scratched," corrected Warren. "It was then prised loose with some instrument—after the disaster."

The Inspector remained in full flight. "Could there have been misreading of the altimeter by the pilot, or simply an error in the instrument itself..."

"I'd rate the chances of an altimeter fault high," argued Warren. "It's pretty certain that he hit the sea at full power and that he was confident that he was flying high enough not to encounter any obstacles."

Major Bates, the Air Force man, said, "My squadron searched all that area with everything we had. Sonar and electronic instruments aren't the whole answer, though. But visual sightings and spottings are difficult in a sea which is murky from all the sand the current brings with it and the mud from all those rivers."

Colonel Joubert thumped the table with his fist.

"This isn't an inquiry into the loss of the *Gemsbok*. That was held years ago," he grated. "It found that the pilot died at the controls—and that is good enough for me. I'm a policeman, and I say there is little proof that this inscription was made by Captain Fairlie's father."

"Take it or leave it, that panel is from a Viscount—probably the *Gemsbok*," replied Warren.

The colonel glared at the two experts, at Tafline, and then let his gaze rest on me. Slowly, deliberately, he lit a cigarette and watched me through the cloud of smoke.

"I don't deny it," he said. "I'll accept that it was the *Gemsbok*." He eyed me fixedly. "Captain Fairlie, the C-in-C gave me a transcript of your interview with him." He indicated the pile of typescript in front of him. There were newspapers in the collection, too, sensationalizing Musgrave's questions about the *Waratah*. "*Waratah*

Found?" asked one headline. "Did Fairlie Brothers have a Treasure "Tryst?" I squirmed at the sight of them. Musgrave had known just the right note to strike for the press.

"There are pages and pages here about your views on the search for the *Waratah*..." He stopped and looked at me inquiringly.

"Yes?"

"Do you not find it strange that after your ship had nearly sunk in that big storm, you were sent a telegram which didn't say anything about your escape, or wish you safe, but only told you to stay away from the *Waratah*?"

"I understood what was meant."

"Did you, Captain Fairlie? Did you?"

"I mean, we had talked about the *Waratah*, we shared something over the old ship."

"What did you share?"

Tafline interrupted. "It was the thing which really brought us together. It was a kind of starting point, our first common ground..."

Joubert eyed us both. "A very strange form of introduction, I may say. It struck me as so strange that I felt it necessary to ask you to come along here today and tell me more. 'Keep away from the *Waratah* until I see you'. Why keep away? What did you intend to discuss about the ship when you met Captain Fairlie again? If you keep away from something, you must know where that something is, not so?"

Tafline blushed and was confused. "It—it was a form of expression. I didn't know Captain Fairlie very well at that stage. I..."

"You were in the area recently where the panel was found, were you not, Captain Fairlie?"

The faces round me turned blank at Joubert's tone of interrogation. It seemed, too, that the friendly surge of professional interest by the civilian experts had dimmed.

"Yes, but..."

"But what?"

I gestured towards the documents on the desk. "I explained it all to the C-in-C. I tried to at the Buccaneer inquiry. I have long believed that the clue to *Waratah*'s disappearance was the answer to safety for oil rigs in that area."

"Quite so, quite so. Yet the telegram says, 'keep away from the *Waratah*.'"

He let the silence fall, and then went on, "I said before, I am a policeman, Captain Fairlie, and in order to get to the bottom of things, we look below what lies on the surface. There are a number of very strange undercurrents in all this. The *juffrou's* telegram is one of them."

"It was just a simple message with no hidden or sinister meanings..." I began.

"What do you say, *juffrou*?"

"It was an everyday thought wishing him well."

Joubert smiled sarcastically. "'Keep away from the *Waratah*'—a very ordinary thing for a young lady in love to say!"

"You're reading all sorts of things into this, colonel!" I protested.

"There is nothing ordinary about a testament being scratched on a sheet of aluminum," retorted Joubert. "It is less ordinary still for someone whom everyone believes was killed in an airliner crash to bequeath his son a non-existent ship. In all my experience, I have never heard of anything like it."

I said, "You've forgotten the watch, Colonel Joubert."

"No, Captain Fairlie, I have not."

The police major chuckled in the background like a jackal at a lion's kill.

"That watch is just the sort of extra fancy touch that rouses a policeman's deepest instincts of distrust. It makes the job look too right, too watertight. If it weren't for that watch, I might have had doubts. But look at it—it's one of those self-winding calendar types and the hand has been set at October 23, 1967. Not you notice, at the date of the crash, July, 1967, but a couple of months later. Very clever, very clever indeed"

I checked my anger. "You want proof—we can easily have the watch analyzed. Or I can tell you myself—there was an inscription from the Air Force Association on the back. It was given to him when he became chief civilian pilot. The wording said something about his wartime raids."

"I don't for a moment doubt it is your father's watch, Captain Fairlie, just as I don't doubt that it is a panel from the *Gemsbok*. What worries me is how all this surfaced all at once, and why. And where that telegram about the *Waratah* fits into it."

"I've tried to explain, I've said over and over..."

Joubert waved his hand in dismissal. "I want to think this thing over—a lot. You'll be hearing from me again." He laughed in his overbearing way. "If you really want people to be on your side, you produce the wreck of the *Waratah*! Until then, you still have a great deal of explaining to do to a lot of people, Captain Fairlie!"

I went cold at the thought. "What do we say to the press?"

Joubert shrugged and laughed again. "*You* say, Captain Fairlie! It's your story. You set the ball rolling."

I turned to Tafline. She was unhappy, withdrawn. Again I wondered, what was all this *Waratah* suspicion and subtle accusation doing to her feelings?

Joubert added, "That pretty face of yours will provide the press with the romantic interest on the story they love so, *juffrou*."

An hour later, stunned by a barrage of reporters' questionings and blinded by a score of bursting flashbulbs, we stood by the great splash of color which is the flower market. She had not spoken since we emerged into the street, but she asked the Malay woman for *kalkoentjies* ("little turkeys")—those tiny exquisite wild gladioli, daubed with colors as if they had just been painted and scented, which come from hidden places of the Western Cape. Because it was winter, they were difficult to obtain in the market, but the woman came back smiling with some of the earliest which had been gathered from some sheltered kloof. I pinned the bunch to her lapel without speaking, and she looked down into the brown-and-yellow splashed center.

"They are like a woman in love," she murmured. "Beautiful by day, and her heart perfumed at night."

Why did my father have to find the *Waratah*? I asked myself resentfully, looking at her lovely face. Why did they have to come between us, those puzzling, bitter, unanswerable questions?

She said, "The *Waratah* is like the albatross hung round the Ancient Mariner's neck—for both of us. It has driven you into a corner, Ian. You are discredited, in danger of losing everything—your career, reputation, esteem..."

The cold fear tugged at my heart as I waited for her next words.

"We can never realize our love properly while we carry this burden."

The numb silence fell between us. I did not want it, but she was right and I knew that she was right.

I was afraid, though, when I saw Greatheart reach for the sword.

She said, "We must go and look for the *Waratah*, you and I."

CHAPTER 11

Touleier planed swiftly down the following sea, rose, and shook herself with an exulting motion as she raced out of the trough under full power of her great racing blue nylon spinnaker. A dollop of cold sea came aboard as she lifted and sloshed past me as I went forward to trim the jib a little so that all the spent wind of the spinnaker would spill into it, just as the mainsail was giving its overflow to the spinnaker itself.

"Watch it!" I warned Jubela at the helm.

Touleier was making a good eleven knots with a bone between her teeth, and I was driving her hard. Her sails were as taut and eager as I to get to the Bashee. *Touleier* liked it that way—she was a thoroughbred and could take what I handed out and, even in the rising sea and fresh southwesterly wind on the port quarter, she did not roll much because of her lean, streamlined hull. She was steady, tense, alive, and seemed to be exhilarating in being taken from her winter confinement as much as I did driving her. Between *Touleier* and myself there was that imponderable rapport which comes sometimes between a man and his ship—perhaps that is why I won the South American race in her—and I understood her every mood. It was this, perhaps, which made me a little particular about Jubela steering her, although he was handling the superb flier magnificently, grinning now and again as she picked up an extra knot or two in a downward plane, or giving a slight correction to the helm as he watched the taut, towering pyramid of canvas above him.

Tafline watched us from the cockpit as we handled the yacht. Like us, she wore oilskins, but no hood, and the wind blew her short hair forward over her forehead. Something of the pure joy of the yacht's speed touched her, too, and relaxed the urgency of our forward flight; she spoke only a little now and then to ask me some technicality of sailing.

Touleier drove for the Bashee.

I had emerged from my unhappy engagement with the colonel and the reporters to the easement of that moment with her by the flower sellers stunned, bewildered, raw, confused, certainly with no idea of repeating my search for the *Waratah*. The fact that the liner lay somewhere accessible, not hundreds of feet deep out of reach in some forsaken patch of sea, beat like a drum in my brain, but equally imperative was the unconcealed hostility of the authorities and their conviction that they had to do with an irresponsible nut. Whether I would ever be allowed to command the *Walvis Bay* again and resume the weather watch was open to the gravest doubt. At any moment I expected to be summoned to Pretoria to account for using the weather ship as a springboard for what the Weather Bureau undoubtedly now regarded as a private investigation of the *Waratah* mystery and nothing else.

Because my whole being was a ripple of hurt nerves, I had responded badly to her suggestion that we should go and search for the vanished liner.

How could we hope to succeed, I asked her roughly, where squadrons of specially equipped aircraft, helicopters and warships had failed? It was barely a fortnight since Major Bates and his men had been over it. Bates had button-holed me on leaving the Conference, and asked my permission to read in the transcript, in the interest of his Maritime Group, my statements about off-shore currents and winds. "Only providing you don't also use it as evidence against me," I had said firmly.

I had used Bates's own words to justify my own reluctance.

"The air-search revealed nothing: Bates himself has said so," I argued with her. "I myself sailed the *Waratah*'s exact course, and I saw nothing, I assure you."

She had paused, in that guarded way of hers, her face buried in her nosegay.

"True," she replied quietly. "There was no island for Bates and his fliers to see, no mysterious underwater cavern, no hulk. But you saw what there was. You saw that ancient ship, sailing against the wind."

I had felt uncomfortable and on the defensive. I regretted having told even her.

"It might have been anything—some sort of optical illusion caused by the waves and the light. One can't start a search on anything as nebulous as that."

"Phillips of the *Clan Macintyre* saw it too," she replied.

"I am not denying it," I hedged. "All I am saying is that it is certainly not substantial enough to approach the authorities. If I came along now, after all that has happened, with a story that I had seen the *Flying Dutchman*, I think they'd clap me in a lunatic asylum straight away. When it came to the point, I couldn't even bring myself to tell the C-in-C. In order to convince them that they should renew the air-sea search, they need some completely down-to-earth, substantial, and tangible facts."

She smiled. "I said, we must go and look, you and I. I didn't mention the authorities."

"What do you mean?"

"*Touleier*."

"*Touleier*!" I expostulated. "But she's laid up for the winter. You can't just go off in a yacht which doesn't belong to you anyway, but to a syndicate! Besides, it's winter, the worst time of the year..."

"The idea came to me during the Conference when I turned and looked at you," she went on. "*Touleier*'s ready for the round-the-coast race in the spring, you told me so yourself. You also said they wanted you to skipper her, although you probably couldn't, if you're on the weather watch. She's got a new suit of sails and that untried self-steering device. Nothing would please the sponsors more than that the winner of the South American race should take *Touleier* on a quick shakedown cruise round the coast while his own ship is being repaired."

I gasped, then I laughed. It might still lie within my grasp to justify everything I had done and said about the *Waratah*.

"It's so simple and so fantastic!" I exclaimed, a little unsteadily.

"Jubela—I could get him to crew with us. It's a big strain handling a fast boat like *Touleier* by oneself, and Jubela knows his stuff. We can expect some rough weather..."

"We want rough weather; we want another big gale," she said firmly. "It's the way we'll find the *Waratah* secret."

"This time I'll take a camera along—a very good camera," I remarked. "If we see anything like my old sailing ship, I can at least bring back a picture for the doubting Thomases."

The thought of the wild sea and frenetic wind sobered my enthusiasm for a moment. "We can count on at least half a dozen winter gales in those parts. However, the one I hit in *Walvis Bay* and the sort of gale which hit the *Waratah* was no ordinary winter gale. But we do know that the storm that hit *Waratah* was followed shortly afterwards by two other exceptional gales. We may be lucky—or unlucky. It's also very different being out in a blow in a small boat like *Touleier* and a ship even of *Walvis Bay*'s size. The going will be rough."

She had touched my hand. "There's probably not a sailor in the whole Southern Hemisphere safer than you in a gale, The Fairlies must have been born in gales."

I felt like adding, died, too.

Touleier's sponsors had been delighted when I put forward Tafline's suggestion. They, at least, did not seem to share the general misgivings about me. Jubela appeared as glad as the sponsors when I found him drinking mournfully in a shebeen at 10 o'clock in the morning.

"The sea is clean," he had said. "And I am like a bushpig in a wallow here."

Now he was in his element; gone was the silence and depression which had marked his final days at the wheel of *Walvis Bay*. I had told him the *Waratah* story and Tafline had been with me. "It is right that one should know the grave of one's ancestors," was all Jubela had replied, "and this ancestor must have been a great sailor."

The mood of the three of us was tight, purposeful, that day when we approached the headland of St. Francis, our last southern gateway to the Bashee, still some 200 miles to the northeast, the final point in rounding the "ankle" of the coast. *Touleier* herself seemed to share that mood: taut, yet controlled; eager, yet aware of the dangers ahead.

I took my binoculars and climbed into the rigging. Astern, the horizon had the peculiar blur of purple-blue characteristic of a southwesterly blow, although I felt sure it would not work up into a buster of the caliber which had nearly sunk the *Walvis Bay*. I had to rely on my own instincts. It would have been fatal for me to have got in touch with the Weather Bureau, and I had no intention of letting Colonel Joubert in on our mission. I had concealed the yacht's departure by slipping out of Cape Town at night, in a growing northwesterly wind. Now, well to the east, rounding that "ankle" of the South African coastline, I was keeping well clear of the land in order to avoid being caught by some of the violent squalls which sometimes sweep down from the high land. *Touleier*'s thrusting spinnaker would snap the light-metal racing mast like a carrot if it were caught aback.

There it was!

I called to Tafline. "Cape St. Francis!"

She swung up nimbly alongside me and looked through the binoculars, and then let them hang round her neck on the strap. She put her face against mine, warm by contrast with the cold southwesterly wind and its threat of rain. The dedicated purpose of the voyage was lightened by my joy at being away to sea with her, and having a splendid yacht underfoot. I think she guessed what I was thinking, for she turned and looked into my eyes, and allowed the roll of the mast to sway her hard against my side.

Touleier raced on.

Unwilling to break the silence, yet reminded of our mission by the sight of that distant landmark, she said at length, "You read the sea like a book, Ian. It is what lies ahead now, isn't it? It would be pure magic, you and me and *Touleier*, if it weren't for the *Waratah*."

I side-stepped it now. I gestured towards some other passing ships. "We're using the standard northward route close to the coast to avoid the Agulhas Current. That tanker out there is picking up the benefit of its southbound flow. That's the way it has always been. Northbound, you keep close to the land, especially in this sort of wind, which sets up a counter-current shorewards."

Without warning, she buried her face in my neck. "Oh my darling, my darling!" she sobbed. "I know all these winds, storms, currents, and the rest are part of the pattern which has been woven into our lives because of...of..." I felt the warm tears against my skin, "But it's you I want, free of all these terrifying shackles..." She choked gently, and I tried to comfort her, and I tasted the salt of her tears on her lips. She took my face in her hands and searched it with her fingertips as if to memorize every line; she kissed me as if her heart would burst until even that lively deck and press of sail became oblivion as we raced towards the Bashee.

There were a hundred things to do to the yacht as *Touleier* sped northwards. After Cape St. Francis, Tafline had insisted, as part of the general state of alertness and preparedness, on being taught the rudiments of helmsmanship, although my heart was in my mouth once when *Touleier* was caught napping by a sharp squall with her at the wheel; the yacht went far over before I could get to Tafline's side, but Jubela saved the situation by letting fly a halyard.

I kept *Touleier* well clear of the big harbor of Port Elizabeth, but beyond we went close to two groups of tiny islands, called St. Croix and Bird, which lie in the big bay of Algoa. In these waters the first sailor ever to round the Cape nearly five centuries ago turned back because his crew mutinied: Bartholomew Diaz planted a marble cross, and it is wrongly commemorated by the name Cape Padrone at the northeastern fringe of the bay. Only in this century, shortly before the Second World War, was the true location of Diaz's cross found slightly to the north.

Now we were approaching the spot. I was trying to use the weak inshore counter-current about three miles out to help *Touleier* along and edge past a race of the Agulhas Current which spills over near Cape Padrone.

There was muddy water under the yacht, a sure sign that the southwester was strong enough to generate at least a slight counter to the big main stream further out.

Jubela was off watch and Tafline sat scanning the sea and the shoreline with my glasses: watching, hoping, tireless.

"An island!"

I threw a quick bight of halyard round a cleat and slithered to her side.

No island had ever been recorded hereabouts.

"There!" she pointed, giving me the glasses. "It's dark against the white."

The bucking deck and my unsteady hands made focusing difficult. Then I saw the tiny cross at the summit.

I laughed. I had not realized how keyed up I really was. My nerves were as stretched as *Touleier*'s rigging.

"Diaz made the same mistake four centuries ago," I told her, disappointed. "The cross is a replica of Diaz' original, which tumbled down and was found in fragments among the rocks below."

"But—it looks like an island!" she maintained.

"That's why it deceived the experts for so long," I went on. "Its actual name is False Islet. Diaz logged that he had planted his cross on an island, and for hundreds of years men searched for an island, just as we are doing. Until an acute historian-detective hit on the secret of False Islet."

She was still game. "No chance of the *Waratah* being ashore there?"

"Not a chance," I answered. "Since the cross was found, thousands of people have visited the place. You can walk from the mainland across a sand causeway to it." I added, to let her down lightly and not dampen her keenness, "It's so easy to be deceived on this coast. In a few hours we'll come to a spot called Ship Rock. Another near it is called The Wreck. If you want to imagine things, the natural topography gives one full scope."

Towards sunset the wind eased and backed to the south. We took in *Touleier*'s spinnaker for the night, leaving her moving well under the American-cut mainsail and jib. We could not be off the Bashee until the following evening at the earliest, if the wind held. In the crowded shipping lane I decided to rig a spotlight high in the rigging to illuminate the sails so that we would not be run down by some unwatchful steamer. *Touleier* held close to the coast and at intervals the lighted resorts stood out clearer almost than the navigational lights. A thin veil of spume from the breakers hung over the cliffs. It was scarcely necessary for me to listen to the radio met. reports to know that the main front had bypassed the Cape—the change of wind direction southwards was a certain pointer that we had nothing to expect, or to fear, from this particular southwester.

As we sat alone in the cockpit—she was half-turned away from me, gazing towards the land—she suddenly said:

"Did you really see the *Flying Dutchman*, Ian?"

She had never spoken of it again since that day when first the news of the *Gemsbok* panel reached us. My stomach knotted at her words. Gone was the quiet pleasure of sailing.

"I told you, I saw a ship, an ancient ship, sailing against the wind."

There was a long pause. She watched the distant coastline.

"You didn't link her in your mind with the *Flying Dutchman*?"

"No."

She got up quickly, turned to me and dropped on her knees. She scanned my face, deeply, tenderly.

"My darling—are you quite sure of what you saw?"

In that moment, I would have traded away a dozen *Waratahs* for her.

I leaned forward and touched a wisp of short hair above her ear. She would not let my fingers go.

"When I was thrown against the rear of the bridge by the big wave," I explained, "I wasn't stunned, My sole concern at that moment was to prevent *Walvis Bay* from broaching to. Nothing was further from my thoughts than the *Flying Dutchman*—or the *Waratah*. My only thought was to save my ship. I grabbed the wheel. Then I saw. It was a ship, and she was close, between *Walvis Bay* and the land. She was darkened. It was all too quick to distinguish any details. I mean, I couldn't distinguish gunports, deckhouses, porthole lights or anything like that."

"No human figures? A man with...with..."

"A bloodied sword?—No."

"It was more an outline, then?"

"She seemed almost on top of us, I saw a high prow and a towering, square stern, and I noticed particularly the way she was heading—southwest. That meant she was sailing right into the eye of the wind."

"The sails, what did the sails look like?"

I paused and considered. "Now you come to ask, I don't

remember seeing any sails. I should, being a sailor. But what struck me most forcibly was the way she was going. Both her stern and bow were quite distinct, both were high and well defined. There was no mistaking them. It was for all the world like one of those pictures you've seen of an old-fashioned caravel."

"And you and Phillips—are the only two who claim to have seen this ancient ship? You are sure there is no other record of her?"

"Certain," I replied. "You might even discredit my sighting by saying that I had been subconsciously influenced by all my delving into the *Waratah* disaster. But Phillips himself—no! When Phillips sighted what he himself called the *Flying Dutchman*, he had no idea even that the *Waratah* was missing. He had brought the *Clan Macintyre* successfully through a great storm. Half his ordeal was already behind him. No, what Phillips saw, he saw in daylight, not at night."

She looked at me sharply, and then helped me slack off the mainsail under the dropping wind, waiting, in her quiet way, for me to continue.

"Let's discount my sighting for the moment. Phillips knew all about sailing ships. He stated categorically that the mizzen of the caravel he saw was raked back, and the foremast forward."

"Your sighting is so recent, and yet Phillips' is much more explicit," she said quietly.

"I can't say I saw the masts or the sails," I went on. "But I saw the hull clearly. The high bow and stern were exactly as Phillips describes them. And she was definitely sailing against the wind. It scared Phillips. He drank cocoa. I felt more like a shot of rum."

"Were you frightened, Ian, like he was?"

"I knew only fear," I replied somberly. "I have tried since, over and again, to try and rationalize it. I still go cold when I have a nightmare and see right ahead of me that dark, old-fashioned hull and *Walvis Bay* about to crash into it. There were seconds only between us and certain death, that I know."

She turned away and spoke so softly that I had to crane to hear what she said.

"I saw nothing, yet I felt it all, hundreds of miles away, that night. It's impossible to describe the feeling. It was the same that first day I came aboard and saw your photographs."

We left it at that. But had I "felt" the *Waratah* then, I would have put the yacht about and nothing would ever have induced me to go in search of her again. As it was, the wind and the sea were quieting; it was a joy to have her close against me in the cold chill as the night wore on. There were no ghosts at sea that night. She was warm, she was alive, she was mine.

The lid of the *Waratah*'s coffin lifted next night, and the ghosts escaped.

At dawn *Touleier* was south of the Bashee.

We had sailed all day northwards, never out of sight of the great forests and high cliffs which come down almost to the water's edge. Far out at sea, even, we could hear the breakers. It is an iron shore. One scarcely ever finds a seashell which has not been smashed by the force of the waves. We both grew more tense as *Touleier* approached the Bashee, and she was very silent. We contented ourselves with minor tasks about the yacht and left unsaid many things. We did not talk about the *Waratah*.

The coastline is cut by innumerable rivers, and each one seems to have an exquisite lagoon at its mouth. In the first dim light I could see solid columns of mist marching down each river to the sea, shaped and squared by the cliffs on either side.

One- two- three flashes.

Bashee Mouth light.

Tafline screamed from below.

For a moment I sat rigid. Her voice seemed to hang against the dark backdrop of the cliffs, the shadowy forests and the river mouth white with breakers.

I raced to the cabin.

She was sitting up on the bunk, wide-eyed, shaking.

"The storm, Ian! That wind...!"

I held her, trembling. In the dim light coming through the porthole I could see that consciousness had not come fully into her eyes.

"My darling, the wind is gone. It's a quiet, still dawn. There's no storm."

"I heard..." she shook her head as if to clear it. "But he stood here, and his oilskins were wet." She buried her face against me. "Thank

God, it's you, my darling. It was only a dream."

I soothed her. But the strange, deep eyes were full of shadows.

"I can see him now, standing by the bunk," she said, smiling a little wryly. "I could hear the wind, and his oilskins were dripping."

"*Who* was standing?" I asked gently, cold at the recollection of Sawyer.

"It was just an ordinary person," she said hesitatingly. "No, not *him*. There was nothing like that. Just a man." She looked at me searchingly. "His face was like yours, a little. I could hear the gale. His oilskins were streaming wet, it's all so vivid. Why, what is the matter?"

It was I who was trembling. She had on almost nothing except a thin slip of a thing; I could see her breasts and her body now where she had pushed aside the bedclothes in her agitation.

Where before I had seen the mystic, the sea-ancestry, the knight with unadorned armor against the panoply of the *Waratah* in the lists. Now I saw the woman.

She sat and held my gaze. She extended her arm to touch me. Not taking her eyes from me, she slipped off the wispy thing. She brought my hands to her breasts in the tender lycanthropy of love. We searched for each other's eyes, lips, hair. Then her lips went cold. Her body lost its fervor to be one with mine.

She drew back. She wept—a quiet, passionless sobbing, a grief as deep, it seemed, as the passion of the moment before.

"We could love, we could forget," she said softly, "but we can't forget, and it would come and take our love away from us. It would only be pretending. You are committed and I am committed. We are not free to commit our love until we find the *Waratah*, I said before, and my body and my heart say it now, until we are free of this burden, we will not be able to realize our love properly."

All I could say, was: "We're at the place now. South of the Bashee."

She ran her hands over her breasts and down her thighs; she clasped them round her knees and hid her face. She gave a last broken, half-sob.

I moved to comfort her, but she shook her head without looking up. "I'll dress and come up to you in the cockpit."

150

As I went to the door, she said in a smothered voice, "When we have the *Waratah*, I am yours."

She was tense, alert, when she came on deck as if being at the Bashee would in itself solve everything. She had come across at once to me at the wheel. She did not kiss me, or stand close, but faced me from the other side of the helm, her hands warm on mine by contrast with the stainless steel circle of the wheel.

"I know now you will never love me less," was all she said.

But as we ghosted through the placid water towards the land, I felt her tenseness and disappointment growing at the sight of the empty sea. With daylight, we could make out the deep cleft the Bashee makes between the forested hills, the signal station on a grassy cliff with more forest for a backdrop, and a group of thatched holiday rondavels nearby.

Then the bubble of pent-up feeling burst.

"It's so *ordinary*!" she exclaimed. "There's just nothing here, Ian!"

I took in the sails and *Touleier* lay in the easy swell, perhaps a mile offshore.

"It's the normality of it like this which breaks down the picture of whatever I saw in *Walvis Bay*'s path that night," I replied. I was tired, drained of feeling. Like that moment at the flower sellers, I hated the *Waratah*. But, again, I knew she was right.

"Yet," she went on, and I still recall her vehemence—"where we are now, maybe right under our keel, a great liner went down and an airliner too. I feel I want to tear the sea apart and look."

Tear apart! I remember her words now: the answer was all too improbable, too simple, when one came to think of it. I wonder if we would have accepted it, had we known then, without having to live it out?

She jumped on the rail and gazed astern, as if to probe that gentle sea for the undefined spot where Alistair had died.

"I didn't expect anything like this!" She was puzzled, angry. "I took it for granted there would be a sinister sea, a sinister setting, somehow. My reason tells me your brother died somewhere right here. You nearly did, too, but I see nothing. We have the most concrete proof that your father sent you a message from 'south of the

Bashee', but where, where?"

She gestured helplessly. One of the big supertankers ploughed south; a coaster was coming up fast behind us, closer inshore.

"The sea has a lying face," I retorted. "I know. I know how savage and remorseless it can be, this stretch of apparently guileless water, and it does cover up the *Waratah*'s secret; we have narrowed it down to here."

She looked at me and said: "Maybe I was wrong to make you come. Maybe I am wrong about the *Waratah*. If I am wrong about her, then I am wrong about last night."

I gave the wheel to Jubela and sat beside her, looking southwest.

"No," I replied. "I am the only person who has seen the other side of the coin and lived to tell it."

"That's what I believe."

"Everything else, all speculation for sixty years, every sea and air search ends here, south of the Bashee."

"It is not enough simply to be here, Ian. There must be something more."

"The murderers of my brother, my father and my grandfather, were never brought to trial."

"What do you mean, Ian?"

"The sea, and the wind."

She gestured at the gentle sea, turning a deep blue-green in the new light. "It seems impossible to credit."

"Except for the Skeleton Coast, there are more wrecks to the square mile along this coast than anywhere else in the world," I replied.

Tafline shivered, and she was silent a long time, staring at the empty sea. Then she said. "If this thing—whatever it is—occurs only at long intervals, what is the use of our coming so soon after it hit at *Walvis Bay*? I was crazy to suggest we come in a small boat like *Touleier*. We're simply risking our necks to no purpose, if the same wind and sea conditions recur."

My thoughts were only half on my reply. The *Waratah* now held to ransom the slim, lovely creature beside me; my throat constricted at the recollection of her a few hours earlier. Find the *Waratah* and find my love! For her sake, for my sake, there must be no mistake! I answered, far from convinced: "It's just the other way round. The bigger the ship, the less chance it has, because it has a much longer length exposed to a wave. A sixty-foot wave would threaten a long ship whereas a small thing like *Touleier* would simply rise to it."

She did not seem quite reassured and did not reply. Then she turned and I found my pulses racing at those deep eyes.

"Darling, perhaps you have already solved the *Waratah* problem and don't know it? Isn't it simply a question of the *Waratah* being overwhelmed by one of those monster waves, despite all the experts said about her stability?"

Her tone made me yearn to play traitor and agree. Reluctantly, however, I said, "The answer to that is, no bodies or wreckage were ever found, and the place was alive with ships within a couple of days. When a big vessel goes down, wreckage would spew out of her hatches; the engine-room boilers would explode."

She broke in hopefully, and I loved her for it. "Isn't it all too cut and dried, just as the experts were about the *Waratah* and her stability?"

I smiled back. "Maybe as an expert I'm in danger of not seeing the wood for the trees. I can only take the picture so far, and no farther. All I know is that a danger area lay right across the track of the *Waratah*, and she went straight into it. Then there came into play some unknown, lethal, death-dealing factor which can swallow up a 10,000-ton liner as easily as it does a modern airliner or a supersonic fighter-jet."

"Do we simply wait around here, then, hoping for this unknown factor to manifest itself?"

My heart sank when I looked at her, but I forced myself to say it. "No. We have to run the gauntlet. That means the southwest. We must get up to Port St. John's. Then, if a gale comes, we must sail the *Waratah*'s course from there—southwest. It's the only way I see if we want to find out."

She came close to me, the first time since the night.

"I don't think I am afraid of dying; I am only afraid of losing you."

We sailed to Port St. John's from a sea as empty as the hour after the *Waratah* had vanished.

CHAPTER 12

It came, plangent and fateful as a distant bell-buoy tolling over a killer reef.

All day we had inched *Touleier* up the *Waratah* coast while the wind stayed light in the northeast. Tafline and I checked, discussed, spotted landmarks like the impressive rock which is called The-Hole-in-the-Wall. It was perfect fair-weather yachting and some of the tension seemed to ebb from us as we absorbed the soporific magic and she ghosted along. We had breathtaking glimpses of black, iron-bound cliffs topped by great forests, for which the territory is famous; we could pick out, by their lofty whiteness like ships' spars, the straight trunks of the *umzimbeet* trees among their darker companions; fragile lagoons came and went at sunset with the chimerical loveliness of an old Chinese print on silk; tree euphorbias hung out stark candelabra of branches against great cliffs and begged to be photographed; here and there the lush strelitzias would over-arch a river mouth with sensuous, tropical beauty, a frame for secret mangrove swamps behind, trodden not by human foot but by the claws of giant crabs as big as soup plates.

The twice-daily shipping forecasts brought a taut expectancy. One is broadcast after lunch, and the other after 11 at night. There was no hint of a gale.

There was a nerve-tingle at dawn when I brought *Touleier* into position off Port St. John's where the *Waratah* and *Clan Macintyre* had exchanged their last signals. We had decided on this just as, lower down the coast off East London, we had cruised over the exact spot

154

where the liner *Guelph* had received her garbled "t-a-h" lamp signal from a ship which was never subsequently identified.

Tafline had asked me to call her when *Touleier* was under the Cape Hermes light. I went to her cabin. She was lying, eyes wide open, waiting for me.

I felt a small nerve kick in her lips as she kissed me and she indicated the heavy sweater and slacks she had been wearing when she left me after the late-night forecast. The apology, the dedication, the promise, were all in her embrace. She held me for so long that it was I who had to remind her that the wheel was unattended.

We went on deck.

She shivered as the flash came from the Cape Hermes lighthouse. It stands, as it did when the *Waratah* passed by, unnaturally bright against the dark cliff on the southern bank of the lovely river mouth. Except for a few thatched seaside cottages, the coastline looked the same as it did on that fateful morning when the two liners parted. She shivered again at the sight of the strange rectangular columns of mist marching down the St. John's River to the sea, shaping themselves to the cliffs on either side. The great Gates—massive, forest-covered twin peaks flanking the river on either side—were shrouded in the early light. Once the mist swirled aside and showed the ruins of an old piled jetty and rusting boiler of some abandoned coaster, relics of the days when the port was still used by shipping.

She whispered, as if afraid to arouse the specters of the past. "Is this the place?"

I nodded.

The sea was empty.

Our shadows dissipated when the sun rose for another fine day. It lulled us into going ashore when a friendly ski-boat came out from the land and offered us a ride. I left Jubela in charge of *Touleier*. We were rowed across the river near the mouth by an African ferry; there was a magnificent up-river view for miles. I think we were both glad to be on land and stretch our legs. We laughed at a ridiculous pleasure launch shaped like a giant swan in poor imitation of something Mediterranean; we speculated over the origin of a twelve-foot sailing ship anchor with gigantic flukes which stood near the old jetty; we saw an old cannon from the treasure ship *Grosvenor*, a mystery of

Pondoland which rivals that of the *Waratah*.

We walked along the riverside road after lunch, and she bought some African beadwork. She was excitedly showing me a tiny rectangle of exquisiteness—each pattern in the Transkei has its message, of love, rejection, birth, death, health—when a car with tourists drew up with its radio blaring.

It was then that we heard the news of a gale warning. "Northwesterly to westerly winds in the vicinity of Cape Point will reach thirty to forty-five knots, spreading eastwards..."

Eastwards! To us! Here was the classic storm pattern beginning!

I caught her arm. The pleasure of the small purchase died in her.

I looked at her, and she looked at me. I remember her now in her thin summer dress standing next to the roughly-planked wooden stall by the edge of the chocolate river, the blue, white and gold beadwork held in her hand. It seemed impossible, in that soft semi-tropical setting, that ice, gales and rollers would start to hurl themselves at the Cape within hours. Was it one of those lethal secondary low pressure systems which hive off the main storm and send the oilmen hurrying to batten down everything to safety and shipmasters to keep anxious watches in the type of weather which has earned the Cape of Storms its terrible cognomen? Would it turn into...?

I left that question unanswered in my mind.

"How bad is it, Ian?" she asked, handing back the beadwork to the disappointed African woman.

"We might know more if there had been a *Walvis Bay* on station," I replied. My mind raced over a mass of technicalities. "It may be everything; it may be nothing."

Upon the outcome hung my career and our love.

"God!" I burst out. "If only I *knew*! If only I could phone the Bureau and ask."

"You could, Ian! It's worth the risk!—don't mention your name or *Touleier* or the fat will be in the fire. You must know more before sailing down the coast."

I punched my fist into my palm in frustration. "The real significance can only be judged when I know more about the upper air winds, temperatures, pressures, and the like. Imagine an ordinary yacht skipper asking for that sort of stuff!"

"Somehow, you must."

I looked at my watch. A quarter to two.

"I've got it! By now the Bureau will have had plenty of time to study this morning's weather satellite picture. That'll give us some idea of what's coming. It isn't the whole answer, as you know, but it's worth trying."

In the old hotel's musty foyer near a glass case of sea relics—huge conch shells, a medieval ship's bottle, a sea-scarred snuffbox whose vignette had been obliterated by long immersion—I took the telephone call which was to mean so much to us. Tafline stood looking out to the river, past the massive wooden balcony supports of old ships' beams as I heard the portents.

"What is it, darling?" she asked, when I had finished.

She had paled, and I kissed the bloodless lips. "It's still too early to say. We must get away to sea. At dawn this morning, the Cape had strong wind and rain, and by ten o'clock it was blowing a gale; the pressure went down like a lift. I think the Bureau was delighted to have a mere yachtsman ask such intelligent questions—they were quite forthcoming. The storm's moving east, at a great rate, towards us. But it could sheer off southwards into the Southern Ocean. Then all we'd get off the Bashee would be some strong wind."

"Shall we know at all in advance?" She, like myself, knew we had to go, yet we jibbed before putting the horse to that cataclysmic jump.

"From the signs we can, and the signs are at sea," I answered. "Here on the coast we should have a northeasterly wind today, and maybe even into tomorrow. You can tell if it's going to be a real buster because the pressure drops while the northeaster blows. Then suddenly the wind will die. Up goes the pressure. The wind shifts like lightning into the south-west, and before you know where you are it's a full gale."

"A *Waratah* gale, Ian?" she asked in a small voice.

"The right thing would be to signal Port Elizabeth as we go south. Yet one word of me being here in *Touleier*, in a gale, and they'd stick me landbound in a desert at the farthest spot away from the sea they could find, if they didn't sack me outright. We must get to sea—now. It'll take us all night to reach our target area off the Bashee. We can hope for that freshening northeaster behind *Touleier* until it drops and gives way to what we're really looking for."

Our ski-boaters had left the village and gone fishing at Second Beach, an idyllic spot at the back of the huge cliff which is Cape Hermes. We hurriedly hired a car and found them on the rocks. They were surprised at our urgency to get to sea, and it was not until the middle of the afternoon that they put us alongside *Touleier*. They did not seem to grasp the significance of the yacht's famous name, and I did not enlighten them.

"Get the mainsail and jib on her," I ordered an equally surprised Jubela.

As we headed away southwest, I explained the weather to him. We crammed on the big spinnaker to make time until dark. Later I intended to clear the decks of all loose gear and snug her down in earnest to meet the gale.

The sun dropped behind the Gates of Port St. John's, and the forests were silhouetted. Tafline had been below a long time, securing and stowing the galley things and double-checking all lockers.

She had changed from her summer dress back into yachting sweater and slacks when she joined me. Cape Hermes was still visible astern, although the lighthouse itself was masked. She sat by me at the helm while Jubela worked forward.

We continued to watch the disappearing headland. Then Tafline left her seat and dropped on her knees in front of me on the gratings, scrutinizing me as if we had been parted for years.

"When I listened to you on the phone talking about the ins-and-outs of the weather I wondered, are *we* not dicing with the devil for our lives? Not the *Flying Dutchman*, but us? Deliberately, presumptuously—us?"

The headland flared brighter, the sun using the river passage for its last rays.

I tried to soothe her fears with more facile explanations of the safety of a small ship in a gale, and how tried and tested *Touleier* was, except for the new self-steering gear. I did not confess my misgivings about it, nor about the tall racing mast. I had watched *Walvis Bay*'s short stubby foremast go half-overboard, and it had been steel, not light-alloy, nor was it under a press of sail.

She did not take her eyes from mine as I explained. Then, as I faltered to a finish, she made the most telling gesture in all my knowledge of our love. She put her cheeks between my hands, and said something to herself as if her heart would break. Then she spread her arms on my knees and buried her face, so that I saw the last sunlight between her short hair and the polo collar. Did she weep? Did she pray? All I know is that she knelt silent a long time.

The yacht drove on.

The day ran out, and the partridge sky became feathered with gold.

We took the racing sails off her at sundown and brought up the tough gale trysail ready for use. Jubela and I worked on the self-steering gear and decided to disconnect it. Both of us had shared the wheel in *Walvis Bay*'s ordeal, and we knew what to expect. Our judgment, in an engine-less craft under sail, would have to be finer than any automatic device if the same thing happened again.

When we had cleared the yacht, I sent Jubela below to rest. Tafline stayed with me, waiting for the late-night shipping forecast. It would give us an idea of the direction of the storm. What I wanted, however, was more technical data which I could get only from Port Elizabeth, but I dared not signal the met. office there. I shelved my dilemma. The wind became fresher from the northeast; the stars were numberless over our heads, and the sea was sweet.

She tuned in.

"There is a gale warning," said the announcer. "Strong northwesterly winds between Cape Town and Cape Agulhas will reach forty to fifty knots, spreading eastwards, with southwesterly forty-five to fifty-five knots later."

"The signs are there, all right," I remarked. "Tonight every oil rig will be battened down, waiting for the worst."

"Why does the wind switch from northwest to southwest round the Cape coast?" she asked.

"Because of the land mass," I replied. "That's why I'm so desperately keen to know what is happening at Port Elizabeth."

She went on hesitantly, as she always did when she asked me about sailing matters, "Phillips was dumbfounded when he saw that old-time ship sailing against the wind. Since *Touleier* has no engine, how do you intend pushing into the teeth of a southwesterly gale?"

The impending storm still seemed very far away that clear, fresh night with her next to me.

I held her hand tightly and explained. "Safe tactics in a sailing ship and a steamer caught in this sort of gale are two different matters. Two windjammers—the *Johanna* and *Indian Empire*—were, in fact, caught on the same day by the *Waratah*'s gale. Both 'hauled out' some seventy miles to sea to get away from the tug of the southbound Agulhas Current. They both crossed the *Waratah*'s course, but they saw nothing, and spent ten days in one position riding the storm. That's what the experts thought Captain Ilbery would have done in the *Waratah*—beat it out to sea as far as he could, to ride out the storm in safety there."

"You still haven't told me what you intend to do."

"If the wind freshens, as I think it will, we'll be off the Bashee by mid-morning. While the weather is fair, I'll get *Touleier* as near to *Waratah*'s last known position as I can. Then—we'll ride out the gale. See what happens. We can't do more, we simply don't know more. It's really trailing one's coat in a sailer. We'll have to play the game off the cuff, perhaps even heave to, if the weather becomes too bad."

Touleier drove for the Bashee.

Jubela called me at first light and I went to wake Tafline to be with me at the radio. I still dared not make a signal. I decided that I would try and intercept what Port Elizabeth was saying to other shipping. If it was bad, the port met. office would be warning the coast. From there, too, had come the C-in-C's "clear-out" order.

I stood for a long while, simply looking down on her asleep in all her loveliness, not daring to bring her to the day of tight tensions which I knew must follow. For I had taken a look round from the cockpit, and the signs were in the sea and sky. The wind had backed northerly and freshened; the tiny fluffs of cirrus cloud seemed high enough to want to compete with the last fading stars. There was no ominous bank on the southwestern horizon yet, the purple sky-bloom which wrote the death of *Waratah*, *Gemsbok* and the Buccaneer. I was uneasy, taut, yet eager for the encounter, but I am glad now that I waited that breathing-space of minutes while my breath fell into step with hers, which the creaking of the yacht failed to disturb.

After I had woken her, she joined me at the radio in the main

160

cabin. On the South American race it had given trouble. When *Touleier* had been hard pressed, there was a seepage somewhere which affected its performance. I am no radio expert, and all I could do then was to try and keep it as dry as possible. The experts who had overhauled it had reinstalled it in the same place, with some extra waterproofing. It still seemed vulnerable to me, however, being close to the overhead skylight. Nevertheless, it seemed to work well enough now.

I probed the wavelengths.

Nothing.

I handed over the tuning dial to her slender fingers. Previously, the instrument had seemed to respond better to her delicate touch than to mine.

She held up a warning hand.

Port Elizabeth met. to *Ocean Fuel.*

"Supertanker!" I whispered.

> 0600 GMT. Pressure 1000 mb, falling. Wind, light northerly to northwesterly, freshening. Sea, moderate northeasterly.

She swung round to me, questioning.

"Yes!" I said. A *Waratah* gale was on the way.

"Listen!" she said.

Port Elizabeth came in again after the *Ocean Fuel*'s acknowledgment.

> Southwesterly gale off southern Cape coast, fifty to fifty-five knots. All lined up here for gale, Advise you to make for nearest port.

She came up to the cockpit and stayed with me until ten o'clock.

We were off the Bashee.

Jubela joined me and she went below. He and I unbent and stowed all sails, including the big mainsail, in the for'ard sail locker. We double-lashed all running gear on the lean, uncluttered deck in order to allow the seas free passage. We checked the self-draining cockpit and the buoyancy tanks. We also frapped the tall mast, Jubela agreeing with me that had it been jointed, we would have been well advised to send down the upper half.

We broke out the small heavy canvas jib in order to keep steerage way. We brought to the ready, as an emergency standby, a still smaller, tougher trysail. In the soft weather of the moment the larger storm sail was scarcely enough to make the yacht ghost along, but it was all we needed as we marked time.

When we were done, I found Tafline below. She had made packets of emergency sandwiches, and wrapped and labelled them individually as meals for the coming days. In a full blow, the galley stove could not be used. She had also filled big vacuum flasks with hot coffee and soup against the emergency.

It was not until later, however, that I found out that her main concern had been to go once again through all the *Waratah* documents, double-wrap them in waterproofing, and re-stow them out of reach of any possible flooding in the galley's special head-high, metal-lined locker.

She was finished by the time the lunch-hour shipping forecast came—thoughtful, tense, saying little.

> There is a gale warning. Strong southwesterly winds between Port Elizabeth and East London will reach forty-five to fifty-five knots later. All shipping is advised to make for port. We repeat, there is a gale warming...

"No order from the C-in-C this time," she remarked.

"It'll come," I replied grimly. "It's the final stage. They want to be quite sure, before putting out an order of such gravity."

The sea still kept its face bland, but the wind became uneasy, gusting fitfully from the northeast. I let Tafline steer the gliding yacht in order to pass the time.

We said little, except once when she asked, "Are we over the *Waratah* now, do you think, Ian?"

"We certainly are right in the area where she disappeared."

She cut in quickly. "What will you do when you find her?"

I was about to answer when my eye caught something on the far horizon.

"Look!"

The line between the blue of the sea and the purple of the storm was scarcely distinguishable. It merged, it fused, trying to conceal its evil in the water it was so soon to corrupt.

She gave a slight shiver, turned to me as if she intended to say something, and then started below.

"I'll bring up all the oilskins."

The barometer started to rise. Soon the uneasy wind would settle into its true channel—the southwest.

The first punch the storm threw at *Touleier* unmasked its lethal intent.

I had put the yacht on the port tack, heading away from the land in the late afternoon. The wind was veering into its storm quarter, but still remained moderate. The sea began to rise, but I was unhappy about the Agulhas Current. It was so strong as to affect the steering: I was glad I had discarded the self-steering device. It required human brains and skill to offset what was starting to happen to the sea and wind. I was anxious, too, about *Touleier*'s position. In theory, I knew that at first she would be driven southwards by the current, but once the gale got under way in earnest, she would be blown back upon her course. By tacking out to sea until it worsened, and then tacking landwards again, I reckoned she would be roughly in the *Waratah* target area when the storm reached its climax, which would probably be next morning.

I explained all this to her.

"There's a point beyond which one cannot go with a ship," I said. "*Walvis Bay* was on the limit. If it gets too bad I'll heave to."

She smiled a little and said, "Brinkmanship? A Fairlie judgement against a gale?"

I nodded, but inwardly I did not share her faith in myself. I carefully counter-checked every point I could think of. It would need everything Jubela and I could muster to keep her afloat. I went cold when I thought consciously about that giant wave which had hit *Walvis Bay*.

With a clap like a rifle-shot the storm jib exploded outwards in an iron-hard concave and blew to ribbons. In a second, it seemed, squares, rectangles and triangles of ripped sail insinuated themselves into the running blocks of the upper rigging. A ten-foot strip, still clinging by one tenuous cringle to an unyielding length of nylon rope, streamed out and flapped savagely against the mast. Then even the tough grommet could take the strain no longer, and the sail wrapped itself round the spreader and upper shrouds. The forestay thrummed like a double-bass.

The squall had struck ahead of the main army of the storm, now ominous and purple-black to starboard. There had been no herald of its coming.

Touleier lay over on her side until the lee deck and cockpit were awash.

Pinned like that and with almost no way on her, anything could happen. And the storm itself was upon us.

"Jubela! Quick! That storm jib! Quick, man, quick!"

Urgently I thrust the helm into Tafline's hands. "Just try and hold her steady until the jib draws. It'll take both Jubela and me to set the other storm jib. One of us will be back as soon as we can."

She was strained, doubtful about her ability to steer in such an emergency. Jubela and I crawled forward along the steeply-angled deck while patchworks of torn, blown trysail snapped and yapped against the mast. I was glad that we had had the foresight to unbend and stow the mainsail; with it, *Touleier* would have been on her beam ends by now.

"Got it!"

Jubela threw me a nod. The smaller, tougher sail was snugged home and began to draw. I slithered to the cockpit and took the wheel from Tafline. The yacht came upright and shied like a startled horse under the drag of the small sail, even, Jubela threw himself flat up for'ard, watched anxiously for a moment or two, and then gave the thumbs-up sign. Water cascaded off the deck. *Touleier* picked up speed rapidly and shook herself clear.

I threw all my attention into watching the yacht, the sea, and the sky. That squall had made it clear, even in this early stage, that no quarter would be given. *Touleier* gave a quick, duck-like shake. The contempt in it for my fears broke our tension for a moment. We both grinned. But *Waratah* was never far from our minds.

She gestured at the sea, "All those arguments by the experts seem

164

so futile when you come face to face with the reality."

"They went for the ship, I go for the sea," I said, knowing well what was on her mind.

"And the gale," she added.

I liked the feel of the tight little craft under me and the confident way she behaved. The wind began to increase with every gust.

Then—it roared into the southwest.

Its onslaught was different from my previous encounter, but again there was the clear distinction between the advancing storm and the darkening land. *Touleier* had the rising sea abeam and started to put her rail under regularly.

We found it hard to talk to each other because of the wind. But I leaned down to her ear, gesturing at the waves.

"*Waratah* wasn't heading into a beam sea like we are doing. She was meeting it head-on. That lessened her problems a great deal."

She nodded, looked astern.

Bashee light.

Touleier's portents were identical to *Walvis Bay*'s.

An hour later, the wind notched up gale force. I estimated its speed at between forty and fifty knots. Icy rain sluiced along the deck. It was pitch dark, and a tremendous cross-sea was building up against the main current. I was a little startled at the way *Touleier* lay over at the crests under the impact of each savage gust, and the rag of sail slatted and roared. But it held. Soon—if the maneuver were to be carried out at all—I must put her on the opposite tack. I sent Tafline below, using the weather forecast which was due as an excuse. Jubela and I roped ourselves tightly to the cockpit in case it was swamped.

I watched my moment.

Suddenly *Touleier* took a deep lee lurch and at the same time she was struck by one of those hilly, sharp-topped pyramids of sea, unlike anything I have ever seen before or since. In a moment she was halfway on her side. I felt the wheel start to lose its positiveness. Water poured over us until I was knee-deep. Jubela was hurled against me, but he clawed himself away in order to give me freedom with the wheel. I tried it to starboard, hoping to bring her head more into the wind. Then I felt the storm jib bite as she rose to the crest, and tons of water were thrown along the unobstructed decks. Seizing the moment,

I put the wheel hard over and Jubela, following my actions, let fly the sheet and then trimmed it for the new tack.

Touleier was round!

Sea surged and gurgled from the self-draining cockpit. Tafline came up from the cabin and looked about her, startled. It was impossible to see her eyes in the dim compass light. Her voice was strained.

"The radio, Ian, it started all right, then something happened...she seemed to go right under!"

I cupped my hands against her ear. "She's all right now. If it becomes much worse, I'll heave to."

The lee deck was completely under water, but *Touleier* was lively and handling magnificently.

"I'll bring you something hot," she called back.

The wind whipped back her sou'wester over her shoulders as she turned to go below. Ballooning out behind, for a moment it made her unsteady on her feet, the thrust was so powerful. Then she ducked out of sight.

I kept *Touleier* under the rag of sail for the next couple of hours. By ten o'clock the wind had risen to a whole gale—sixty knots! Its roar was appalling and it was locked in violent combat with the Agulhas Current. It threw up sharp, deadly pyramids of water which spent themselves by falling bodily on the yacht's deck. Tafline reported the skylight over the radio broken, and Jubela crawled forward and secured a square of tarpaulin over it. If they had warned shipping away from the coast, we certainly had no chance of hearing it. I was soaked. She brought us relays of hot soup and coffee. At times the clash of the current and gale under her rudder made the yacht almost unmanageable. I had not the slightest idea of her position. While the wind had still been usable *Touleier* had, I knew, beaten some miles to the south of the Bashee, but it was certain that she had been driven back since.

I decided to heave to.

I went below to tell her of my decision, leaving the wheel to Jubela.

On deck, my ears had been numbed by the thunder of the gale and the cold; here, in the confined space of the cabin, the waves added their drum-like crash against the hull to the general uproar. It was impossible to move across the place—streaming wet from rain and seawater jetting in through the tarpaulin-lashed skylight—without using the grab-handles. The motion was jerky, uncertain, unpredictable, violent; a sudden pitch or staggering roll could easily break a limb if one did not hang on.

Tafline was very pale. "Darling—is this the end? Are we sinking?"

I wanted to hold her, comfort her, chase the shadows from those lovely eyes. All I could do was hang on against the wild, erratic motion.

"Far from it," I answered. I did not say, it will be worse before the night is over.

She shuddered, looking at the untidy mess swilling about under the yellow oil lights. We had disconnected the battery supply and drained the acid from the cells, in preparation for the storm.

"Was it worse—in *Walvis Bay*?"

"Yes, but different," I reassured her. "*Touleier*'s like a cork, she's under sail. *Walvis Bay* plugged into it, nose-down. In the whaler, I was able to hold the *Waratah*'s course, but any set direction now is out of the question."

"No wonder they pray, 'for those in peril on the sea'."

"I'm heaving her to," I explained. "There's nothing to be gained by trying to sail. It will make the motion easier, perhaps."

She stared hard at me, and then asked in a small voice, "This doesn't mean you're abandoning the *Waratah*, does it? I'd rather go on, come what may. If it's for my sake..."

"The question of speed worried me greatly, but I don't think it is a factor. You see, the *Waratah* was steaming at thirteen knots, *Gemsbok* was flying at over 300, and Alistair over 600. I can't see any connection. I feel sure that *Touleier*'s being hove-to won't make any difference. If it—whatever it is—is to come, it will come, whether we are under way or not. From the way the yacht is behaving, I think the storm center must be close. The entire storm moves strangely fast. In twenty-four hours one of these blows could have spent its main force."

"Over!" she echoed. I saw how near breaking-point she was.

I said gently, "If the gale sticks true to form, it will reach its peak sometime tomorrow morning."

"Morning!" she gasped. "Will the yacht—can we—take much more?"

"She's in good shape," I replied. "There's not much damage so far."

She held my gaze. "While she goes, I go—please remember that."

I remember that now, too.

Before we put the helm up, I inched forward along the streaming deck on the lifelines and placed oil bags on each side of the bow. While I took the wheel, Jubela did the same over the counter. Immediately there was relief from her laboring, and she began to ride more comfortably. I got in the jib, and we hove her to on the port tack, streaming a sea anchor. The yacht shipped huge quantities of water; the lee rail and deck were constantly awash. Meanwhile the dollops started to come over the stern, too. I attributed this to the head-on clash of the gale and the current. I was very anxious lest the self-steering gear should be damaged and tangle with the rudder, so we put another oil bag in an old fish basket and ran it out on a deep-sea lead, which was the only spare cordage we could find. The lines were stowed in the sail locker, but we could not risk flooding her forward by opening it. The makeshift bag served its purpose. Now the yacht rode more confidently, although I could visualize how terrifying in daylight the seas would look from wave-level in the cockpit.

By midnight the gale was still increasing and a massive cross-sea threw the yacht about like flotsam. We double-lashed our minute storm jib to save it; high in the rigging the remnants of the first storm sail unraveled themselves, strand by strand. *Touleier*'s head held well into the wind. As the violence and the din grew, I debated whether I should attempt bending a tiny trysail high up aloft, but I discarded the idea because of the danger of climbing the arching, jerking mast. There was the danger, too, of getting her long mainboom in the water. If she broached to and were pooped, nothing could save us.

Through the rest of the night, Jubela and I alternately stood short helm watches until we could bear the breaking seas, the rain, and the icy wind no longer. Frozen, we came below, and Tafline fed us hot coffee and soup and her emergency sandwiches. Rest was impossible and the bunks were soaking. It was safest to wedge oneself on the floor gratings between foam rubber cushions off the lockers and cling on when a more violent shudder shook the hull in every plank.

When it was light, the sea presented an awesome sight. Tafline came into the cockpit when it was my turn to relieve Jubela. The roar of the gale made speech impossible. I saw her give the same quick intake of breath, half-sigh and smothered exclamation, she had done when she first saw the wrecked deck of the *Walvis Bay*.

The forward strike of the southwesterly gale, with its savage accompanying run of sea against the great current, had created an ocean of pointed hills which boiled and leaped high on either side of *Touleier* and fell over both the yacht's rails at once. Rain swirled in solid, icy sheets. The demented wind whipped off the summits of the wave-hills and bore them bodily aloft, higher than the mast, in a white shower of salt. The mast spreader, stays and blocks were white—not with salt but with threads of canvas stripped from the sail we had lost in the initial stages of the battle. Despite the oil bags, *Touleier* was swept fore and aft continually. The cockpit drainage could not keep pace with the inflow, so that there were never less than a couple of feet of water round one's knees. *Touleier* was still full of fight, although the lurches to lee that she gave as she reared to the crest of the waves were even more frightening on deck than they seemed below. There was no question of steering her among this watery valley of a thousand hills. She cavorted, swung, pitched, rolled and dipped all in one motion, it seemed. The oil bags were working well; we had renewed them an hour or two before. Without them, it appeared impossible that *Touleier* could have survived the storm.

I took the wheel from Jubela, and signaled him to go below. Tafline was in the cockpit, crouched against the cabin woodwork out of the wind, securely roped to the grab-handles by the door. My eyes were full of blown spray and rain.

I therefore never saw the thing that hit us.

I had been guiding the kicking rudder—that violent cross-sea made her wild—to try and keep her head towards the eye of the gale. It must have been about half past eight. Only dim sunlight lit the awesome scene. *Touleier* took a deep lurch and at the same moment she was struck by a heavy weather sea. She seemed to be thrown sideways into another mountain of water. She went over at an impossible angle. The mainsail boom plunged under. Before I had time even to realize what was happening, I was up to my armpits in water. The yacht lay down, completely on her beam ends, with her keel showing between the waves.

I went cold with fear.

Touleier dropped like a stone.

Here was the same sickening drop I had known in *Walvis Bay*. The whaler's head had been pointing into the storm and she had been under power; now I had under me a yacht without headway, lying on her beam ends with the long mast and submerged storm-jib acting as further make-weight to prevent her ever coming up again.

I could not see Tafline. All that held me to the yacht was a bight of nylon fixed to the lifeline. My mouth and eyes were full of water and oil from the bags.

Down the yacht dropped.

The cabin door flew open as Jubela threw his weight against it from the inside. He was in shirt and trousers only—he must have stripped off the oilskins to dry them—and as he came out, the wind ripped the shirt from his back and whirled it away into the scud-filled sky.

I spat and retched oil and seawater. "An axe! Get an axe, man! Cut it away!"

He seemed stunned, unhearing. Frantically I chopped my right hand into the left palm to show what I meant. He saw, and ducked away.

I saw Tafline's terrified face. She, like myself, was roped fast to the lifelines. She cowered, half-crouched, half-squatted, on the inner edge of the gunwale planking which now lay parallel to and half under the water, instead of upright.

Still *Touleier* lay over. Still she dropped.

The stern started to slew from the greater weight of water aft in the cockpit. The rudder was beyond human control. Her head began to come away from the run of the sea. The next wave would send her stern-first to the bottom.

Jubela, naked to the waist, broke from the cabin with an axe and raced up the weather rigging, now lying almost flat with the sea. I saw him hack at the tough light-alloy of the mast just above the spreader. It bent, but did not break.

The bow started to corkscrew and the stern gurgled deeper under me. I yelled frantically to Tafline to get rid of her lifeline. If the yacht went down, she would take Tafline with her to the bottom.

Jubela doubled back along the rigging and switched his attack to the stays and rigging-screws on deck. I do not know whether it was luck or shrewdness or desperation, but at his second stroke one of the main shrouds parted; a second went and he dodged its backlash; then the rest seemed to part all at once. The mast crumpled, snapped, broke free. A twelve-foot jagged stump was all that was left.

Relieved of the mast's weight, I felt the first touch of life come back into the hull as the buoyancy tanks fought back. Jubela felt it, too, and hacked again and again.

Touleier started to rise off her side. But she still continued that awful downward fall, like dropping in a bottomless air pocket.

Jubela turned to leap forward to cut away some of the trailing wreckage.

He stopped and froze. He pointed ahead with the axe.

He turned and screamed at me, his face stunned with shock.

I could not hear the words, but his meaning was clear from the frame of his lips.

"A ship!"

The wind eased momentarily.

The air-pocket drop stopped.

The death-dealing pyramids of water held back from giving their final *coup-de-grâce* to the floundering yacht.

Touleier pivoted back on to an even keel. Hundreds of tons of water cascaded free. Rigging trailed overboard from the truncated mast.

Tafline, too, saw Jubela's shock. She scrambled on to the cabin roof towards him. She and Jubela could see. I could not, from the low level of the cockpit and the trough of the sea.

She turned and called. My astonishment at hearing her vied with my amazement at what she said.

"A sailing ship! Dead ahead!"

I yelled to Jubela to cut away the overside clutter before it pierced the hull. He paid no attention. He stood transfixed, staring.

Again I shouted at him. He did not carry out my orders. Instead, he slid aft to me at the wheel. His face was grey with fear.

"I...have never...seen...a ship...like it!" he jerked out. "Umdhlebe!"

Umdhlebe!—something strange! The smell of death about it!

I shoved the helm into his shaking hand. I freed my lifeline and jumped up alongside Tafline.

She pointed.

There was no mistaking Phillips's description: there was the high bow, pointing into the eye of the gale, and the squat, square stern. But she had no masts. Water creamed and broke over the bow. Between bow and stern the hull was rounded, disproportionately long, like a whale's back.

A burst of spray hid the caravel.

"It's impossible!" I got out. "I've never seen a ship like that except on a picture..."

She gripped my arm and said unsteadily. "There *is* a ship. A whole ship. A big ship. It's nothing to do with that old-fashioned bow and stern. It's lying caught between them..."

"Dear God! What sort of a nightmare is this!"

"It's not a nightmare, and it's not a caravel," she jerked out. "It's an island! It's an island shaped like a caravel, Ian! And it's got a ship on it—upside down!"

Touleier rose to the next crest. We could hear each other. Here was that merciful, unnatural lull *Clan Macintyre* had known, the lull which had saved *Walvis Bay*.

I made a shambling run to the stump of the mast, grabbed it, and gave her a hand to me.

Touleier lifted.

"Look, Ian! The bow and stern don't rise to the sea! They're steady! They're—rocks!"

Across the welter of sea, a few cables away, I saw what Phillips had seen, what I had seen under *Walvis Bay*'s bows.

A smooth hill of rock, one end shaped like the bow of a medieval ship and the other in perfect imitation of the stern, reared itself above the confused, grey sea. Between the extremities, it fell almost to water level, and seen from a distance, in the confusion of a gale and impending darkness, it presented the perfect silhouette of a caravel. Phillips had sighted it between himself and the land, against the backdrop of a dim sunset. It must have been a mere silhouette, and distant. What, I asked myself hastily, had caused Phillips to add that he had seen masts? Had it been some trick of the light, or had his overwrought, tired brain simply added them as a natural adjunct to the hull? Or, more simply still, was it that, against the shore skyline, where the great forests hang on cliffs above the sea, a trio of the huge, white, spar-like *umzimbeet* trees had provided the puzzling addendum?

In front of my very eyes now was the exposed rock into which *Walvis Bay* had nearly crashed headlong. In a flash I saw why the sea had not struck down the weather ship after her hideous downward drop, or *Touleier* a few minutes before:—the ship-shaped island provided a perfect lee, a powerful natural bulwark, against the force of the gale and the run of the sea.

We stared unbelievingly at the rock, an island unmarked on any chart.

But it was not upon the rock that our eyes were riveted.

She gave a half-sob and buried her face against my shoulder.

It was the ship.

The barnacle-fouled hull was mortised so deftly between the "bow" and "stern" of the rock that it seemed part of it; indeed, its regular line enhanced the resemblance to a deck between the two projections. Its roundness, curved inward and upward, added to the manmade appearance. At the "stern" the deception ended with brutal plainness.

Two huge screws projected into the air.

The ship was upside down.

A steamer, keel and screws in the air, lay sandwiched between the two rock eminences some hundreds of feet apart. The island seemed scarcely wider than the steamer's beam.

When I spoke, I did not recognize my own voice. "We'll get a jury stay rigged on to the mast and go closer and look."

She bit her lips fearfully and looked at the hulk.

"How...?"

173

I turned to go aft. I stopped dead. There had been nothing for me but that fatal little caravel-shaped island ahead.

Until now. Then I saw.

Behind the yacht towered a grey incline of sea. It was high enough for me to have to look up and see the waves bursting and racing. *Touleier*, sheltered from gale and sea, was in comparative calm.

I held her, frozen, round the shoulders.

"A valley—a valley in the sea! We've toppled down a valley..." I pointed to a sort of shallow valley formed in the sea itself.

The stunning simplicity of it was incredible. The violence of the sea created a sort of hollow in its surface. The gale brought with it a massive run of the sea in the opposite direction to the Agulhas Current, and the two opposing streams banked up and formed a hollow. Something in the undersea topography must have helped, this being over such a limited area. This "seamount" was a needle-like pinnacle which reared up from the ocean floor, and only an exceptional gale uncovered it, sixty feet deep not high! Normally it was no danger to ships, but a *Waratah* gale bared it, and it turned into the *Flying Dutchman*! Then when the gale eased, the Agulhas Current became master again, the valley and the seamount disappeared, and so did the *Flying Dutchman*...

"Quick! We must be quick, Ian, before it disappears! We must see that hulk!"

Jubela and I hastily lashed up a jury stay from the mast stump to take a rag of canvas. Tafline brought my camera from below.

Touleier edged closer to the hulk on the seamount. It gave us a lee which became progressively smoother, the closer we approached.

The high promenade deck which had caused so much controversy lay crushed and concertina-ed under the 10,000 tons deadweight. Somewhere, too, under the telescoped superstructure, on which the whole weight of the ship rested, was the ruin of the single high funnel with its once-proud insignia.

The camera's electric flash cut across to below the air eighteen-foot double screws, sea-fouled and trailing seaweed.

She called out the name, upside down, emblazoned on the stern. "*Waratah*."

CHAPTER 13

"That fantastic roll of hers, when she dropped down like we did, must have been the death-stroke. She must have rolled right over, clean on to the seamount, and come to rest lodged as we saw her. No wonder there were neither wreckage nor bodies. The weight of the ship trapped everything underneath. Her upper decks were completely crushed. All the loose gear the world debated about for so long must be lying under all that weight."

"It must have been all over very quickly," Tafline said quietly. "They had a merciful end, those 211 souls."

"Three minutes, some expert worked out. They reckoned at the time that had she capsized, it wouldn't have been longer than that. I expect, too, that in a storm like that everyone was below decks. All the bodies are probably still inside—or what's left of them."

The hulk had a complete unreality for me. I could not credit that this was the ship whose every detail I had studied for so long. It reminded me of my first visit to the *Cutty Sark* at Greenwich dry-dock. As a boy, I had studied her plans, knew every interior layout, every deck, as if I had trodden them myself. Then came the day when I went aboard. It was at once familiar and strange. Now I looked with the same new-old eyes at the crushed, corroded hull resurrected from its sea-grave by the extraordinary phenomenon of gale and sea.

Astern, the power of the gale held back the incline of water, so willing to engulf the *Waratah* as of old; here, in the shelter of the seamount's lee, we could hear ourselves speak, although the storm thundered by on either flank, giving a curious, disembodied effect to our presence, like being in a capsule—aware, seeing, fearing, but at the same time partially divorced from it.

Touleier lifted and heaved too much to allow us to bring her safely more than perhaps a quarter of a cable's length from the wreck. Moreover the wind was masked by the immediate lee effect of the seamount, so that the way was almost off her. I was gravely concerned about the mast and the trailing clutter of rigging.

Yet I was drawn to the thing which I had sought so long.

The exorcism had begun. It was not over.

T must know still more about the *Waratah*.

She, too, wanted it and said, "There's the airliner, your father's message. He must have been here too!"

What awful secrets still lay hidden in that rusted hulk, its propellers so grotesquely turned to the sky? The swell seethed and swished, enveloping the wreck to the first line of cabin ports, tight closed, as they must have been that same day sixty years ago, against the ancestor of the gale which again today had laid its offering on the altar of a sea which could not yet wholly claim its dead.

Tafline shuddered, a spasm of fear.

Jubela shuddered, too, and would not reply when I explained rapidly to him in Zulu. I had grabbed his oilskins and sweater for him from the cabin and he pulled the sou'wester hard over his forehead, pretending that handling the yacht needed all his concentration.

I made up my mind.

"Bring her round—handsomely now," I told him. The yacht handled clumsily with the trailing debris alongside; the way the mast stump whipped at the flap of the tiny jib brought my heart into my mouth.

"Clear away that mess as quick as you can," I told Jubela further. "Keep a tight watch. I'm taking the dinghy to have a look..."

Tafline helped me inflate the rubber coracle from an air bottle while Jubela got busy on the wreckage with an axe.

"Her boat deck used to be fifty-five feet above the sea," I said, "but it's flat now, so there'll not be as much as that to climb. With all those barnacles and growths on the hull, it should be easy to find footholds."

"What about...?" She pointed at the hovering incline of sea.

"The gale's holding steady," I replied. "So long as it does, the water should stay where it is. We must be quick. Every minute counts. It's now or never, to see the *Waratah*. Watch out especially when we get to the keel, the wind could blow us off our feet."

Leaving the yacht in Jubela's care—he seemed to want to concentrate on physical tasks to avoid looking at the dead monster towering above us—we made for the stern. It looked easier to climb than any other part of the hull. We had a rope to lash ourselves fast to the decaying screws against the pluck of the wind.

We paddled to the nearest porthole. My heart raced. I tried to look in. The glass was opaque with green growth. Even my strong flashlight would not penetrate it.

Disappointed, we dipped and splashed our way to the rudder. Lying inverted, the old-fashioned counter, designed before the cruiser stern became fashionable in passenger liners and showing clearly its affinity with the days of sail, provided us with an easy first step up towards the rudder pintles. Higher still were the propellers.

I edged in. Tafline's face was hidden by her sou'wester. The swell receded. Unexpectedly, she stood up and jumped lightly on to the counter. How many years was it since human foot trod that fated hull? She stood poised for a second, then swung round to face me. She pushed back her sou'wester. I see her still: her face radiant, the short hair light against the old dark hull.

She tapped each heavy brass letter, green from years of immersion, with her right toe.

"*W-a-r-a-t-a-h*" she spelled out, never taking her eyes from my face across the couple of feet of heaving water.

She held out her arms.

"Come to me."

I jumped. She put her lips close to my ear, and for a moment the caravel-rock, the sea and the wreck ceased to be.

"I have the *Waratah*, and now I have my love."

Then she eased me a little from her, and the question was in her eyes.

"Yes," I said. "We must look further."

Had it been like an ordinary wreck, perhaps we should not have chosen to go on. But, because the hull was completely intact—tribute to those Clydeside builders who had claimed to be among the world's best—it had a shutoff quality, unlike the piteous rends, torn plating, or broken back of a ship aground on a merciless reef. The long, sinister, corroded hull, doubly odd because of its lack of upperworks, lay there, its ports closed, waiting.

There was nothing to stop us.

I had brought a boathook and a length of rope, but for our initial progress up the incline of the counter they were unnecessary. The clusters of barnacles gave us adequate foothold. We were able to stand comfortably when we reached the rudder, holding on to the huge slab of rusted metal. This was braced by four massive transverse strips of iron, each about four inches wide and nine feet apart, so that it was a relatively easy matter to use them as footholds to the eighteen-foot screws towering above our heads, their bronze still surprisingly bright against the general shabbiness of the hull.

I used the boathook to haul myself up on to the first pintle, reaching down and helping her up beside me on to the narrow iron shelf. From this higher position we were able to see for the first time something of the seamount behind the ship. The rock was covered in thick marine growths; she started momentarily at a movement, but it was only one of a colony of outside rock lobsters. How long would the seamount stay above water?—long enough to make it part of the air-element which was so alien to it and so kill off the teeming life of lobsters, mussels, barnacles and other rock-and-sea creatures?

She gave a gasp at a movement above us. I whipped round, my nerves strung to breaking-point. A magnificent albatross, holding himself skillfully against the wind, came to rest above one of the propeller shafts and then plucked eagerly among the sea-creatures.

We breathed again. We pushed on.

I secured the boathook over the next pintle, and we climbed yet higher.

My eyes went automatically to *Touleier*, so safe—for the moment—in the lee of this rock-and-metal hill of death and enigma. My sailor's heart skipped a beat at the sight of the seas which boiled behind her, and on either side of the seamount. We were held in a tight, ephemeral cell of safety. We could not see a defined line where the sea-valley began or ended. We were protected, where we stood, from the blowing spray and lash of wind, but I feared that when we got higher further exploration might be impossible because of it.

How long could, or would, the phenomenon last?

Precious minutes were racing by.

We had to see the top of the hull!

I bent to help Tafline. In doing so, my line of vision was through the gap between rudder and hull.

"What is it, Ian?"

I stopped transfixed. She could not see from where she was.

A fuselage, one wing attached and the other piled upright against the side of the hull, lay in a crumpled, untidy heap on the far side of the wreck. The tail-section had snapped half-off and the airliner lay broken-backed across a rock, as if a giant had begun to break it across his knee and then grown tired of the game and cast it from him.

My hands were shaking as I hauled her up, I pointed.

"Four engines!" she exclaimed.

I found my voice. "Airscrews! Alistair's was a jet!"

Some of the propeller blades were broken off and others were wrapped round each other and the turbine casings.

"*Gemsbok*!" she exclaimed. "*Gemsbok* and the *Waratah*—crashed together!"

I craned forward to try and see more. "Those experts were right about her going in at full power—look! They said she first touched something and then slewed round. Dad must have been sitting on this side, nearest to us, and the wing on his side came off in the final moments of the crash and landed up against the hull of the ship."

"How could he have come alive out of that?" she exclaimed. "Ian, he must have had some time to have cut loose that panel!"

"He crashed at night, remember. Maybe that would account for the peculiar writing."

"Do you see anyone, in the immediate shock of a crash, calmly setting about chopping off a piece of the aircraft? And then, of all things, deciding to make a testament out of it? He must have seen the name *Waratah*, and that would need daylight. That means the seamount must stay above water for a good few hours..."

I agreed. We felt safer to go on.

She took a firm grip of my hand and leant out to see as far beyond the hull as she could.

"Ian! Ian—there are *two* tails! There's another against the side of the ship!"

Cautiously, fearfully, I eased her back to safety on the slippery shelf to enable me to see. One slip would have been fatal; our precarious perch was twenty-five feet above the rocks.

I extended my range of vision by using the boathook. I, too, peered out round the bulge of the stern. That high tail was unmistakable. The Buccaneer!

It projected from the hull slightly forwards of where I judged the bridge must be and almost on a level with where we were standing. Only the tail was visible. There was no sign of the rest of the machine.

I edged myself back on to our narrow place of safety.

"It's Alistair's plane," I said numbly. "The tail sticks out of the hull up for'ard. The jet must have gone right through this rotten old hull like a bullet. Only twenty feet higher, and he'd have missed it!"

We stood silent, shaken. The gale roared past and the sea probed at the base of the hulk. The earlier radiance in her face was gone. I was filled with a sick hatred for the wreck.

"Let's go back, Ian! Haven't we come far enough to know all we want to know? Remember what Alistair himself said—what if you do find the *Waratah*? All there'll be is a lot of skeletons! Among those skeletons are your father and your brother..."

I poised myself uncertainly on the slippery foothold. At that moment I held her life in my hand. I did not know it.

What made me go on?

I could not answer that any more than what brought her that day to the dockside and *Walvis Bay*. In retrospect, however, I think it was that the blank, rotting hull provided no way into the *Waratah* mystery, not so much even as an open port. It was a shape, a thing, a hulk, and even in the moment of discovery, it shut itself fast.

"To the top—only," I replied. "From there we can see along the whole length of the keel. It won't take a couple of minutes."

The massive struts from the stern to the propeller shaft tunnels, which bulged unnaturally big once one was against them (normally they would be deep under water and not seen) gave us an easy passage to the keel. We were careful when we lifted our heads above the level of the hull and exposed ourselves to the gale. Another albatross appeared magically out of the spindrift and coasted down to settle near the remnants of the Viscount. This time she did not admire but shuddered—had the birds once feasted on human flesh as well as on the delicacies the seamount brought from the deeps?

The long level of the keel stretched away; the salt and wind stung our eyes. Tafline pointed at what appeared to be a larger accretion of deep-sea things round a rusted stump of metal. It was the only projection along the ship's bottom.

I pulled her down close to speak into her ear.

"Engine-room ash chute. Burnt coal from her furnaces was dumped through it into the sea. It goes right through the ship, clean through the watertight compartments and into the engine-room itself."

"What is that supposed to be, then?" She indicated the metal stump.

"It's a loosely-hinged metal cover to the chute. The mechanism is simple. When the weight of the ash discharged from her furnaces was greater than the sea pressure thirty feet below the waterline, the chute opened automatically. Experts thought it might have stuck open and allowed the sea to flood the ship from the engine-room."

She screwed up her eyes and looked along the spume-swept hull. "Then why don't we open the hatch and look inside?"

We had found entry to *Waratah*. It was as simple as the device itself.

We inched along the keel at a crawl to the outlet, which faced sternwards to form a final outcurve of the interior passageway. This "lip" of metal, now heavily encrusted and black with rust and immersion, was about two-and-a half feet high, roughly curved with a kind of primitive streamline like a ship's ventilator. Where it met the hull there was a metal hatch cover, about three feet wide and four feet long, hinged at the forward end. The small half-cupola of the lip also acted as a brake to prevent the hatch cover from swinging open too wide. It would come to rest at an angle of about sixty degrees when fully extended, the speed of the ship providing a natural motion to sweep the spent ash clear. It was simple and ingenious.

I reached with the boathook and got a grip on the "lip". The crawl along the flat broad bottom had been more difficult than dangerous; I remembered how the wind had plucked away Jubela's shirt.

We crouched behind the little cupola.

The hatch rectangle and surrounding jamb appeared much more rusted than the metal of the hull itself, caused no doubt by white-hot coals and cold water. There was a continuous discharge down the chute.

Also heavily rusted was a big eye-bolt set into the hatch cover, to which was attached a broken length of cable. I could not locate the aperture where this cable entered the hull because of the growths and corrosion, but it was clear that the trap could be pulled open at will from the inside, if there was need to get rid of the ash quicker than by the automatic way.

She crouched, simply looking at the hatchway. Her eyes met mine, and they were full of unspoken questions.

"I'll try," I said, going to the eye-bolt. "The odds are that the hatch is rusted solid with the hull by now. The metal round here in continual contact with the white-hot ash would deteriorate far quicker than the rest of the hull."

I gripped the eye-bolt.

She stopped me. "Open that, and perhaps you open a Pandora's Box. Remember Alistair's words: maybe a lot of skeletons only!"

It was so tantalizingly near.

"If it's no go, it's back to the yacht," I replied.

I tugged. The hatch cover moved.

"It's quite loose! Give me a hand!"

She hung back, tense, uneasy.

"We needn't go in. We can shine the torch and see if we can spot anything."

Together we lifted the metal cover about eighteen inches, but there was no way of keeping it open. I unscrewed the metal top of the boathook. We tugged the hatch open again. I jammed it with the boathook top.

The gale, ventilating the passageway, swept up to us a deep-sea smell of water and decay, a curious musty odor of rotting metal. The chute, we saw, widened slightly a little further in. It ended about fifteen feet down against a round watertight bulkhead door, clamped shut.

The torch beam also showed a narrow metal ladder, red-brown with rust, clamped against the side of the chute.

I played the beam to the bottom.

At the end of the ladder, against the floor formed by the bulkhead, hung two uniform jackets.

One was white, the other blue.

She gripped my arm, and gave a sharp intake of breath, half-sigh, half-exclamation.

One of the jackets, on whose shoulders the green mold showed against the white material, was an old-fashioned naval uniform with a high upright collar. The once-gold epaulettes were also green with mold, and the brass buttons were as dim as the ship's name on the stern.

The other jacket was fresh blue. Its goldwork on the shoulders and sleeves was dimmed, but not completely tarnished.

I flicked the beam on to the insignia on the sleeve.

It was a captain's jacket of the South African Airways.

My hand was shaking so much I could not direct the light. I gave it to her. She brought it back to the white jacket.

The collar was embossed with two blue anchors. The sleeves had the insignia of a merchant marine first officer.

She played the light over it inch by inch. I don't think either of us breathed.

She held it steady.

"There's something sticking out of the top pocket!"

I craned forward as far as I dared. It was a black-covered notebook with a pencil in the spine.

I found my voice.

"My father and my grandfather's jackets!"

"Your father must have scratched the panel down here! He wasn't blind or hurt—he was down there in darkness, next to his own father's jacket!"

"It must have got stuck on something—it only floated free when *Walvis Bay*'s storm finally loosened it!"

The question seared both our minds. Would the probing flashlight next reveal two ragged heaps of bones which were my kith and kin?

It would be my duty to see them first. I took the torch from her.

Holding it at arm's-length down the shaft, I explored the corners below the jackets.

An old-fashioned miner's safety lamp with a gauze screen was in one corner. There was a scatter of matches round it.

"They used that sort of lamp in the old coal-burners' bunkers," I said in a whisper, as if in the presence of the dead. "Same as in the coal mines. It's a Davy lamp—couldn't cause a coal-gas explosion..."

"Ian! We must have those two jackets! Try and reach them with the boathook!"

I snatched up the long pole. Without its metal claw on top I could not unhook the jackets.

"I'll go down."

"No! No!" She held me tight. "No! Don't! Let me! That rusted ladder won't take your weight..."

We argued; we lost life-ebbing minutes; she won.

I ran a bight of rope under her arms and eased her down. The first step held, but the second gave even under her slight weight. My heart was in my mouth. Step by step, she edged her way to the jackets.

Then she was there.

She looked up and called. "This old one is so fragile, I'm almost frightened to lift it."

Before I could stop her, she unhitched the rope from under her arms and tied the notebook securely with it. I yanked it up. I pocketed it without looking.

My anxiety to get her out of that fate-filled tunnel and my haste made me fluff the rope on its return. The loop which I had hastily remade for her shoulders caught on the rusted rung which had snapped under her weight.

I jerked the rope.

The noose narrowed. It stuck tighter.

My hands started to sweat. I redirected the flashlight beam. I saw her upturned face above the polo collar of her sweater. For a moment, her eyes-looked into mine.

I gave the rope a savage jerk.

It gave.

My arm shot wildly sideways, free of tension.

It swept away the boathook prop.

The hatch cover crashed shut.

All I knew was a stunning blow on the head, a crash, and a clatter.

How long did I lie there sprawled among the barnacles—five, ten minutes?

My first consciousness was of that inescapable deep-sea smell— my face was among the sea-things; second, of blood streaming into my eyes and salt on my lips; third, the stunning, overwhelming agony of mind which drove away the mists from my brain—she was trapped in the *Waratah* tunnel where the other Fairlies had died!

I grabbed the eyebolt and yanked with all my strength.

It did not move.

I looked round for a lever. The boathook top and torch were missing—that had been the clatter into the chute I had heard as the hatch cover knocked me senseless.

The long wooden shaft of the boathook was there, however, and I thrust it through the eyebolt to lift it. The effort brought a wave of nausea and a blinding stream of blood into my eyes.

I pried it. The shaft snapped.

In frantic desperation I knelt down and shouted her name. There was no answer. I cupped my hands and shouted again, trying to penetrate the slab of rusty metal.

Then I saw. The jamb which had been weakened by white-hot ash in *Waratah*'s lifetime and by over a half century of corrosion after her death had given way under the slamming weight of the hatch cover. The slab had sunk an inch or two into the rotten metal, jamming it tight.

A cold horror which had nothing to do with my stunned state came over me. I grabbed and tore at the eyebolt until the ragged metal ripped my hands.

Still the hatch stuck fast.

I knew what I had to do. But first she must know that I had not forsaken her, I beat a rat-tat with the broken boathook shaft on the hatch cover. Had I not been so engrossed, I would have noticed that the wind had eased—that is why I heard.

Her signal came back faintly—a muted rat-tat.

I gave one final despairing tug at the unyielding eyebolt.

Jubela! I must have his strength, an axe, some sort of lever to prise open that hatch!

I turned and got down on all fours, crawling back along the keel towards the stern. Now I realized the wind no longer plucked the way it had done. I got half to my feet and made a shambling run towards the rudder. The dinghy bobbed at its foot.

I hung back.

I hadn't the rope or the boathook now. How was I to bridge the nine-foot gaps between the giant rudder pintles? I climbed clear of the hull proper along one propeller-shaft tunnel. I let go, holding on by my hands alone. My feet groped for a foothold on the lower pintle.

It was out of reach.

I glanced down in desperation. Forty or fifty feet below was the dinghy and the sea. Three or four feet from me was the slime-covered pintle.

I let go. I came down half-sideways. I fought for balance. I snatched at the thick blade of the end-on rudder, and held on. I steadied myself. I was safe.

I wiped the blood out of my eyes and swallowed my nausea.

Frantic, I dropped again, slipped, grabbed, from pintle to pintle. Four times more my life hung on a thread above the kicking sea. Then I was in the dinghy, paddling for *Touleier*.

Jubela stood hanging on to the makeshift stay he had rigged, astonished.

Before I was halfway to him, I shouted, "An axe! Get me an axe, a crowbar, a boom—anything! Quick! Quick!"

I knelt to the paddle, glancing up only to see my direction.

Jubela clutched the dinghy's grab-lines.

He, too, did not see it coming.

The sea burst over us.

The gale had eased! The sea was rushing back! The "valley" was filling! The seamount was submerging!

I had a glimpse of Jubela tottering on the deck. Then he was thrown into the welter of foaming water. My back fetched up against something hard. I clutched it fast as the sea fought to tear loose my grip.

Touleier was borne away, half-submerged, in a foam of sea, like a paper boat on a pond.

THE HOLLOW SEA

* * *

Five days.

Five dawns.

Five days of undetermined merging of day and night.

Five days of gale.

Five crucifying days of agony.

How far I was blown that first day, I have no idea. In the first desperate hours after *Touleier* was blown away from *Waratah's* grave—the wild despair burned acceptance into my mind: her grave, too—I fought to get the yacht's head round to go back to her by bringing up the big mainsail from the locker and bending it to assist the rag I had managed to set in place of the jib. The rudder was jammed because the mainboom had crashed on to the self-steering gear, and the first wild wave fused the two as if they had been welded. I saw the rudder was hopeless. I decided to steer her by sails. The fact that every moment I was being blown further away from her goaded me to a strength I did not know I possessed. There was no sign of Jubela. I presumed he must have been swept away and drowned in that first onrush of returning sea.

Each recalcitrant stay, each intractable sail gasket, each impossible sheet, I fought with a frenzy which ignored the pain of my blood-raw hands as the nails were torn from the sockets of three of my fingers and a thumb. In the end the gale won—that awful, thundering attrition from the southwest which resumed in full blast after the lull. What chance had I, one man, when a crew of race-proven, storm-toughened seamen were needed, against the fury of the gale when trying to break out a bolt of canvas which seemed to have all the devils of the deep lodged in its folds?

I failed.

I wept when the sail blew away into the white, driving gloom of salt and spray. I could not see a boat's-length ahead. I fought for hours after that to try and rig the jib as an emergency, but it, too, was ripped away into the sea-murk. Every time I managed to bring her head round, the yacht would start off in an eccentric circle because of the jammed rudder, until the gale and sea would catch her and throw her bodily to the northeast—away, away, each desperate mile, from

187

the *Waratah*'s grave.

When I realized I could do nothing to handle the yacht, I set about trying to get the radio to work. The rawness of my wounded hands was made worse by spilt acid from the cells, which I refilled and changed, at first with hope, then with despair. The set remained as mute as the hour she had reported it dead.

On the third day, when I ate the last of the emergency sandwiches she had made, and drank the last unpolluted water from the tanks, my frenzy turned to exhaustion, and then to calm—a kind of numb, uncaring calm. My reason told me I was in as almost severe straits as she the moment that steel lid shut on her upturned face; my heart told me it did not matter, and that soon we would be together again.

So I read the pitiful little log between black covers which she took from Douglas Fairlie's pocket and caused her own doom.

I read of the *Waratah*'s doom.

S.S. Waratah.
9 p.m.
July 27, 1909

I write this in the presence of Almighty God, to whose protection and mercy I shall go when it is finished, in the certain knowledge that I have only a little time to live. That I am alive, is a miracle, for around me tonight are the bodies of over 200 of my fellow-beings—passengers, captain and officers—in this ill-starred ship. I interpret this small reprieve from death as His grace to enable me, in my extremity, to record how the *Waratah* met her end.

We sailed from Durban at approx 8 p.m. yesterday. I had the first watch today. I was surprised, before it was light, to have Captain Ilbery join me on the bridge. He wished me a formal good morning and then stood looking out ahead.

"As an old sailing shipmaster I must sniff the first wind of the day," he said with an attempt at a smile, but it was clear to me he was very uneasy about something. I had never known him be like that before.

"What do you make of it?" he asked me.

I was surprised that he did not address me by my rank, He was always meticulous about this, especially in front of the crew.

"Coming up for a southwesterly blow, sir," I replied.

Captain Ilbery kept on looking to the southwest, as if he expected to see something there. The sea was rising, and once or twice the ship put her head down. We had had trouble loading 250 tons of coal into the well-deck bunker at Durban and we could not get the ship upright. Now I resolved to get the well-deck coal below as soon as the day watches came on duty.

Captain Ilbery went to the extreme forward section of the bridge. He seemed to be studying the well-deck.

To lighten his unease, I used a windjammer expression as a joke.

"No need to whistle for a wind, is there, sir?"

The Captain did not reply, but started towards the chartroom companionway. Then he said, "Come below a moment, will you, Douglas?"

I was so startled by his use of my Christian name that I left the bridge and followed him without giving orders.

Again, in the chartroom, he used my Christian name. Even when he had officiated at my wedding aboard *Waratah*, he had only half-managed to get it out.

"Douglas, what do you make of it?"

The thought crossed my mind, how many great storms has he ridden out, and what is so special about this capful of wind from the southwest?

"It seems to be working up a bit from the southwest, sir," I replied. "There's not much to it at the moment. We had a bit of a blow from the same quarter outward bound round the Cape, you remember..."

"I don't mean the storm, man—I mean the ship," he retorted with a vehemence which was so strange from him. "The ship and the storm together, if you like."

"It's not a storm yet, sir," I pointed out.

"It will come," asserted Captain Ilbery. "One develops an

189

instinct, a sixth sense, about these things. It's coming—a big one. This ship has never been in a Cape buster before, Douglas."

"I'd feel happier if that well-deck coal were below for the sake of her stability," I answered. "The sea is working up, and she has an odd sort of dead feel to me."

Captain Ilbery seemed relieved that I shared with him the unspoken fears we both felt about the ship, her stability, and her incredible roll and lurch.

"Do that then," he said. "Get it stowed below as soon as you can after daylight."

"Can I compensate the ballast tanks as well?" I asked. "I would like all the weight I can find as deep below her center of gravity as I can put it."

Captain Ilbery eyed me gravely, and was about to say something when a messenger came from the bridge.

"Steamer fine on the port bow, sir. Overhauling her."

I went to the bridge, but Captain Ilbery stayed. A ship called the *Clan Macintyre*, bound for London, signaled us. We exchanged formalities, It was off Port St. John's.

Shortly after *Waratah* had passed *Clan Macintyre*, Captain Ilbery returned to the bridge. He was formal, which showed he had reached a decision in a difficult situation. There are not many captains who would have the courage to risk censure by running from a storm which had not yet developed into anything special in a crack, well-engined 10,000-tonner.

"I am going to do what my sailing-ship instincts tell me," he informed me. "Haul out, Mr. Fairlie."

I set course as he directed, and *Waratah* headed seawards across *Clan Macintyre*'s bows and across the scend of the sea—its run was now strongly from the southwest—while the wind rose to a full gale. The new course, taking the sea on her starboard bow, brought several heavy seas aboard and drenched the coaling gangs I had set to work.

Shortly after 10 o'clock—it seems scarcely credible that it happened a brief twelve hours ago—*Waratah* was struck by a heavy beam sea. She hung at the end of her roll in her characteristic way until I was convinced she would never come back. She lay in that position for perhaps five or six seconds, and then yawed off course landwards. Her recovery from the roll had been so sluggish that I feared that the worst had happened below.

Within seconds, I had an emergency call from the chief engineer. Hundreds of tons of coal had shifted in that awful roll and were lying against the ship's steering rods, jamming the rudder. I sent to Captain Ilbery to come to the bridge while I ran to the engine-room.

That is the reason why I am alive tonight.

With the rudder jammed, the ship's head swung round, away from the safety Captain Ilbery had so wisely sought. The ship listed badly to starboard. It was now blowing a full gale from the southwest. The sea had worked up with alarming rapidity. The speed was still on her when I rushed from the bridge to the engine-room.

It is hard to write of a man one has seen burned to death before one's very eyes. Vinney, the engineer, was waiting for me. The engine-room was a holocaust. Vast quantities of coal were lying across the steering rods and this would have to be cleared before the ship could be brought under control. Already two coal trimmers were not accounted for. The roar of steam being blown off drowned the senses. Vinney had also emptied the main furnace ash chute as a precaution.

It is impossible for me now to estimate times, or say how long I had been in the engine-room, but the engineer and I were on the catwalk by No. 2 boiler furnace making hurried plans to clear the coal when the disaster happened. I am still too dazed to give a coherent account of it, but do this I must, for this is my final task.

One moment Vinney was beside me; the next, the entire furnace seemed to tip forward as the ship's bows dropped at an angle so unlikely that it seemed to deny she was a craft on the surface of the sea. White-hot coal spewed from the furnace over the engineer and two stokers. I did not even hear them scream, it was so sudden. In a moment, it seemed, the whole engine-room—furnaces, engines, bunkers, boilers—turned upside down. At the same instant there was a tremendous crash and a rending noise whose like I have never heard before. Even now, nearly twelve hours afterwards, I have difficulty in crediting that this 10,000-ton ship capsized, turned completely turtle.

I found myself hanging on to the catwalk railing staring upwards through the metal tunnel of the ash chute which had been emptied. Had the engineer not dumped its contents at the first emergency, a cascade of white-hot ash would have written the same fate for me as for him. Scalding steam and smoke made it impossible to see across the inferno of the engine-room; the roar of escaping steam boomed and reverberated between the metal walls of the compartment like non-stop thunder.

As I groped to haul myself on to the inverted catwalk, I was confronted with another impossibility—I was looking at driving storm clouds across the sky through the chute opening! The cable to the ash chute hatch had been left unsecured in the haste to empty its contents and the watertight bulkhead intersecting the tunnel about fifteen feet from the bottom had swung wide of its own accord.

My movements were instinctive. My sole thought was to escape from the roaring, thundering, searing engine-room before the boilers exploded. Everything was lit by the red glow of the flaming coal which had been ejected from the furnaces, and I coughed and gasped for breath in the swirling smoke. I had no conscious appreciation in those desperate first minutes of the nature of the disaster which had overtaken the ship—all I knew was that she had capsized completely. In the baleful light I saw a trimmer's lamp attached to the catwalk rail. I took it and climbed up into the ash chute. I closed the bulkhead behind me so that when the boilers exploded, I would be shielded against the concussion.

At that stage I considered that the ship, after turning over, was floating upside down with her keel in the air. I think I first intended to swim clear of her, but when I put my head outside the open hatch for a moment, the sight of the boiling sea and insane wind drove me back, terrified. I tugged the hatch cover closed by means of the cable and lit the trimmer's lamp. Better to have at least a floating wreck under one than be cast adrift on that awe-inspiring sea. I tried to pull myself together.

The catastrophe overtook the ship at between 10 and 11 this morning, but it was not for fully an hour afterwards, sitting here in the ash chute in a state of numbed shock, that I came to realize that my first reconstruction of it, namely, that the vessel was floating upside down, was wrong. Shortly after I entered the chute there was a violent, grinding movement like an earthquake which brought terror to my already overwrought nerves; I thought the ship was settling and that the boilers would explode when the sea reached them. This cataclysmic noise drowned even the racket and vibration of the screws turning in empty air above my head, The grinding and rending threw me from side to side in the chute. I was too terrified to try and open the hatch again. When the violence and movement stopped, I came to the conclusion that the ship must have been settling down on some solid object, crushing the superstructure as she did so, with that nightmare of noise.

The boilers did not explode, as I feared. I felt the screws start to slow, and then stop, as the steam pressure fell away. I blessed Vinney's foresight for throwing open the steam safety valves.

I am not sure now whether the noise, or the silence which followed, were more terrifying. I found courage at last to try the hatch again. I thought it had jammed, but the significance of it did not come home to me until I cautiously screwed open the bulkhead door through which I had come from the engine-room. A jet of compressed air and stale smoke whistled in, but before hastily screwing it shut, I caught a glimpse below.

The ship was full of water!

In this moment of my extremity—the light is beginning to flicker for want of air and my breathing becomes more difficult as the tunnel's oxygen is spent—I know that I am sealed alive in a ship which, for some reason which I cannot

193

explain, is neither afloat nor ashore.

Later: Breathing very difficult. No point in prolonging my life further. Ship rocked and heaved. No. 1 hatch burst, I think. I will douse the light now to have use of the last of air for what I must do, namely, open the lower bulkhead to the flooded engine-room, and go through. I will then seal the chute behind me with this account to tell how the Waratah met her end, so that the sea will not be able to reach it.

Under my grandfather's signature was scrawled, "Read this. Will scratch message for Ian on panel cut from *Gemsbok*—Bruce Fairlie, captain, SAA Viscount *Gemsbok*, July 19, 1967."

I took the black-covered notebook, embossed with two blue anchors of the famous line, wrapped it in oilskin, and buried it deep among the other *Waratah* things which Tafline had so carefully stowed in the waterproof galley locker.

The frenzy of the gale made it almost impossible to write *Touleier's* log. I resorted to a kind of cryptic telegraphese to try and rush down on paper, amid the violent kicking and jerking of the hull, something of what was happening. Often I had to wait five minutes or more between individual words because of the bucking. To try and fix the yacht's position was out of the question.

A flicker of hope came to me on the afternoon of the fourth day.

I saw my chance. There was a lull in the gale in the late afternoon. If I could get rid of the mainboom wreckage locked in the self-steering gear, I might still save the yacht. Not until I chopped at the gear with an axe did I realize how weak I was. I had had no food since the last sandwiches nearly two days before. The salt-contaminated fresh water had made me vomit. My feeble strokes simply bounced off. I switched my attention to the stump of the mainmast, whose heel was starting to thrash. Somehow I managed to fix it, but it cost me a left hand stripped of flesh to the bone of the thumb and two fingers.

Before I could attempt more, the gale resumed in full fury.

That night I gave up hope.

In the morning, *Touleier* was still afloat.

I did not think it possible for her to take any more punishment, or that there was anything left to carry away. But at dawn I was jerked from my semi-coma by a crash and a gust which even in my sinking brain stood out as more violent than anything I had yet encountered. It took away the stump of mainmast and mainboom wreckage. The starboard cabin ports were blown in and water cascaded into the shambles of a cabin.

I did not want to die down there, cowed, beaten, alone. I wanted to die with a curse on my lips at the southwest wind, facing it, feeling its plucking challenge on my face at the end,

I tried to say goodbye to her at the bunk where we had had the magic of that other dawn off Pondoland, looking down on her loveliness, but a lurch crashed me to my knees, and as I sprawled I prayed, oh Christ put an end to my thoughts like the southwest wind, will the agony never end? She said, while the *Waratah* mystery is unresolved, I cannot be yours. Now it is resolved, and very soon she shall have me.

I dragged myself on deck to die.

CHAPTER 14

The persistent slatting, rattling of the sail reached down into my coma.

My last spark of consciousness cursed the southwest wind. Could it not leave me to die even in peace? The roaring in my ears told me that the end could not be far off. My fading sea-instincts told me it was not the wind which was roaring—maybe I noted subconsciously that it had fallen. Perhaps that is what caused me to force open my eyes and wonder why, then, a sail should slat, when there was no wind?

The downrush of air forced oxygen into my unwilling lungs and I tried to get to my feet to cut loose that maddening slatting sail. As I grabbed one of the cockpit handles, the roaring increased, the wind increased.

A man hung in space over the socket of the mast.

The big Super Frelon helicopter hovered over *Touleier*, its rotors slatting and banging. All round the yacht the sea boiled in minor imitation of the gale. I tried to focus on the helicopter—one of the big long-range French-built craft the South African Air Force uses for troop-carrying—but all I could distinguish before a fit of giddiness swept me off my feet was the five-pointed roundel representing the Castle of Good Hope.

When I drifted back to half-consciousness, I was aware that an airman was fixing a "horse-collar" device under my arms preparatory to signaling the helicopter to winch me up. It was the thought of her, those priceless *Waratah* documents which were now all the living things I had left of her, that made me seize the grab-handle and hang on fast.

"Take it easy, chum!" exclaimed the airman. "We're here to help you. You'll be all right once we get you aboard."

I heard a megaphone shouting above the racket of the rotors, but I was too far gone to know what was being said.

"*Waratah*!" I mouthed. "In the galley. Top locker. I don't go without them!"

The pain in my hands jerked me to full consciousness. I could see the horror and pity in the airman's eyes as his glance went from the cut in my blood-matted hair to my hands.

I pulled myself together. "Down there—a lot of documents," I managed to get out. "Bring them, and I'll come. Don't...don't...for Christ's sake don't leave her to sink! She's all I...I..." I couldn't formulate the words. "*Waratah*" I articulated carefully. "*Waratah*, man!"

He cupped his hands and shouted something to the hovering craft, and then signaled. He went below and came up with the documents she had wrapped in oilskin. Some of them were blotched and stained with blood and lymph from my hands.

"This it?" he asked, as if speaking to a child.

I nodded. "That one with all the blood—is that a little black notebook?"

He unwrapped it quickly. It was.

A fresh wave of nausea overtook me. I could not uncurl my fingers from the grab-handle.

The airman made another hand signal to the Super Frelon.

He said, "We're putting an automatic Sonar buoy on board—continuous homing signals, and then we can pick her up later—okay?"

I wasn't aware of being winched up into the helicopter. My first recollection was of lying among what appeared to be innumerable big fuel drums in the padded interior of the craft. The airman was pouring something down my throat.

Major Bates knelt next to me. He grinned when he saw me conscious. "Our flight paths seem to cross a lot." He saw my hands. "You should stick to steamers."

It was the mention of steamer that brought me sitting half upright—*Waratah*!

Bates said tersely, "Can you sit up? Can you talk?"

I nodded.

He told the men who supported me, "Carry him up forward and put him in the co-pilot's seat next to me. Give him something to eat. Coffee—put a shot of brandy into it."

Bates was at the controls when they brought me to him, a man helping me on either side. Already I could feel a touch of warmth coming back into my body.

"Get this off—urgent—priority," Bates dictated to the radio operator. "I've got Fairlie, alive, also yacht *Touleier*." Give the position." He spoke over his shoulder to the man who had rescued me. "Did you put that automatic buoy aboard her?" He nodded and Bates went on. "It's not only your sponsors who would not forgive me for abandoning that little beauty in mid-ocean."

"Mid-ocean?"

Bates waved through the Perspex canopy. "See any land? Four hundred and thirty miles out to sea."

I started to get my thoughts straight as the food and drink had their effect.

"I didn't realize anyone knew we were missing."

Bates gave a short, mirthless laugh. "Maybe people are getting wise to Fairlies popping up and then vanishing. I got a standby alert the day after the gale began. The papers were full of you—again. You gave them just the cream on the coffee that they love. Fairlie lost in search for lost father. All the rest of it. The whole works. The whole country's buzzing with you."

He looked at me penetratingly, kindly. I sensed a difference of attitude from my frigid reception before by the authorities.

"Can you answer some questions? Some of them will be tough."

He looked away and issued a string of orders.

Tafline. That is what he meant. I cringed.

"Give me a moment," I replied uncertainly. "Tell me more from your side first."

"That man Jubela of yours should have a gold medal," went on Bates, not looking at me. The Super Frelon was moving ahead, fast.

"Everyone wants to give him one."

"I saw him swept away and drowned," I said weakly.

"A British tanker picked up Jubela barely a couple of hours after that," resumed Bates. "He'd got himself a rubber dinghy—the yacht's, I suppose? The tanker radioed that *Touleier* was lost—the hunt was on. We knew almost exactly where to go."

"South of the Bashee." My words were almost involuntary.

"It wasn't the yacht only," Bates added grimly, "Your man said you'd found the *Waratah*."

The cold agony of it flooded back.

"I did."

Bates glanced sharply at me. "What he had to say so electrified HQ that I took a chopper that same afternoon and risked my neck to bring Jubela ashore from the tanker to tell us what he knew." He smiled. "I've learned to fly some since meeting the Fairlies. What Jubela said galvanized us still further, when we got him ashore. Apparently he'd been shouting his head off aboard the tanker for them to do something."

I could hardly frame the words. "About—what?"

Bates said levelly. "Jubela saw you come back alone, without..."

I could not say her name.

"He knew that something terrible had happened to her, but he didn't know what. He guessed she was trapped somehow when you came yelling for an axe. He'd also seen the name *Waratah* and said you'd told him about her."

"I explained to him about my father and grandfather," I interjected.

"It was nothing to what he gave the papers," Bates went on. "I felt really sorry for your police pals trying to cope." Then he resumed rapidly, refusing to let me speak. "The tanker picked up Jubela drifting in his dinghy miles away to the southwest of where he last saw you. The search was easy, after that. A couple of frigates went first, and they worked back from where Jubela was found. One of them got a sounding which looked good. By that time Jubela had told us about the seamount, but it was outside the scope of ordinary sounding equipment. Next day we got the survey ship Africana with her special equipment down from Durban, It was a piece of cake. She found the seamount, spot on."

I broke into a flow of words. "And the *Waratah*?"

"That submerged seamount confused the echoes from the metal hull of the *Waratah*," replied Bates. "The survey ship reported that it was, in fact, an isolated, narrow, needle-like pinnacle jutting up hundreds of feet sheer from the ocean floor, so narrow..."

"It was just wide enough for *Waratah* to lie on top of it," I said. "Her beam was only fifty-nine feet."

"In the wide ocean, you'd have to run slap into a tiny thing like that before you'd locate it," remarked Bates. "We also established that the seamount lies between the usual northbound and southbound routes the ships use; a sort of no-man's-water."

I remembered how Douglas Fairlie had written that *Waratah* had yawed off course when the rudder jammed.

"Jubela's story about your lady friend being trapped aboard the hulk had the whole world by the ears," Bates said. I did not like the way he would not look me in the eyes when he spoke about her.

"They sent down divers and frogmen. They found the wreck, upside down, sixty feet below the surface."

I waited. I could not ask.

"They tapped the hull. They got an answer near an old hatch."

I sagged forward in my seat and Bates shouted for assistance, but I waved them away.

"She's alive?"

"This morning, five hours ago, when I took off, she was alive," Bates answered tersely. "Just. Immediately they found the hulk they got an air-line down to her—fired it through the hatch with an explosive bolt. Water, too, fortified with this and that to keep her going."

I thumped my hands, which they had bandaged while Bates talked, unfeelingly on the armrest of my seat. I did not even feel the pain.

"Why don't they get her out?"

Bates stopped me. "There is only one man who can tell them how to get her out. We had to find you at any cost."

I choked and turned away. I held up my shattered hands to Bates. I could not speak.

200

But he went on. "They found *Touleier*'s mainsail the day after she was missing—like Jubela, it had drifted away southeast, away from the seamount. Some rigging wreckage, too."

"We cut away the mast."

"The experts argued that where the wreckage had drifted, there also would the disabled yacht drift. That's the way Jubela went in his dinghy. But I had read what you told the C-in-C about the search for the *Waratah* and how the cruisers followed the current and looked southeast. I argued. I reasoned. When I quoted you they were dubious. I tried to tell them their search was making the same mistake as for the *Waratah*. I was out over the sea every day. I wanted to fly northeast, away from the search area which they had plotted. I remembered your telling the C-in-C about two old steamers which had been disabled near the Bashee and didn't drift southeast at all, but northeast?"

I nodded. "*Tekoa* and *Carnarvon*. *Tekoa* landed up near Mauritius after six months."

Bates went on. "The search drew a blank, of course. They called it off officially yesterday. I put my big oar in, for the hundredth time. At last they agreed to let me take this old bag and search northeast. The gale blew itself out on the coast a couple of days ago. See those fuel drums in the rear? The Super Frelon can take a company of troops but I loaded her up with fuel instead to get maximum range. I spent half last night estimating your probable drift to the northeast—if you were still afloat."

The big machine, the calming sea below, and the broken rearguard of storm cloud hurrying away seemed as unreal as the two uniformed jackets under our torchlight.

I started to explain about the ash chute. "When will we land?"

"About mid-afternoon."

"Then tomorrow we can get her out."

Bates swung away from the controls and his eyes locked with mine. "Fairlie, there is no tomorrow."

I was stunned, confused, still unable properly to grasp the fact that she was not dead.

"But she's alive and she's got air and water—you said so yourself."

Bates's voice was edged. "I had to find you today. There is a new southwesterly gale due in the *Waratah* area tonight. I don't have to say any more, do I?"

I sagged in my seat. "Surely they can keep the air and water lines going until it is past!"

"You'll see for yourself when we come over the spot," said Bates, his voice gentle. "There's a whole flotilla of ships at the wreck. Frigates, survey ship, salvage pontoons. They can't keep salvage pontoons at sea in a gale. To start with, they haven't got engines. The lifelines would snap in a seaway anyway. Unless we can get her out this afternoon, they'll have to cut the lines..."

"That's impossible!" I shouted.

The radio operator came behind us, handing Bates a signal. The pilot ignored my outburst.

He said sharply, "If you want to save her, talk, and talk fast, man! Tell the salvage boys the setup, the layout, the technicalities. Only you know them. Put in every tiny thing you can remember—it may be important for the boffins. Dan here will transmit in relays what you have to say. I'm pushing this old flying hencoop as hard as I can. Talk!"

While Bates flew, Dan knelt by my seat, taking notes to radio ahead to the salvage teams. I explained how the ash chute led into the interior of the *Waratah*, the hatch and its mechanism, how it had jammed shut, how the watertight bulkhead sealed the tunnel from the engine-room.

The Super Frelon roared on.

I dared not look at the southwestern horizon. I dreaded that purple-blue smudge whose arrival would mean the end of the salvage operation. I tried to put from my mind the horror of her being trapped in that chute for five whole days, not knowing whether it was day or night, haunted by those two ghosts, one in a white jacket and the other in a blue. I banished the awful nightmare from my mind which was part of my frenzy aboard *Touleier*—that she would put an end to it all as they had done.

I fell into an exhausted doze after the stream of radio signals, questions and answers, technicalities, for I was awoken by Bates's hand on my shoulder.

"There!"

The Super Frelon was dropping fast from about 1500 feet. Ahead lay the line of the coast, the curious cleft of the Bashee Mouth, unmistakable. About ten miles offshore, I judged, a cluster of ships lay in a tight circle—three frigates, the survey ship, a couple of long salvage pontoons, cumbersome and low in the water, and a cluster of small craft. On the outer fringe, hovering like cubs round a lion kill as if afraid to get closer, were more small craft; ahead, at a safe distance too, were two light aircraft.

"Press!" snorted Bates. "See how they keep away? That's your Colonel Joubert's work. He's got a guilt complex about you the size of Table Mountain, and he's trying to work it off by being tough with everyone not immediately connected with the salvage operation. Flew specially from Cape Town to superintend things." He gestured at the circling aircraft. "I just hope they don't try and come too close as we go in. They'll do anything for a picture, and you're about to give them one in a moment."

"Me?"

"You, at the end of a winch line," responded Bates. "My orders are to drop you aboard *Natal*—she's the one nearest the survey ship."

"*Natal*!" I echoed, dismayed. "Lee-Aston!"

Bates laughed. "You'll find a lot of attitudes towards you have changed! That includes Lee-Aston. All the big brass are waiting for you aboard his ship."

"Thanks," I said, but he cut me short and pointed at the horizon.

"Don't thank me yet," he said quietly, "There's your old enemy."

The purple-blue smudge lay low on the horizon.

"It doesn't look good," he said candidly. "I've been getting special met. reports every hour. While you were asleep, the whole storm front seemed to pick up speed. It's heading towards us, fast. There's already a full gale off Cape St. Francis."

Here, in the sunlight and warmth of the helicopter cockpit, it seemed impossible that she should be entombed down there, sixty feet under icy water.

I craned to try and see through the waves, but Bates said, "You can save yourself the trouble, chum. You simply can't see through that murky water. Here we go. Stand by."

"What's the rescue plan, major?" I asked. "Surely you're part of it?"

"There's no plan—yet," replied Bates. "They're waiting for you. Everything depends on you. Her life." He must have seen my face, for he added quickly, "I shouldn't have said that. But you've got to face it. An hour ago the odds were fifty-fifty. Now they're sixty-forty against. In another hour..." he indicated the grape-purple southwestern horizon. "I'm dumping this old grasshopper on a private field over there by the river which we took over as an emergency landing strip. I'm getting myself a trim little Alouette in her place."

They lowered me by winch and "horse collar" on to the frigate's stern.

Jubela was first at the cable. He could not speak. He took me, still suspended, in that curious high-up armshake he had given me the night I saved his life in the Southern Ocean. It was only when I saw the look on the sailors' faces who released me from the device that I realized how I must look:—I was still in my sea-stained, torn oilskins, and my hair and five-day beard were clotted with blood from the gash over my eyes. I held my bandaged hands clear, high away from the winch wire. Perhaps the two seamen thought I was a stretcher case, but it was Jubela who took me under the arms and guided me for'ard under their direction.

They rapped on a door.

"Come in!"

The men round the captain's conference table looked as startled as the seamen. Lee-Aston, in faultless white, came forward, hand extended. He stopped at the sight of my bandages and blanched.

"I think I owe you more than I even thought," he said quietly.

It was Colonel Joubert who pulled out a chair and fussed over me as I sat down.

"The thought of that pretty face down there kills me," he said in a cracked voice. He turned away. "What a bloody fool I was! Anything in my power to do now..."

Lee-Aston didn't waste any more time.

"Malherbe, Navy salvage," he said crisply, introducing a sandy-haired lieutenant-commander, "Jansen, Search and Rescue, Matthews, frogman. We've got the idea of the layout of the wreck and the chute

204

from your signals. We haven't much time."

Malherbe looked at his watch. "It's 3:30 now. By five I must cut the airline."

He fired the question savagely. "What is holding that hatch?"

I explained quickly.

"We could blow it with a light charge, then?" said Malherbe.

"And kill her in the process," retorted Matthews. "My frogmen couldn't get her out in time before the water rushed in."

"The hatch isn't the real problem," interjected Lee-Aston. "We've known for days that she was under it. We didn't know what sort of compartment lay underneath."

Malherbe said, "We thought maybe there was a whole watertight compartment. "That's why we delayed. You can't mount a salvage operation to lift a 10,000-ton ship in a couple of days. It would take months, even if it were possible."

"She's right within our grasp, as it were," said Lee-Aston. The voice was cool, controlled, but I saw his right fist contract until the knuckles were white against the bone. I knew then what was going on inwardly with him.

"The problems are enormous," he added. "I've no doubt that the frogmen could lever open that hatch, even without having to use explosive. But, before we can get her out, the chute will fill with water. We simply can't get her clear quick enough. She'd drown in sixty feet of water. She must be terribly weak into the bargain."

Jansen, Search and Rescue, said, "My boys will pick her out of the water the moment she surfaces. I'll put a ring of rubber dinghies in the sea immediately over the hatch, with frogmen at the ready in every one of them. There won't be any delay."

Lee-Aston leaned back. He said crisply, "I think you know, Captain Fairlie, that I was one of a court of inquiry which sat to investigate a collision between one of our new subs and a Frenchman at the entrance to the Mediterranean."

"I don't want to know about subs. Let's get on with saving her," I broke in.

Lee-Aston was unruffled. There was even a slight grin on his face. He looked round the conference table.

"Subs mean rescue."

"What are you driving at, commander?" snapped Malherbe.

"You've got the perfect escape route in that chute, perfect for the buoyant ascent method of escape they use in modern subs! It's very simple: a man climbs into what we call a trunk, and seawater is let in until the compressed air pressure inside equals that of the sea pressure outside. Then he opens the hatch and simply steps out. You don't need a mask—or any breathing apparatus at all. The man in the trunk breathes air which has been compressed by partially flooding the escape trunk from the sea. Once he's outside the hatch and moves towards the surface, sea pressure decreases and the compressed air in his lungs starts to expand. He can't suck in water if he wanted to. He can't drown. It takes less than ten seconds to come up from 100 feet down. At sixty feet, it's perfectly safe."

Malherbe thumped the table. "Just pump in more and more air until it's compressed inside the chute!"

Matthews jumped to his feet. "I'll get my team down there right away. They can lever open the hatch as the air inside equals the sea pressure outside."

"Not so quick!" snapped Lee-Aston. He looked at his watch, "How long before you can raise the air pressure in the chute to equal the sea's, Malherbe? We can't afford to fluff it now. It's a matter of very delicate checks and balances. Your frogmen will have to open the hatch at exactly the right moment, or else the chute will flood, or there won't be enough pressure to eject her. If the frogmen can't open the hatch, you'll have to stop pumping compressed air or you'll burst her lungs inside the tunnel. Jansen, get your men spread in a circle round the probable area of ascent. You'll have to pluck her out of the water smartly—she's very weak." He spoke to an aide. "Tell Major Bates I want him overhead in a helicopter in—" he looked inquiringly round the tight circle of faces "—fifteen, twenty, minutes?"

"Eighteen," replied Malherbe, who had been scribbling calculations on his pad. "Eighteen minutes exactly. By then the pressure in the chute will equal the sea pressure outside the hull."

Joubert caught my eye and gave me a tentative thumbs-up signal. He grinned hesitantly.

The other men started to get to their feet, but Lee-Aston held them back.

"Captain Fairlie, gentlemen. Where do you want to be when the pressure goes critical, captain?"

The austere captain's compassion warmed me. I wanted the new-found sympathy and understanding I had found round the table, but I also wanted to be alone if...if...I dared not frame my fears.

"Bates. With Bates."

"Tell Major Bates to pick up Captain Fairlie in ten minutes' time from the stern platform," Lee-Aston ordered the aide.

"Aye, aye, sir."

Lee-Aston stood with me at the stern. Jubela was alone on deck, staring as if mesmerized at the buoy marking the wreck. A galvanic ripple had passed through the circle of waiting ships from the conference table. Five yellow rubber dinghies, their grab-lines dripping, disposed themselves round the spot where the solitary orange-yellow wreck buoy bobbed in the rising sea.

Beneath it was Tafline.

Frogmen pulled on their black rubber wet suits and flippers, and I could see them checking times. Three of them hoisted scuba air bottles on to their shoulders and two had heavy crowbars.

Upon these men's deftness would hang her life—in twelve minutes.

The compressor's note quickened.

They were pumping the air into the chute which would kill or save her.

As if to mask the sound, Lee-Aston said, "It is a very well-tried method, Captain Fairlie."

I wondered how long I could go on talking.

"Won't the compression burst her lungs inside the chute?" I managed to say.

"No," replied the level voice. "It's not nearly high enough, at sixty feet, for that. Coming up—you're absolutely safe from drowning, I assure you. You can't hold your breath even if you tried. As you come up the air expands—it comes out as bubbles."

I saw Bates's little Alouette approaching,

"Don't imagine you'll see anything happening beforehand in that murky water, even from the air," warned Lee-Aston. "She'll come out and up in a cocoon of air, and the first you'll know of it will be a few air bubbles from her lungs preceding her."

The Alouette swept in.

Lee-Aston said, "Look at your watch in nine minutes."

It was only then that I realized his own desperate anxiety under the cool exterior. My hands were bandaged beyond the wrists. I had no watch.

Lee-Aston waved the sailors aside and himself adjusted the "horse-collar" round my shoulders.

The winch tugged. He stood back and saluted.

Bates was alone in the cockpit. The others of the crew stayed in the rear compartment. He did not say anything, but held out his left wrist with his watch.

Six minutes.

I was grateful I could no longer hear the compressor. We came round in a tight circle. I saw a line of bubbles. Bates checked me.

"Frogmen. There won't be anything before the time."

From the low altitude of the helicopter, I had a wider view of the horizon than from the frigate's deck. It seemed that the advancing purple storm bank was only a few miles away.

Bates came round again and hung in the center of the circle of yellow dinghies. The frogmen, two to a dinghy, did not look up from watching the enclosure of water.

The helicopter hung.

There was nothing in the murkiness below.

Bates held out his watch, wordlessly.

Zero!

"There she blows!"

The thin line of bubbles, like a torpedo wake, were different from the strong cascades emitted by the frogmen.

Bates dropped the Alouette like a lift to about twenty feet above the water.

In the middle of the erupting water, I saw the short hair, the polo collar, the patterned shoulders. Frogmen seemed to dive from every quarter to support the white face against the dark sea.

Bates was grinning. "Get down there on the horse-collar—you first!"

In the rear they stood aside, too, and in seconds I was hanging above the sea.

I looked down and she looked up.

Tafline.

ABOUT THE AUTHOR

Geoffrey Jenkins (1920–2001) was a South African novelist, journalist, and screenwriter renowned for high-stakes adventure tales grounded in meticulous research and a deep feel for Southern Africa. Born to Daisy and newspaper editor Ernest Jenkins in either Pretoria or Port Elizabeth, he showed early literary promise, receiving a special eulogy at seventeen for his historical work *A Century of History*, introduced by General Jan Smuts.

A winner of the Lord Kemsley Commonwealth Journalistic Scholarship, Jenkins served as a war correspondent during the Second World War and worked for several years on London's Fleet Street, where he became friends with James Bond creator Ian Fleming. Fleming admired Jenkins's imagination and once encouraged him to develop a Bond story; although Jenkins's completed manuscript *Per Fine Ounce* was never fully published, fragments have since appeared on the official Bond website.

After the war Jenkins settled in Rhodesia, marrying fellow writer Eve Palmer in 1950. Together they produced respected nonfiction about Southern Africa before Jenkins turned to fiction. His debut thriller, *A Twist of Sand* (1959), became an international bestseller, translated into more than two dozen languages and adapted for film.

Over the next three decades he produced a distinguished body of novels, including: *The Watering-Place of Good Peace* (1960; revised 1974), *A Grue of Ice* (1962, U.S. title *The Disappearing Island*), *The River of Diamonds* (1964), *Hunter-Killer* (1966), *Scend of the Sea* (1971, U.S. title *The Hollow Sea*), *A Cleft of Stars* (1973), *A Bridge of Magpies* (1974), *South Trap* (1979, paperback *Southtrap*), *A Ravel of Waters* (1981), *The Unripe Gold* (1983), *Fireprint* (1984), *In Harm's Way* (1986), *Hold Down a Shadow* (1989), *A Hive of Dead Men* (1991), and *A Daystar of Fear* (1993).

Blending the rigor of journalism with the sweep of cinematic storytelling, Geoffrey Jenkins secured a lasting place among twentieth-century thriller writers.

LOOKING FOR ACTION & ADVENTURE
AUTHOR ALAN CAILLOU
DELIVERS !

ADDITIONAL ACTION & ADVENTURE
FROM ALAN CAILLOU

DON'T MISS ANY OF MICHAEL KASNER'S HARD HITTING MILITARY NOVEL SERIES

BLACK OPS

Formed by an elite cadre of government officials, the Black OPS team goes where the law can't - to seek retribution for acts of terror directed against Americans anywhere in the world.

3 BOOK SERIES

Armed with all the tactical advantages of modern technology, battle hard and ready when the free world is threatened - the Peacekeepers are the baddest grunts on the planet.

4 BOOK SERIES

CHOPPER COPS

America is being torn apart as criminal cartels terrorize our cities, dealing drugs and death wholesale. Local police are outgunned, so the President unleashes the U.S. TACTICAL POLICE FORCE. An elite army of super cops with ammo to burn, they swoop down on the hot spots in sleek high-tech attack choppers to win the dirty war and take back America!

4 BOOK SERIES

FROM CALIBER BOOKS
www.calibercomics.com

CALIBER
BOOKS

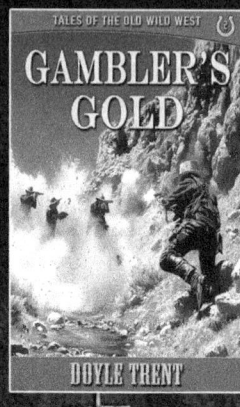

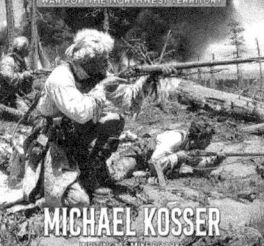

FROM FANTASY AND SCIENCE FICTION
AUTHOR ROLAND J. GREEN
THREE EPIC SERIES

FROM CALIBER BOOKS IN PAPERBACK AND EBOOK

DON'T MISS ANY OF NEIL HUNTER'S NOVELS FROM CALIBER BOOKS

Reporter Les Mason is completing an expose on the Long Point Nuclear Plant. But before he can finish he dies an agonizing death. The doctors are baffled—and there are similar cases to follow...Chris Lane, his girlfriend, and organizer of the Long Point Protestors, discovers Mason's notes, and decides to find out for herself what the plant has to hide.

2 BOOK SERIES

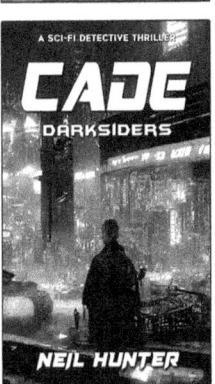

In middle of the 21st century America – over-populated decaying cities are ruled by hi-tech gangs pushing every vice and wastelands are controlled by bands of mutants. Ordinary citizens are oppressed and face a hopeless future. But Marshal T.J. Cade is a new breed of law enforcer. Teamed with his cyborg partner, Janek, Cade takes on these criminals and works in the gray areas of the law to get the job done.

3 BOOK SERIES

The village of Shepthorne England wasn't being gripped, but strangled by a winter's blanket of heavy snow and Arctic temperatures. The trouble began innocently enough with a massive pile-up of autos on frozen roads leading to and from the village. Then, from the sky, a military transport plane with its top secret cargo of devastation crashed down towards the center of the village. Hell was just beginning to touch Shepthorne and its unsuspecting citizens...

FROM CALIBER BOOKS

CALIBER BOOKS

www.calibercomics.com

www.ingramcontent.com/pod-product-compliance
Lightning Source LLC
Chambersburg PA
CBHW072052170626
46813CB00004B/1317